MY ROOMMATE'S
Girl

by JULIANNA KEYES

Visit our website at www.juliannakeyes.com.

Cover design by Khoi Le
Formatting by Polgarus Studio

ISBN 978-0-9950507-5-4

First Edition June 2017

1

In hindsight, the story ends the moment it begins. I park in front of the apartment building, my new roommate, Jerry, comes out to help me bring in my meager belongings, and everything is fine. Then he says, "This is my girlfriend, Aster."

I look at Aster and I'm done.

So if you think about it, Jerry kind of started it.

From our few text exchanges, I know that Jerry, like me, is a third year student at Holsom College, a reputable-if-not-notable school just outside of Seattle. He's pre-med, a meticulous recycler, and, if today's outfit is any indication, a fan of polo shirts and the color purple.

"Hey," Aster says, sticking out a hand as she props open the door to the building with her hip. I hoist my over-stuffed duffel bag higher onto my shoulder and take her hand, forcing myself to let go after a few seconds.

"Hey. I'm Aidan."

"I know. Jerry told me all about you. Come on up." Jerry had a lighter load and took the stairs, but Aster presses the button for the elevator and we get in, making the quick trip to the second floor. "Do you live here, too?" I ask, trying not to sound hopeful.

"No," Aster says as we step out into a quiet hall with pale gray walls. "I'm on campus. This is it." She stops at door 211 and holds it for me to pass through.

We enter just as Jerry goes back out for more stuff, and Aster leads me past a tidy living room and down a short hallway. It's my first time living off-campus, and though I'd only seen the place in pictures, it's already better than the two years I spent in Holsom College residence. The walls aren't made of stained concrete, the floors aren't covered in stained carpet, and, well, there aren't any stains anywhere. The walls are still clean, the wood floors still shiny, the appliances still functioning.

I got into Holsom as part of a scholarship program that gives troubled kids a second chance, and when it became apparent that my second chance was being jeopardized by the distractions of life on campus, I'd managed to convince the program director to let me use my room and board credit to rent a room in town instead. Now here I am, January third, new year, new home, new blonde distraction.

Jerry's previous roommate left his furniture behind, and I've inherited a queen size bed and a slightly lopsided desk. Combined with my duffel and milk crates, it's the most I've ever owned. "This is nice," I remark, taking things in as Aster lingers in the doorway. "Way better than residence."

She smiles. "I know, right? Nothing is stained."

She has a shoulder-length blond bob and clear, makeup-free skin. Her white T-shirt sets off her natural tan, and her torn jeans and bare feet make her look like she'd be more at home on a surfboard than a college campus. The dip in the V-neck of her

T-shirt gives me a glimpse of cleavage I will think about for many nights to come.

I don't have a type. I like all girls. Short, tall, thin, curvy, light, dark, and everything in between. Aster lands on the naturally pretty part of the spectrum, straight white teeth, clear blue eyes, and, when I pass her on my way to collect more things, a tiny smattering of freckles across her nose.

She smells like laundry detergent.

I'm still smelling it after Jerry and I have carted up the rest of my belongings, and I'm still thinking about it when he offers me a beer and toasts with, "To roommates."

Jerry seems like a nice guy, but he's my total opposite. His hair is dark, mine is dirty blond. His arms are tattoo-free; both of mine are etched in ink I started getting when I was fifteen. Jerry's here because his dad's a doctor; I'm here because the judge told me if I didn't go to college I'd be going to jail instead. He said lifting cars and lifting weights weren't the only things I could do, but that's all I had to look forward to if I didn't take the once-in-a-lifetime opportunity he felt strangely compelled to offer me.

I'm not an idiot. I took it. I took the scholarship they probably could have given to some kid who wasn't faking his gratitude. But hey, I figured I'd made a living taking things that weren't mine—why stop now?

"How were your holidays?" Aster asks, perching on the arm of Jerry's chair. The living room has a leather couch and two club chairs, and I'm on the couch opposite the two of them, trying not to eyeball Aster's cleavage.

"Just fine," I reply, sipping my beer. "Yours?" To stop myself from staring I turn my attention to the front window. The January sky is gray, its pale expanse carved up by the bare branches of the tree that looms outside. In the summer, when it's leafy and green, it's probably pretty. Right now it feels like prison bars. I'd only spent a few nights behind them, but it was enough to convince me I'd taken a wrong turn somewhere right around the time I stole my first car.

Jerry wraps up a story about spending Christmas with family in Portland, and I missed whatever Aster said. Their politeness makes me feel antsy, like more of a black sheep than I already am. They're the smiling, sweet people you see in catalogues, modeling corduroy and sneakers. I'm...not.

A shrill ring interrupts and Aster gives a little jump. "Shoot!" she exclaims. "Sorry." She stands and pulls a phone from her back pocket, answering on the third ring. Her voice grows muffled as she disappears down the hall.

"So," Jerry says. "You back to class tomorrow?"

"Yeah."

"The break was nice."

I nod along, like I didn't spend it in residence with a kid from Taiwan. He didn't speak much English but he had some awesome video games, so that helped pass the time.

"You said you, uh, play Frisbee baseball?" Jerry asks when the silence becomes awkward. "I didn't know that was a thing."

I try to appear pleasant and conversational, but it's not easy. I don't fit in at Holsom, and I definitely don't fit in with purple polo shirts. "Me either," I say finally. I hadn't heard of the sport until I was informed that part of my scholarship requirement was that I have at least one "approved" pastime and a part-time job.

Now I play Frisbee baseball at one of the campus gyms every Thursday and pull three shifts a week at the library.

"Aster's good at sports," Jerry says when Aster pads back into the room, her bare feet quiet on the hardwood.

"I'm okay," she says, returning to her spot next to him. "I can run without falling down. What do you play, Aidan?"

Hearing her say my name has an odd effect on me. Most people call me by my last time, Shaw. For some reason it makes me want to sit up a bit straighter, put the beer away, be better. But I don't.

"Nothing," I reply. "Not really."

Her brows pull together in confusion. "Oh."

"He plays Frisbee baseball," Jerry offers, suddenly uncertain. "On a rec team?"

I feel bad. I'm not really a dick, I just don't like small talk. Or a lot of talk.

"On Thursdays," I make myself say.

Aster scratches her knee through the torn denim, echoing Jerry's words from earlier. "I didn't know that was a thing."

"A lot of people don't. We're always short players."

Jerry perks up a bit, seizing the chance to show me what a good roommate he is. "Aster could fill in for you, if you wanted." Then he turns to Aster. "And if you wanted," he adds.

If she's annoyed at him offering her services, she hides it well. "I'm free Thursdays. Just call me, if you want me." Then she laughs. "To play," she corrects herself. "If you want me to play with you."

She presses her hand to her chest, drawing my attention there yet again. My stomach tightens, then my thighs, my arms.

Everything pulls in tight, anticipating my next move, the way it did whenever I found the car I'd been sent to steal, sitting there, innocent, waiting.

No clue what was coming.

And no way to stop it.

2

I'm smoking in front of the gym when Aster arrives on Thursday night. It's dark and cold, the sky clear. The parking lot is half full of cars, and Aster weaves between them as she walks up. She's wearing a puffy yellow jacket zipped to her chin, a red hat pulled down low over her ears. She's the brightest thing in the lot.

I stub out my cigarette on a trash can and toss the butt away, nodding at Aster when she's close. "Hey."

"Hey. I didn't realize you smoked."

"Only sometimes. Don't tell Jerry." The apartment building is non-smoking, but I only smoke when I'm stressed, so it wasn't an issue. The fact that I stressed all day at the prospect of seeing Aster for the first time since I'd moved in, *is* an issue.

"Your secret's safe with me." She smiles, but I swear I see her nose wrinkle a little bit when I reach past her for the door. I'm wearing a hoodie over my T-shirt and sweats, and now I pull it off as I follow her inside, hoping the smoke doesn't cling to my skin.

The building has two gymnasiums and a small pool, and the air smells like chlorine as we walk down a hallway lined with orange lockers. The gym doors have been propped open to encourage spectators, none of whom ever turn up.

"That's us," I say, pointing toward a small group of people in white mesh jerseys on the far side of the room. "Thanks for coming."

"No problem," Aster replies. She pulls off the red hat and shakes out her hair, the thick, shiny strands falling neatly into place. She's a foot in front of me and I take a second to admire her ass in the black workout tights, her lean legs, graceful walk. I meant it when I said I like all kinds of girls, but I've never been with a girl like Aster. A girl who looks like she goes on ski holidays with her wealthy family and reads books to blind kids in her free time. Someone who's totally comfortable smiling and shaking hands with my teammates and introducing herself, saying her name, Aster Aster Aster, so many times it turns into a chant I can't get out of my head.

Frisbee baseball isn't terribly different from actual baseball, we just use a disc instead of a ball, but Aster listens politely as Shamus, our Irish team captain, outlines the rules, then takes her position in right field as we begin. My team is called the Shamrocks, courtesy of Shamus, and our opponents are the Scare Bears. I'm playing third when the first player comes up to bat, eyeballing Aster. There aren't a lot of Frisbee baseball teams at Holsom, so they immediately identify her as a newbie and predictably hurl the disc in her direction. She jogs back ten feet, waits for the disc to drop, and catches it easily before tossing it back in. One down.

The next batter tries the same thing, this time a shorter toss, aimed to drop in front of her. It skitters across the ground and she runs in, scoops it up, and fires it into second, catching the runner as he tries for a double.

Two down.

Okay, maybe Aster looks like a girl who skis and reads to blind kids *and* plays Frisbee baseball.

The third player isn't intimidated by the last two plays, and whips the disc into right field. It soars high and deep and Aster breaks into a sprint as she tracks it. The disc is coming down but still has momentum, and the runner is already rounding second. It's an easy home run until Aster leaps into the air, one arm extended, and snatches the Frisbee. She lands on her feet, takes two steps to slow her speed, then casually jogs back in. Our team waits there, deeply impressed, and I'm standing at the back of the line to high five her as we return to our bench.

"What the fuck?" I mutter into her ear as she tosses the disc to the other team's first baseman.

She bats her lashes at me, too deliberate to actually be innocent. "What? Isn't that what I was supposed to do?"

"How many more secret skills do you have?"

She grins and blows a piece of hair off her forehead. "No secrets here, Aidan."

* * *

The first inning wasn't beginner's luck. Aster is a fucking all star. She "hits" well, runs smart, and fields like a genie. There's nothing she can't do. Shamus is drooling over her by the time we get to the bottom of the fourth, and he's fully in love with her when we win 13-8. Though she'd offered, I'd had no intention of actually asking Aster to play with us tonight. It was only Shamus's pitiful email pleas begging us to find a female player for the game—and the dearth of response from the rest of our teammates—that prompted me to ask Jerry if he'd invite Aster on my behalf. He'd been more than happy to help. In fact, Jerry is always happy. He's the most upbeat, positive guy I've ever met. He's so upbeat he circles right back around from happy to annoying to kind of mystifying. It's also why I told myself not to invite Aster to play—it'd be one thing to lust after Jerry's girl if he were an asshole, but it's quite another when he's so, well, nice. The kind of guy a girl like Aster would fall for. The kind that's nothing like me.

The team goes for drinks after each game and I normally bail, but tonight Shamus invites Aster and she accepts. "You coming, Aidan?" she asks.

It's on the tip of my tongue to say no, but hearing the invite come from Aster takes away any impulse to reject the offer. Maybe I can consider socializing with my teammates penance for jerking off to the image of my roommate's girlfriend three times in the four days since I last saw her.

We get dressed and trek across campus to a small Irish pub, Shamus's favorite. There are ten of us, so we grab a couple of tables and stick them together while Shamus goes to order the first round. He returns with a couple of pitchers and a server follows with a tray of glasses, and in less than a minute we've all got a glass of beer and a fake smile as we pretend to listen to Shamus's toast.

I'm sitting next to Aster, and I don't hear a word of what Shamus is saying. When everyone echoes the toast I just mumble something, touching my glass to that of the guy next to me, and the girl next to him, then, finally, Aster's. Our fingers bump and she notices the four letters crudely etched into my knuckles: R-I-D-E.

"Ride?" she reads, automatically reaching for my other hand. I want to pull it back, keep it out of sight and not offend her, but there's really no way to jerk away without doing exactly that. Instead I let her enfold my rough hand in her smooth one, her fingers curling mine into a fist so she can read the second word. H-A-R-D.

"Ride hard." She looks at me. "Ride what?"

I try not to stare at her eyes. They're cornflower blue, a shade I know because they used to grow in this weird little patch in the field behind our home when I was a kid. It's a color I associate with being young and carefree and happy. A color I haven't seen since one of the bookies my dad failed to pay burned down our house.

"Ride whatever," I make myself say, the words scratching my throat. I take a sip of beer like my only problem right now is dehydration.

"Jerry said you don't have a car."

That's true; I'd borrowed one for the hour it had taken me to pack up my stuff from residence and cart it over to the apartment. "There are other things to ride."

"Motorcycles?"

She's too close. I can see her freckles, count the tiny strands of hair that cling to her temples, damp with sweat.

I've never had a girl this close to me in a bar that wasn't waiting for me to make a move, or planning her own move. All of my instincts are urging me to put down my glass and take

Aster's hands and put them on my crotch and show her just how hard I like to ride. It might offend her. Or it might turn her on.

Only one way to find out.

"Are we going to see you again, Aster?" Shamus asks, promptly slicing the tension in two. Or maybe the tension was all in my mind, because Aster has no trouble turning away from me to focus on him. I try to listen to the conversation, to hear Aster say she can play again if we find ourselves short, but I can't. Coming here was a bad idea. A table of chaperones and I can barely control myself. Story of my life.

I down my beer and Shamus reaches for the pitcher to pour me another. "No, thanks," I say, waving him off. "I have to get going."

"Oh," Aster says, sounding surprised even as she gets to her feet. "I'll come with you."

"I can walk you home," Shamus offers quickly. "If you don't want to leave right away."

I wince when I see how stupidly lovestruck he is.

"That's okay," she says. "Aidan lives with my boyfriend, and I'm going to their place."

I wince again when I see Shamus's heart break into a million little pieces, shattering all over the table. "I see."

"Thanks for having me," Aster adds, pulling on her red hat. "Nice meeting you all."

A chorus of goodbyes follows us out of the pub and into the frosty night air.

"I didn't realize you were coming over," I say when we've taken a few steps in silence.

"I'm not. I just didn't want to hurt his feelings later."

"Ah."

"Do you think I embarrassed him in front of everybody?"

"No," I tell her. "I'm sure he's used to being rejected."

She laughs. "Ouch."

"At least now he knows you're off limits, so if you come back, he won't keep hitting on you." For my peace of mind, as much as Jerry's.

"That's true."

I glance at her. "Which way to your place?"

"You don't have to walk me."

"Of course I do. It's dark. I'm a gentleman. Or couldn't you tell?" I hold up my tattooed knuckles.

"How could I forget?"

We walk across the quiet campus, winding between the sleepy buildings and bare trees. Street lamps buzz softly overhead, the sidewalks already glistening with frost.

"How long have you and Jerry been together?" I ask. I'd wanted to ask Jerry about Aster all week, but couldn't figure out how to work it into conversation without it sounding like I was wondering if it would be difficult to break them up.

"A little over a year," she answers, brushing a piece of hair back off her face. Her cheeks are pink with cold, making her even cuter, more wholesome, more not my type. But my dick is just not getting the message, and when I sneak a peek at her ass, it blatantly ignores my instructions not to think about it.

"We met at move-in last year," she adds. "We pretty much started dating right away."

"Lucky guy."

"What about you? Jerry didn't mention if you had a girlfriend."

"No. No girl."

"What about Missy?"

"Who?"

"Missy? On your team? She played second base and jumped into your arms after your home run?"

"Oh. Missy. No. Not her." Missy has been flirting with me since she joined the team in September, but I've never taken her up on her offer. I have to play with those guys every Thursday, and I don't want to hook up with Missy and then see her pouting week after week because I didn't call.

And though I hardly know her, I know Aster's a girl who expects a phone call.

And Jerry's the guy who calls her.

"This is me," she says, stopping in front of a tall concrete building. "Thanks for walking me."

"Any time."

"And thanks for inviting me. That was fun."

"Why do you live here?" I blurt out. "And not with Jerry?"

"I'm an R.A.," she replies. "A resident advisor. It covers the cost of dorms and meals. I could use the money. And...it was too soon to live with Jerry."

"Sorry. None of my business." Though I file away the fact that if she needs the cash, maybe she doesn't go on ski trips with her wealthy family. She probably does read to blind kids, though.

"That's okay. Also, he steals money from my wallet."

"What?"

She laughs, the same sound I haven't forgotten from earlier in the week. The same one I hear when I'm jerking off. "Just kidding. Jerry's great. You're going to love him." She waves and pulls out her keys. "Good night, Aidan."

I step back. "'Night, Aster."

3

For the next six days, I manage to think about Aster a little less. I only jack off to the thought of her ass in the air and my hands in her hair three times. It's an improvement over last week.

All of my hard work is promptly undone when I let myself into the apartment Wednesday night and find Aster alone on the couch. There's a pizza box on the cushion next to her, her bare feet crossed at the ankles on the ottoman. The visual of coming home to Aster hits me stupidly hard, and I tell myself the heat I'm feeling is just the contrast from the cold air outside. That the *want* tugging at my insides is just hunger.

But it's not.

"Hey," I make myself say. I turn around and take off my coat and boots, trying not to show how happy I am to see her.

"Hey," she replies. "Sorry for just being here like this. Jerry was supposed to meet me for dinner but he got stuck at the lab and I'd already ordered the pizza."

"Totally fine."

The kitchen and living room are divided by a small counter,

so I can still see her as I fill a glass with tap water and down it in three swallows.

"Do you want some food?" Aster asks. "Jerry's going to eat at the lab, and he said to tell you to help yourself if you're hungry."

I try not to appear too "hungry" when I look at Aster and wonder what else Jerry is willing to share.

I should tell her no. I should say I ate and go into my room and close the door and put on headphones and forget she's here. But I've never been good at resisting temptation, even when it's wearing an oversized Holsom sweatshirt and faded jeans and seems to be legitimately enjoying *Bridget Jones's Diary*.

"I'll have some pizza," I say, grabbing a napkin from the counter. "But you've gotta change the channel."

"This movie's a classic."

"It's not." I take the spot on the far end of the couch, the pizza between us. I can practically feel her scrutinizing my white button-up shirt and dark pants, far from my usual attire of jeans and old concert T-shirts.

"Did you have a late class?" she asks.

I grab a slice of pizza. It's pepperoni and mushroom and it's still hot. My mouth waters and I take a bite, glancing at Aster. It's not a secret that I have a job, but it's not something I advertise. My job at the library is in stark contrast to the tattooed knuckles and bad attitude.

"I was working," I say around the food. "At the library."

"Oh. I didn't know."

"I never told you. Change the channel."

She picks up the remote and scrolls through the options in the guide. "I'm just being nice because you're new," she informs me.

I grin. Aster's being nice because she's a nice person. "And when I'm not new? What happens then?"

"All this hospitality goes right out the window."

"Uh-oh."

"It's as terrible as it sounds."

"Does Jerry know you're cruel?"

"Nope. He came with me to see *Bridget Jones's Baby* in theater."

I groan and stuff the rest of the pizza in my mouth. If that's what it takes to get a girl like Aster, maybe I've been jerking off to the wrong girl. "Jerry needs some guidance."

She smirks. "Are you going to be that guide?"

"If I ever find him watching *Bridget Jones* by himself, I'll have to step in. No real man watches that movie willingly. And he only watches it for a girl if there's a blow jo—" I catch myself way too late. Aster's blue eyes widen and she freezes, a piece of pizza extended toward her pretty mouth. "I'm sorry," I say hastily. "I forgot who—"

Then she laughs. And laughs. And laughs.

She drops the pizza back into the box she's laughing so hard.

"Poor Jerry," she wheezes, wiping her cheeks with the back of her hand. "I just had to buy his popcorn."

I snicker, relief making me weak and stupid. "It's none of my business," I say, even though I want it to be my business. I want to take Aster to a chick flick and make her pay for it with filthy sexual favors afterward. I want to find out if she'd be offended by it.

"I think you'll be a good influence on Jerry," she says after a second. She's focused on the TV again, settling on a *Big Bang Theory* rerun.

I almost choke. "Did you say a *good* influence?" Not once in my life has anyone ever called me a good influence. I'm not sure I've ever even been called *good*, period. And I'm not sure how to feel about it.

"Yeah," Aster says. "He's so focused on school that he sometimes forgets to have fun. Maybe you'll rub off on him."

"What do you do for fun, Aster?"

She glances at my knuckles and rolls her lips contemplatively. "Lots of things."

I try not to curl my hands into fists, try not to show her how I have to work so fucking hard not to reach over there to touch her, just to see if I can.

I might have been wrong about the money. I might even be wrong about the blind kids. But Aster's a nice person, a good person. She's not going to fuck me if she has a boyfriend.

So the boyfriend will have to go.

4

The middle of next week, I come home to find Jerry studying in the living room. He's alone, for once. Normally I have to see him and Aster cuddling or looking way too happy together as they eat dinner or lock themselves away in his room. I never hear them banging through the walls, but I'm not desperate enough to think they're sitting in there reading scripture, either.

I wish.

"Hey," I say, hanging up my coat.

"Hey," Jerry replies. He closes his textbook. "How was work?"

"Just fine. Ready for the weekend."

"I hear you."

"Yeah?" I grab some leftover takeout from the fridge. "When was the last time you went out?"

He doesn't even lie. "I don't remember," he admits. "It's been a while."

"Come out on Friday," I say, like it's just occurred to me. "A friend of mine is getting married and we're having a bachelor party."

"Getting married?" he exclaims. "How old is this friend?"

"Twenty-three. He's a fucking idiot. We're going to give him one last send-off before the ball and chain get tied on."

"That's young."

I eat another mouthful of cold chow mein. "Real young. You and Aster headed that way?"

"For marriage?"

"Yeah."

I wait for him to say no, this is college, they're having fun, it's not permanent. Instead he says, "Maybe once I finish med school and I'm working. I don't want to tie her down when I have nothing to offer."

A little shiver of guilt snakes through me, but I ignore it. "You'll have lots to offer—in ten years. For now, live a little. Come have a beer on a Friday night."

"Okay," he says reluctantly. "You're right. I'll come. Thanks."

I throw the empty takeout container in the trashcan across the room, sinking the three-pointer. "Thank *you.*"

* * *

Jerry tries to wear a *tie* to the bachelor party. He comes out of his room at ten on Friday night, no doubt having sat in there for the past two hours, wondering when we were supposed to leave. I told him around ten, but he didn't think it was possible to start something so late. I swear Jerry's an eighty-year-old man in a twenty-one-year-old body.

"Take that off," I tell him when I spot the polka dot tie. *Polka dots.* Jerry might be nice and on his way to becoming a doctor, but I'm not sure those facts can make up for this tie. I'm doing Aster a huge favor by intervening here.

At least, that's who I tell myself the favor's for.

"What?" Jerry asks, automatically touching the tie. "This tie?"

"Yeah. It's a bachelor party, not a horse race."

"I haven't been to a horse race in forever," Jerry says. "Have you—"

"No. Tie off."

He reluctantly undoes the tie, folds it carefully, and rests it on an end table. I'm sitting on the couch, wearing jeans and black button-up shirt, my combat boots propped on the ottoman as I eat a bowl of popcorn. I told him this wasn't a drink-expensive-scotch-and-smoke-cigars type of deal, but I don't think he believed me until now.

"And untuck your shirt," I say.

"But that's so slopp—" He breaks off when he sees my face. He's got his sea green shirt tucked completely inside his khakis, and it takes him twelve full seconds to pull it out. There. At least he looks like a semi-youthful person. Or at least a bank employee who's finished work for the evening.

"All right," I say, getting to my feet. "Let's go."

I can tell Jerry's nervous as we make the twenty-minute trek through the cold night to a dive bar called Bender just off the edge of campus. Bender is the anchor of a plaza of seedy businesses, all of which are open twenty-four hours. Pawn shop, sex shop, money lending. Everything a guy could ask for.

I grab the door and noise pours out, the battle of old rock music warring with drunken revelers and a recap of a rowdy football game. Jerry pauses for a second before entering, probably uttering a quick thank-you-God he's not wearing the tie.

The bar is small and tightly packed, and so dark I probably wouldn't have located my friends if I couldn't hear them. They've commandeered three tables and a booth in the back corner, near a hallway blocked by a flimsy beaded curtain. They haven't been here for long, but the table is already littered with empty shot glasses and baskets of greasy food.

"Shaw!" someone bellows, and more shouts follow.

I lead Jerry to the table and pull out two chairs near the curtain. "Hey," I say. "This is my roommate." I make the introductions and Jerry does a commendable job of not appearing too alarmed at the company he's being asked to keep.

I enrolled at Holsom as part of their Promise & Potential Program, and that's how I met most of these guys. Boasting tattoos, piercings, muscles, and perma-scowls, we work at the library, the bakery, and the campus daycare. My friend Wes did two years in prison for his part in a small scale drug operation; now he can change a dirty diaper in ten seconds flat.

Not that anybody will tell Jerry this.

I see a couple side-eye glances at the khakis, but no one comments. They don't know about Aster or my ulterior motive for this evening, they think I'm just bringing Jerry out for a good time. And I am.

A fresh round of shots arrives and I expect Jerry to ask for a glass of white wine, but he grabs his glass and joins in the toast for Brix, the unlucky guy getting married in a month, and downs the whisky like a pro.

I keep pace for the next two rounds, then switch to water. I've got a small buzz, but Jerry's cheeks are flushed and his eyes are glassy and he's not half as tense as when he arrived. He even laughs at T.J.'s story about threatening to break the fingers of a student who claimed his cinnamon bun was over-baked and tried to get a refund.

"That bun was not over-baked!" T.J. shouts, pounding the table. "It was moist!"

We shout our agreed outrage and I can practically see Jerry making a mental note never to visit the bakery.

"Hey, boys," coos a familiar voice, soft but seductive enough to wind through the testosterone-fuelled noise.

"Hey, Sin," comes the chorus.

"Sin?" Jerry echoes as she steps through the curtain and puts her flawless, mostly-bare body on display.

"Sindy," she says. "Sin for short." She bends to whisper in his ear. "Or long."

"Huh?"

Brix gives me a strange look. I've told them most of the truth about Jerry: he's my roommate, pre-med, nice guy, a bit uptight. Definitely not a guy who's paid for sex, or seen someone else pay for sex. I've never paid for it myself, but if you've been to Bender, you've seen guys—and gals—slip through that beaded curtain after Sindy and slide back out with a satisfied smile on their face. Hence tonight's prime seating arrangements.

Sindy sinks into a free chair and crosses her legs, monitoring Jerry's face the whole time, sizing him up. He's a little drunk, a little confused, and a little turned on.

"I haven't seen you here before," she says. She leans in, arms pressing into her torso to emphasize her fantastic rack. She wears a sparkly gold bra that leaves little to the imagination, and I can almost see the shiny fabric reflected in Jerry's eyes.

"Um, it's my first time," he manages to reply. "I'm normally… studying." He's having a hard time keeping his gaze off her chest, though he's doing a commendable job of trying.

"Hey," Brix says, rapping on the table to get my attention. "You wanna watch your friend get his rocks off or play pool?"

"That's a tough one," I say, standing. "But I guess I can kick your ass before your new wife takes over."

Half of us move to the far side of the bar with the pool tables and dartboards. I see Wes talking to some sketchy guys in the corner, but tell myself to stay out of it. We all got our spot in this program for a reason; it's probably nothing.

Brix reserved a table and now he racks the balls and takes the first shot. "Should we make this interesting?" he asks, reaching for his wallet.

"No," I say automatically. I've done a lot of bad shit, but I never gamble. *Never.*

"Right," he drawls, smirking as he sinks his first ball. "Because you're afraid of losing."

"Ha." I scoff as he misses his next shot, then pick up my cue. "I'm doing you a favor. You'll see."

I know these guys well enough to call them my friends, but not well enough to talk to them about the situation with Jerry and Aster, though I have a hard time concentrating on the game when across the room I see that Sin has moved into my chair to be closer to Jerry. She's got her hand on his bicep and her head tossed back as she laughs at something he said.

T.J. comes over with another round of shots and I hesitate before taking one. Alcohol only gets me into trouble. Women get me in trouble. *I* get me in trouble.

Fuck it. It's Friday. I'll sleep through the weekend and be back on the straight and narrow come Monday.

Three games of pool and another five—or was it eight?—shots later, I can't even remember what straight and narrow means. We stumble back to the table, mocking Wes's failed attempts to pick up women and his insistence that he "didn't want to, anyway," and find Jerry and Sindy squeezed into a booth together.

A half-eaten basket of carrot sticks sits in front of them, as well as an empty bottle of white wine and two glasses.

Oh, Jerry.

I sigh inwardly, thinking tonight's game plan might be a little harder to execute than expected, then perk up when I notice that Sindy's only got one hand visible. The other is hidden beneath the table, doing something that's making Jerry have a hard time finishing his sentence.

"How long have they been in there?" I ask T.J. T.J. went from high school straight into prison, and came to Holsom after he got out early for good behavior. Now he's an art history major who makes a mean focaccia.

"Too long," he replies. "He still doesn't know that what Sindy's offering ain't free. At least, it never has been."

Sindy's a business woman at heart, skilled in one of womankind's oldest trades, and even as I'm thinking how best to insinuate myself into their party for two and convince them to take things into the back, Sindy links her fingers with Jerry's and tugs him out of the booth toward the beads.

She parts the shiny curtain and giggles sexily as she pulls on his hand, and at the last second he turns to look at me, the same look I must have had when I stole my first car. The look of someone who knows he's going to do something bad, maybe even *wants* to do something bad, even as he understands there will be consequences.

Then he lets Sindy lure him out of sight.

"Damn," Wes mutters. "That guy? Really?"

"C'mon," T.J. says. "Look at those khakis! When else is he going to get laid if he doesn't pay for it?"

He's not paying for it, I think.

I am.

5

I wake up with a splitting headache. The weak sunlight slipping past the edge of the curtain feels like daggers piercing my skull, and I groan and cover my face with the pillow.

Eventually I lift the pillow and check the time on my phone: just after eleven o'clock in the morning. I don't have any plans for the day beyond shuffling to the kitchen for some aspirin and crawling back into bed. That's as far as I can make it.

It takes another ten minutes before I manage to get my feet on the floor. I fell asleep in my jeans and now I pull on a T-shirt as I plod down the hall to the kitchen. Jerry's already there, looking as shitty as I feel. His dark hair sticks up every which way and his skin has an unhealthy gray tinge. He's wearing a Holsom hoodie and a pair of boxers, staring morosely into a glass of orange juice.

"Hey," I mutter, my voice hoarse. I fill a cup with tap water, fetch three aspirin from the cupboard, and down them with one swallow.

"Hey," Jerry replies. He may appear sick, but he just sounds…sad. Especially sad for a guy who got laid last night.

I know the answer, but still I ask, "You all right?"

He doesn't look up from the juice.

"Want some aspirin?"

A tiny head shake.

Okay, I'm starting to feel bad for the guy. Not so bad that I don't intend to go through with the rest of my plan to have Sindy bump into Aster and Jerry and spill the beans on last night's encounter, but bad all the same. Bad on top of bad.

"Did you have a good time at the party?" I ask, joining him at the counter. "In spite of the hangover?"

He slowly raises his red-rimmed eyes. "No," he says, his voice surprisingly firm. "I didn't have a good time. I had a horrible time. It was… *I* was…horrible."

I've known Sindy for the three years I've been in town, but we've never hooked up. Still, no one she's been with has ever described her as *horrible*. Quite the opposite.

"I thought you hit it off with that, uh, waitress."

"She didn't work there. She was hanging out. She was lonely."

If only he knew.

"She was hot."

He meets my stare. "That's not supposed to matter. I'm not supposed to do anything about it."

"So you two…?"

He scrubs his hands over his face. "She…" He gestures to his crotch, and I infer the rest.

"That's it?" I press. "Just a blow job?"

"That's it? That's *it?* That's everything! That's too much! When Aster finds out that I— That I—" He breaks off sadly. "That'll be it."

Never mind that I plan to make sure she finds out, I still ask, "How would she know about it?"

He gapes at me. "I have to tell her."

Now I gape. "You're going to tell your girlfriend you let another girl blow you?"

"She's going to know something happened!" he moans. "She'll be able to tell right away and I can't lie to her. I love her. And now she's going to hate me."

I can't believe Jerry's going to do the rest of my dirty work for me. Another hint of guilt stirs, but I squash it. On the one hand I'm sympathetic to the guy's situation, but on the other hand…he *got* the blow job. I just…helped.

"Maybe she'll understand," I offer lamely. "Maybe she'll forgive you."

Jerry scoffs. "Why? Why would she do that? Have you seen her? Have you met her? Aster is amazing. She's a million miles out of my league. She has no reason to forgive me."

"She loves you."

He shrugs and sips his juice. "It won't be enough. This is going to break her heart. Even if she managed to forgive me, I could never forgive myself."

Jerry's very sincere self-flagellation is starting to make me seriously uncomfortable. I haven't bothered trying to convince myself that my motives here are anything other than selfish, because they're motivated by the simple desire to have something that isn't mine. But Jerry's feeling bad enough for the both of us, and my conscience is starting to take note.

"Hey," I say, reaching over to awkwardly pat his shoulder. "Just give it a day or two. You feel like shit right now, but maybe you'll think differently on Monday."

"Have you ever lied to someone about something this big?" he asks. "Broken their heart?"

Now it's my turn to study my beverage. "No," I lie. "I haven't."

He sighs. "Then you can't understand."

* * *

On Sunday night I'm watching the final minutes of a crappy football game with Jerry. Everything about this weekend has been crap, particularly because Jerry feels truly awful about what happened and I've been too hungover to leave the apartment to escape him.

"Do you play any sports?" I ask.

Jerry shrugs. "Nah. I played some growing up—Little League or whatever—but my dad's a surgeon and one night I got a pitch inside, swung, and hit my hand instead. Broke it. After that my dad said if I wanted to be a doctor I had to take care of myself first, so that was the end of sports."

"Do you want to be a doctor?"

He nods. "Yep. It's all I've ever wanted. You?"

"Definitely not a doctor."

"What's your major? You never told me."

"Social work." The degree hits a little too close to home so I'd dodged the question during our roommate interview, but I'm still feeling bad about my last lie, so here we are.

"That's a degree?"

"At some schools. At Holsom."

"Is that why you picked this place?"

"Ah, yeah." Okay, just one more lie. The judge picked it.

"That's cool," Jerry says. "Any—"

A quick knock interrupts, followed by the sound of keys jangling and the faint creak of the door. Aster has keys, but she still always knocks before she comes in.

"Hey," she calls, peeking inside. "Everyone alive?"

Jerry straightens from his slouched position. "Yeah, we—I—What, um, what are you doing here? Right now?"

"Calm down," I mutter from the corner of my mouth.

He stops talking.

"You said you were sick," Aster answers, holding up a brown paper bag. "I brought you chicken soup."

Jerry's mouth opens and closes helplessly, and with every movement I'm convinced he's going to announce his guilt and, by association, mine.

"Chicken soup!" I exclaim loudly. "Isn't that great, Jerry?"

"Ah…yes?"

"I brought enough for two," Aster says, grabbing bowls from the cupboard. "In case you both had this same *mysterious* illness." I see her roll her eyes as she ladles soup into the bowls, and in my whole life, no one has ever brought me soup when I was sick. I thought that was a myth promoted by soup companies.

Jerry's guilt is almost tangible. I can feel it slithering over me, tightening around my neck, making me feel ill when I'd been feeling pretty close to fine. Or maybe it has nothing to do with Jerry at all and everything to do with the guileless, sweet, gorgeous woman who brought us soup we don't deserve.

"What's wrong?" Aster asks, glancing up when we haven't moved from the couch after a minute. "I know you can't be enjoying that football game."

Her uncertainty propels me to my feet. I don't want her to feel as bad as we do, though I'm not sure I have much sway in that regard.

"I'll take the soup to my room," I say, picking up the bowl. "You guys can catch up. Thanks for this."

"Of course," she replies. "Feel better." Her blue eyes meet mine and there's something there, something sweet and smart and vaguely mocking.

I disappear down the hall to my room, closing the door behind me and leaning against it. I don't know why I feel so wrong. This is what I *want*. I want Jerry and Aster to break up. I want Aster to be free to fuck someone else, and I want that someone to be me. And I'm pretty sure I'm about to get the first part of my wish. I just didn't expect it to feel like this. I didn't expect her to bring me soup while I played a sleazy part in breaking her heart.

I eat the soup standing up, then, when I don't hear dishes breaking or raised voices, I grab a textbook and finish my reading for tomorrow's class. An hour later I hear them talking as they come down the hall, Aster still happy, still oblivious. The voices fade as Jerry's bedroom door shuts.

We share a wall and the last thing I want is to hear them going at it, so I pull on some headphones and try to concentrate on my reading. Problem is, I can't read and listen to music at the same time, and if I close the book all I do is picture them having sex to my soundtrack.

I pull off the headphones and slip out of my room. I wash the bowl and spoon, then settle on the couch to find an old sitcom rerun. It's just after eleven o'clock. Hopefully Jerry and Aster fall asleep soon and I can go back to my room and think about something else.

The final credits are scrolling down the screen when I hear Aster's raised voice, then Jerry's desperate one, the sounds muffled by the closed bedroom door. Then the sounds get a lot louder because Jerry's door is opened and Aster is telling him to shut up. "Stop talking!" she shouts, her voice breaking. "How could you? How could—" She hiccups. "How could you do this? *You,* Jerry? I don't—" Another hiccup. "I don't—I can't—"

I try to keep my attention on the television, but I don't stand a chance. Aster hurries down the hall toward me in jeans and a yellow T-shirt and socks, the picture of innocence as she grabs her coat from the chair and shoves her feet into rain boots. She reaches into her pocket and pulls out her key ring, untangling our apartment key from the bunch and hurling it into the kitchen before she storms out. The door gives a heavy, final slam behind her, and for a long second, the apartment is dead quiet.

Then I hear it. A tiny sniffle, a tinier sob, then the soft click of Jerry's bedroom door closing.

I did it.

They're done.

6

I don't see Aster all week. Jerry doesn't talk about her or the break up, just wisely assumes I figured it out on my own.

One of the flaws in my genius plan was underestimating the power of my own guilty conscience; another one is forgetting that Aster and I have no reason to cross paths if she's not coming to my apartment several nights a week. I don't know her class schedule—hell, I don't even know her major—and I while I know where she lives, I have no reason to be in or around that residence. So…shit.

At Frisbee baseball on Thursday I'm lacing up my sneakers when Shamus sits on the bench beside me.

"Hey," he says.

"Hey."

He links his fingers together over his knees and peers around the gym, a real-life example of how not to succeed at being casual.

"Is something wrong?" I ask reluctantly. "Do we have enough players?"

"Yeah, we have enough." He manages to make that sound

like a bad thing. "I asked your friend Aster to play again, but she said no."

I try to ignore the twist in my stomach at the sound of her name. No, at the sound of her name spoken with Shamus's Irish lilt. My stupid plan has another flaw: Aster would never have cheated on Jerry, but now that she's single, there's no reason she can't hook up with Shamus, using a bit of his Irish luck to mend her broken heart. Especially when he apparently has her phone number and I don't.

I am such a fucking idiot.

"Maybe she's busy," I hear myself say.

He exhales. "I don't think that's it. She looked kind of depressed. Still gorgeous, though."

This time I can't ignore the twist in my stomach or the alarm that slices through me. "You saw her? In person?"

"Yeah. We have a class together. We'd just never spoken until you brought her out to play that time."

Oh my God. I opened the door for *Shamus* to walk through? No. *Fuck* no. I was going to take some time to figure out how best to reach out to Aster after the break up, but that's no longer an option if Shamus is planning to make the same move. Shamus, who *didn't* pay Sindy to destroy a relationship. Shamus, who may be keen and annoying, but is also not a world-class asshole.

"I don't really know her," I say. "She's my roommate's girlfriend and they're always…going at it."

Shamus's face falls.

"Like, hardcore," I add. "Sometimes I have to leave the apartment."

"Oh." He cringes.

"I wouldn't mind meeting a girl like that," I continue. "But a completely different one."

"What about Missy?" Shamus asks.

"What?"

"What if you went out with Missy? She likes you."

What the hell is it with guys I'm trying to sabotage being nice to me? And why the hell does it feel so shocking to have someone be kind?

"Not her," I say quickly, just as Missy jogs over and drops her bag at the far end of the bench. She winks at me and I turn back to Shamus. "She's not my type."

He nods. "Sure. Okay. Me either."

And I know we're both still thinking about Aster.

* * *

I'm still thinking about Aster when the game wraps up two hours later. We lose, and I notice her absence in right field for reasons that have to do with far more than her fielding ability.

The team goes out for drinks afterward but I bail, blaming an essay I've got due tomorrow. It's an icy, drizzly night, the sidewalks shining with frozen rivulets of water, trees dripping raindrops onto my shoulders with a steady thud.

Instead of walking home I navigate my way through the dark, quiet campus toward Aster's building. I don't know what I'm going to do when I get there—or which floor she lives on—I just let my feet lead me and figure I'll decide the rest when I arrive.

The building lights are warm and welcoming as I approach, a couple of students shivering in front as they come out for one last smoke before bed. I'm itching for a cigarette now, but the memory of Aster's wrinkled nose kills that idea. I'm not even sure I'll get to see her, but if I do, I don't want to smell like an ashtray.

Before I even have time to come up with a plan, I hear my name.

"Aidan?"

I turn to see Aster approaching the building, her arm around the waist of a very inebriated girl.

"Hey," I say, hurrying toward them and helping to relieve some of the girl's weight. "Everything okay?"

Aster grunts. "Obviously not. Help me get her inside, please?"

"Yeah. Of course."

One of the smokers gets the door for us and we squeeze through. Aster jabs the up arrow on the elevator, then looks at me over the girl's slumped head. I'm expecting her to be angry, like she's learned of my part in her pain, but instead she shrugs and makes a "What can you do?" face.

Right. Aster's a resident advisor. She's got other people's problems to deal with in addition to her own.

We get the girl to her room on the tenth floor, where her roommate promises to keep an eye on her and call Aster with any problems. We step into the hall and Aster runs her hands through her damp hair. Her cheeks are flushed pink from the cold and exertion, and though she's wearing the yellow jacket again, she doesn't seem quite as bright as I remember.

"So," I say awkwardly. "How are you?"

She shrugs, trying to look tough. "All right. You?"

"All right." An uncomfortable pause. "I saw Shamus tonight at the game. He said he asked you to play but you were too... depressed."

Her brows raise. "Depressed? Wow. That's a strong word." Then her tough girl image wobbles. "I mean, maybe it's not the *wrong* word…"

I resist the urge to reach out to touch her, to do something, anything, better than what I've already done. "I'm sorry about…everything." If she only knew.

Aster wipes a stray raindrop off the tip of her nose. "It's not your fault. Did you come here to check on me?"

I try not to notice how blue her eyes are beneath her dark lashes, spiky with rain. How pretty she is. But it's fucking impossible. "Maybe?"

"That's nice, but it's not necessary."

"I know. But you brought us chicken soup the other night, and now here you are taking care of drunk students… Who's going to take care of you?"

That'd be her cue to bat her lashes and say, "You can take care of me, Aidan!" but that's not what happens.

"I'll take care of me," she says matter-of-factly, turning to push against the fire door to the stairwell. "Come on. I'm one floor down. Do you want some coffee? Tea? That's really all I can offer. I drank all the wine, but I have a kettle."

"A kettle? I didn't know they treated R.A.'s like queens."

She smirks at me over her shoulder, but I notice the way she's gripping the stair rail, like she's just barely hanging on to her composure.

"This life is nothing if not glamorous." She exits onto the ninth floor and I trail after her into the hallway, finding the same trampled green carpet and white cinderblock walls I left behind.

We pass a couple of students and Aster greets them by name.

39

Though we're third years and they're likely firsts, Aster still seems like their boss, their older sister. I grew up fast; I've felt older than everybody my whole life. We have something in common.

"This is me." Aster unlocks the door to the corner unit and I follow her inside. It's bigger than the other rooms I've seen; a room meant for two being occupied by just one, an R.A. perk. There's a queen bed pushed into the corner, the covers rumpled. A desk, a bar fridge, a wardrobe and a dresser line the walls. It's a typical dorm room, including the recycling bin topped with two empty wine bottles and a garbage can overflowing with candy bar wrappers.

Aster smiles sheepishly. "It's been a rough week." She pats her stomach. "I'm going to stop, I swear."

"Whatever helps."

Her bravado drops for a second. "It's not helping," she admits, lower lip trembling. "It sucks. Have you ever been cheated on?"

"No."

"Ah. Well. Lucky you."

For some reason I have the inane urge to say something in defense of Jerry, even though that's in direct conflict with my plan.

She plugs in the kettle and grabs two mugs off a shelf, setting them on top of the bar fridge. If I'd tried to predict what Aster's room would be like I'd have guessed something light and frivolous, lots of reds and yellows. But this place is strictly functional, books in stacks on the desk, a laptop beside them, an overflowing laundry basket in the corner. There's no artwork, no photographs, no personal touches. The curtains are pulled back to reveal a view of the street and the small copse of trees beside it. It doesn't feel anything like the bright and shiny Aster I expected.

"Have a seat," she says, gesturing to the desk chair. She takes off her coat and hangs it on the doorknob, so I take off mine and drop it on the floor next to my gym bag.

She's wearing a long-sleeve shirt with jeans, the silhouette of her body highlighted by the streetlamps outside. She grabs a hair elastic from the desk just as the kettle starts to bubble, and pulls her damp hair into a ponytail. She doesn't offer coffee again, just puts a teabag into each cup and fills them with water. I can count on one hand the number of times I've had tea before, but I'd drink anything if it gave me an excuse to stay here.

"So." Aster sinks onto her bed and slumps against the wall, cradling the hot mug in her hands. "Life sucks."

"I'm sorry," I say again.

She blows onto the tea, a tiny billow of steam rising. "I never even saw it coming," she admits, chagrined. "Like, I never had a clue. When he told me, I thought he was joking. He kept saying, *Seriously,* and I just couldn't believe it."

"It was out of character," I hear myself say.

"Ha." She scoffs. "If someone cheats, it's not out of character. It's out of line. Out of bounds. Out of the realm of possibility. He's just another guy who looks like one thing but acts like another. I've had enough of that."

"What did you think he would be?"

She arches a brow. "Oh, I don't know. Loyal? Decent? Honest?" She sips her tea and winces at the burn. "Well, I guess he was honest."

"There's that."

"I keep trying to be angry," she says, eyes trailing over my shoulder to the window. "I keep trying to think of ways to get revenge, but…"

No *but*, I think. Get revenge. Fuck somebody.

Fuck me.

"But I'm just so sad," she says, her voice breaking. "Isn't that stupid? I'm so…fucking…sad."

I say *fuck* a lot. I don't even think about it. But hearing the word come out of Aster's mouth, contrasting with the simple clothes and the tea and that composed demeanor, it sets off a chain reaction inside me. Like a line of dominos falling, shattering every illusion I thought I had. Aster is perfect. Aster is sweet. Aster is flawless.

And Aster is human.

"Have your friends been checking on you?"

She shakes her head. "My friends were Jerry's friends. Or rather, his friends became my friends. Now they're just his friends again. They're not mean about it, they're just…gone."

I swallow. "That's rough." I want to ask about the friends she must have had before they met, but it seems mean, given the circumstances.

"At least you're here."

"Well, you were nice to me when you didn't have to be. Bringing the soup and stuff."

"Why wouldn't I be nice?"

"I don't know. Why would you be?"

Something in her gaze softens, pitying and assessing at the same time. Seeing pieces of me she's not supposed to see. And almost as though she recognizes this, sees my armor locking into place, she looks away and grabs a tissue.

"I'm so silly," she says, wiping her nose. "I'm super emotional and I never am. Never used to be, anyway. But here I am, crying over some guy."

"That's normal," I say. "It's…healthy."

Banging a guy for revenge is not.

Screwing someone over to make yourself feel better is not.

When I first saw Aster, I thought she was above me. If Jerry thought she was out of his league, then she's ten million miles out of mine. But seeing her here now, in this plain room in her plain clothes with this gross tea, I don't think she's anything I thought she was.

"Have you ever been skiing?" I ask abruptly.

Her eyebrows pull together in confusion. "What? Skiing? No. Why?"

"Do you read books to blind kids?"

Now she laughs. "What?"

"You just seemed like someone who would. When I first met you."

She laughs louder, like a release valve has been turned, letting out some of the pressure that's been building since Jerry broke her heart.

Since I broke it.

"I guess I was wrong," I say, cursing myself and my stupid judgments.

"Not completely," she says, dabbing at the corner of her eye. "I read to kids at a library a few times, but they didn't have to be blind. Anyone could come."

"You did? Seriously?"

"Yeah," she says. "Do you like me better now?"

I drink my tea to hide my smile. "Yeah," I mumble, trying not to sound too…sincere. Too eager. "I like you just fine."

7

I can't say I've been friends with a girl before. Not *real* friends. Not even "I'm just doing this until she lets me fuck her" friends. But now, somehow, I find myself doing *friendly* things with Aster. Studying at the library, meeting up for lunch, getting groceries.

As *friends*.

Jerry doesn't know about this, of course. Aster wants him to think she's moved on and practically begged me to keep our friendship a secret; I want to keep this on the down low so Jerry doesn't start putting two and two together and realize I'm moving in on his girl.

Tonight we're at the library, sitting opposite each other at a table in the classical literature section, laptops open. I have a paper due at the end of the week and Aster—who's a criminology major, I learned—is reviewing notes for a quiz tomorrow. I'm so wrapped up in my writing that it takes the moans a second to interrupt my thoughts.

I freeze and listen, fingers hovering over the keyboard, and a second later I hear it again: a soft female moan. Of pleasure.

I peek at Aster over my screen. She's hunched over her laptop, just the top of her hair visible.

Another moan.

Not from Aster.

My heart sinks in disappointment even as it grows two sizes when Aster lifts her head and her eyes meet mine.

"Am I imagining that?" she whispers, covering her mouth with her fingers.

Another moan.

"Definitely not," I whisper back. To say I'm disappointed Aster's not sitting across from me with her hand down her pants would be a phenomenal understatement. It's been a whopping ten days since we had tea at her place and if I thought it was painful to lust after her when she had a boyfriend, it's ten times harder to lust after her when she *doesn't* have one. Because now there's no reason we're not fucking except…we're not.

The moans rise in volume and frequency, breaking off with a tiny, stifled yelp that signifies an orgasm. Aster's gaze darts to the long rows of books to our right as a male groan rattles through the room and we twist in our seats to locate the sound.

"Yeah, like that," he murmurs, voice carrying in the otherwise quiet space.

"Fuck," I mutter, dropping my face into my hands.

I haven't hooked up with anyone since I moved in with Jerry a month ago. I might not do commitment, but I'm a one-woman man until I get the girl. Then it's onto the next one. And right now the only girl preoccupying my thoughts is Aster, whose cheeks are flushed as she hears the guy's raspy breathing, the wet sounds of sucking, his guttural encouragements to the girl going down on him.

I think of Sindy.

I think of Jerry.

I look at Aster. She's got her hands steepled in front of her and she's examining her unpainted fingernails. I wonder if this is turning her on. It's turning me on. I wish that was her mouth on my dick, my hands in that silky hair, my voice ordering her to take it.

The guy comes with a satisfied cry, deafening in the quiet library.

I'm so hard it hurts.

I try to swallow but my throat is too tight. I would give anything to fuck Aster right now. Do anything. Say anything.

"I'm not even jealous," she whispers.

I freeze. "What?"

"Of them," she says, pretending not to notice the couple scurrying out of the book stacks ten feet away, still adjusting their clothes. "I don't even wish that was me."

"You...don't?"

"No. Since Jerry told me he, well, you know, I haven't even been tempted. Haven't thought about it."

"Like, at all?" My dick is throbbing and my ego is stinging. We've hung out half a dozen times and she hasn't even thought about fucking me? Hasn't even *contemplated* it? Here I am working out extra and taking care shaving and *she's not noticing?*

"I tried. Shamus asked me out and we had lunch, but I—"

"Wait." This keeps getting worse. "You went out with Shamus?"

"Yeah. And he was so sweet and funny and all I could think was, *It doesn't matter.* People are assholes and I'm just...done."

My eyebrows shoot up to my hairline. "Done with…sex?"

"Yeah. Sex. Love. Everything. What's the point?"

I dart a glance back toward the library hookup spot. "Orgasms?"

Aster sniffles. "Maybe I'm broken. Isn't that stupid? It's not like I've had a wonderful life and nothing bad has ever happened, but this is the first time I didn't see it coming."

I try to forget about my dick and concentrate on what she's saying. "What kind of bad stuff?"

She sighs and shuts her laptop. "It doesn't matter. I guess Jerry was just another lesson I had to learn."

I gather up my things and keep pace as she exits the library, the February night dark and cold. "You need exposure therapy," I say, my breath billowing in front of me in a white cloud.

"Exposure therapy?"

"Yeah. You should be exposed to the thing that scares you, so your brain understands there's nothing to be afraid of."

She stops in her tracks and narrows her eyes at me. "Are you suggesting I watch people have sex?"

I try not to laugh. I also try not to come in my pants at the idea. "No. I'm inviting you to a wedding. It's this weekend, down in Lawrence. Come with me."

"That sounds like an awful idea."

"That's why you should do it. We can confirm whether or not you're really broken."

"Who do you know that's getting married?"

"My friend Brix. From the…" I trail off, but it's too late.

"Bachelor party," Aster says. "Where Jerry cheated on me."

"But back to the wedding," I begin.

Aster's eyes are flashing with anger. "Maybe you should tell your friend Brix that his marriage is destined to end in destruction and failure and his heart will be replaced with a bottomless pit of bile and hatred."

I try not to flinch. "I'll be sure to include that in my toast."

"I really don't think I'm the right person to invite to a wedding, Aidan."

"On the contrary. Every terrifying thing you're saying is exactly the reason you should come. And it's on Valentine's Day—do you really want to be half a mile away from Jerry when you could be in beautiful Lawrence, Washington?"

She finally looks intrigued and not just disgusted. "That's a better reason than exposure therapy."

"Call it whatever you want. The wedding is Saturday afternoon. We'll drive down first thing in the morning and drive home late that night. And maybe by the time we get back, you won't be so depressed and scary."

That earns me a laugh, her smile making her ten times prettier. And even though I'm still the asshole half-responsible for this mess, I also feel like the asshole that just might clean it up.

8

At eight o'clock Saturday morning, I pull up in front of Aster's building and find her waiting with a carry-on suitcase in one hand and a thermos in the other. My original plan was to catch a ride to the wedding with Wes and T.J., but I'd bailed on the idea when Aster agreed to come, opting to rent a car so we could be alone for the trip. And the plan is already worth it. Even in faded jeans and that yellow jacket, she's the prettiest girl I've ever seen, and it's impossible not to smile as she climbs in.

"Good morning," she says as I pull away from the curb.

"Is it? Or is it a bile and revenged-filled morning?"

She smirks and sips her drink. "Well, it's still early."

"How's your week been?" I take the turn off campus for the freeway, and a few minutes later we're on our way to Lawrence. The day is cold but sunny, the roads clear and quiet.

Aster tells me about a girl who tried to prank her ex-boyfriend by using a fan to blow flour under his door, but accidentally got her hair caught in the fan and tried to run away with it still attached to her head. There's another story about a drunk kid who came home, forgot where he lived, and tried every door on

50

three floors until campus police got thirty-seven reports of attempted break-ins and came to catch the would-be bandit.

I listen as she talks, her story-telling funny and wry. She takes her job seriously but not too seriously; she cares, but not in a motherly way. More like she's been down some of those roads and she wants to point kids in a better direction.

"You remember the other night?" I ask, switching the radio station when it turns to static.

Aster sips her coffee. "Which night?"

"The one where you said you hadn't had a wonderful life, bad things had happened."

She's quiet for a second. "I didn't say bad things happened."

"You sure?"

She gnaws on her lip. "I just meant I'm too old to be naïve. So a guy's an asshole. I shouldn't be surprised. He was too good to be true, anyway."

"How so?"

"You first."

"What do you mean?"

"Asking me to tell you about Jerry is like asking me to tell you I had a winning lottery ticket and I lost it. So you go first. Tell me something painful and embarrassing about yourself."

"I don't buy lottery tickets."

She's not impressed. "Uh-huh."

My free pass to Holsom comes pretty close to winning the lottery, but even though I'm not the most impassioned student, there's nothing I wouldn't do to keep it. Still, I'm not about to tell Aster about my shitty upbringing and my even shittier life choices. I didn't have amazing parents, but they tried. There's a large period in my life where I didn't try at all, and that's nobody's fault but mine. That's what the judge said. It was up to me to make better choices—could I?

I peek at Aster.

The judge would not approve of this.

"Um…" I clear my throat. "I'm afraid of the water. I fell into a pond once, trying to retrieve a tennis ball, and nearly drowned."

She frowns at me. "How's that painful and embarrassing? Did it happen last week?"

"No, I was five."

"Then it doesn't count. Try again."

I rack my brain, trying to think of something I can actually admit to. "I've been sprayed by a skunk," I announce.

Aster turns in her seat. "What?"

"Yeah. Worst fucking thing."

"What happened?"

I sigh and rub the back of my neck, remembering. "I had a, uh, job interview later that day…" It was an assignment to steal my first car, but she doesn't need to know that, "…and I had a bunch of nervous energy, so I went for a run. I had my music on, wasn't paying attention, and at the last second I saw this skunk scurrying across the path, three little baby skunks in front of her. I came to a halt but it was too late—she turned tail and sprayed me. Horribly. Intensely. It was awful. If you could die from a smell, I'd be dead."

Aster's laughing her head off. "What about the interview? Did you go?"

I grimace. "Yeah. I went. I read online that tomato juice helps with the smell, so I bought a dozen tins of juice, filled the tub, and sat in there for an hour. It didn't help at all. I had a red tinge when I went to the interview, which lasted all of two minutes."

That part's true, too. Teddy covered his face and told me I stank, then gave me a piece of paper with the car information, told me to bring it to the garage in twelve hours, and instructed me to start wearing deodorant. He didn't buy my skunk story.

"So you didn't get the job?" Aster guesses.

"No," I lie. "I didn't get it."

"Poor you."

"Yeah." I wait for lightning to strike me dead. "Poor me."

We drive in silence for a minute, and I know Aster's thinking she might get away with not answering the question. I consider giving her the out, but after another thirty seconds I say, "Your turn. I showed you mine; you show me yours."

She huffs, then sighs in resignation. "Jerry never did anything wrong," she says, picking at a spot on her jeans. "Like, really never did. And it wasn't even annoying. He was just *so* good. He was always on time. Always called when he said he would, or if he was going to be late. He picked nice restaurants and let me decide what movies to watch. When we first met I had a sore neck because I'd been sleeping in a lumpy bed all summer, and when he learned about it he bought me one of those foam things for my mattress and a special pillow."

"He just wanted to get into your bed."

She shrugs. "At least my neck stopped hurting."

"So he's punctual and generous. That's not unheard of." I can be punctual and generous, if that's all it takes.

"Imagine if you'd gone to that job interview, and it was a job on Wall Street that was going to pay you a million dollars a year," she says. "And you walked in smelling like ass and they shook your hand and hired you anyway. That's unheard of."

"That's different," I argue. "You don't smell like ass. Any guy would want you. Jerry's not remarkable, he's *alive.*"

Aster arranges her empty cup in the holder between us, stalling before she answers. "He was special to me," she says softly.

My heart twists in my chest. One day in second grade I came home from school and didn't see our dog tied up on the porch like normal. When I asked my dad where she was, he didn't bother to lie and say she ran away, he said he gave her to someone as collateral on a loan he'd taken out. When he paid it back, we'd get the dog back.

I had to see another family walking Daisy around town for the next eight years.

So I know how Aster feels. And now I know how my dad felt when I sobbed myself to sleep, punished for someone else's bad judgment and selfishness.

"How old are you?" I ask, changing the subject.

She lets me. "Twenty-one. You?"

"Twenty-two. I worked for a year before I came here." I'd actually been on parole and not allowed to leave the state of Oregon, where I grew up, but close enough. "Point is, you're young. And if you want to work on Wall Street, there's someone out there who'll hire you."

"I don't want to work on Wall Street."

"I know. What do you want to do?"

"I want to be a divorce lawyer."

I assume she's kidding, then sober when I realize she's serious. "Oh—really?"

"Yep."

"Are your parents married?"

She slants me a look that says the topic's off limits. "No. Yours?"

I give her a look that says the answer may be different, but the unpleasantness is the same. "Yep."

Her lips quirk and she peers through the windshield. "Great day for a wedding."

9

The wedding venue is a small white clapboard church two blocks from the beach. The day is absolutely freezing, icy sea water adding a damp chill to the air and filling my lungs with cold.

"Eek," Aster squeals, fishing her bag out of the backseat and jogging in place as she waits for me to grab my things from the trunk. "How do you know when you have hypothermia?"

I shudder, tasting salt on my tongue when I inhale. "Let's go."

We hustle to the quaint building, a cutesy sandwich board propped out front to advertise the Lewiston-Hershey wedding, and pass through the double doors into a foyer with a table set up with a guest book for signing. I scribble my name but Aster declines, saying she doesn't really belong here.

"It's probably better you don't write anything," I say, putting down the pen. "You'd probably frighten the other guests."

She's gorgeous when she smiles, no trace of whatever shadows I'd glimpsed in the car.

"Shaw!" a deep voice booms.

I turn to see Wes approaching, already in his dress pants and white shirt, collar unbuttoned. He's Brix's best man and they arrived last night to get things ready for today.

"Hey, man."

We hug, then he turns to Aster expectantly.

"This is my friend," I say. "Wes, meet Aster. Aster, meet Wes."

"Nice to meet you," Aster says, shaking his hand.

"You too." The look he gives me implies I will be grilled about this later.

"There's a waiting room just down the hall," he says, pointing. "We've got some snacks and stuff. Wedding starts in an hour, so if you want to relax, you can do it there. Take your time, get dressed, and we'll call you out when we're ready."

"Thanks. Will do."

He studies Aster one last time before returning to the chapel to continue preparing.

"Shall we?" I lead the way to the waiting area, where T.J. and a few other friends are already hanging out. In suits and ties and holding dainty glasses of champagne, they're hard to recognize as the guys I saw at Bender a few weeks ago.

I make the introductions, and everyone looks at Aster and looks at me, then looks at each other. It's not just that she's so obviously *better* than us, it's that I keep calling her my *friend*. They know "friend" is usually code for "I'm working on her," but she's not the kind of girl I've "worked on" before, so they're confused. So am I, if I'm being honest.

"I'm confused," T.J. whispers when Aster leaves to get changed. "Is she really your friend?"

"She is."

"But…why?"

I scowl at him. "Why wouldn't she be?"

"Because you're you?"

That's a fair point, but it still stings. "She doesn't know much about me," I admit. Some girls might judge me for being at Holsom as part of this type of scholarship program—hell, some girls might be turned on by it—but I meant it when I promised the judge I'd make a fresh start at Holsom, and I can't do that if I keep dredging up the past.

Wes and Brix rush in and swivel around, searching for something. "I heard you brought a *friend,*" Brix says. "Where is she?"

I glare at Wes. "Really?"

"Is she a parole officer?" he asks. "Undercover cop? Bodyguard?"

"None of the above. She's a student and she's my friend."

"You don't have female friends."

"I could totally—" I can't finish the lie. "Well, I do now."

"How long have you been working on her?" Wes asks.

"I've *known her* about six weeks," I say. "And I'm not working anything. She's just…"

Everyone's jaws drop and they gawk over my shoulder, instantly forgetting me. I turn to see what they see: Aster, in a fitted knee-length black dress with a plunging neckline, shiny red heels, and lipstick to match. Aster, who's breathtaking in jeans and a T-shirt, now looking like a million-fucking-dollars.

"Whoa," Wes whispers.

Brix is the first to break the silence, stepping forward with his hand outstretched. "Hi," he says. "We haven't met. I'm Brix. I'm the one getting married."

"Nice to meet you," Aster says, fixing him with that perfect smile. "I'm Aster. Aidan's friend."

"Aidan," Brix repeats with emphasis. "Aidan's *friend.*"

"That's right."

"Ahem." I intervene, prying Brix's hand out of hers. "None of these guys have actual friends," I explain. "They don't know how to act around normal people."

Her mouth quirks. "I'm used to it."

She wears a long, fine gold necklace that dips into her spectacular cleavage and it is killing me not to reach out a hand and follow that sparkling chain to God knows where.

"Let's go take our seats," T.J. says. "Someone in this room has found a woman who thinks she can tolerate him. I'm talking about Brix, of course."

"Ass," Brix says, punching T.J. in the kidney.

"Ass," I second, punching him in the arm.

T.J. yelps and scurries out.

"I should have told you they were immature," I tell Aster as we follow them into the chapel.

"That's okay," she says. "I can handle myself."

* * *

The wedding goes smoothly, everyone behaves, no one objects, and thirty minutes later we're on our feet, applauding as Brix and his new bride stroll down the short aisle, hand-in-hand and grinning ear-to-ear.

I met Brix on my second day at Holsom, and in three years I've never seen him as happy as he is now. I'm not quite as poisoned against the thought of love and marriage as Aster, but

I still think they're too young to make such a big commitment. Still, their happiness is contagious and everyone in the room is infected.

Wes and T.J. are happy because there are a couple of cute—and single—bridesmaids waiting to dance with them at the reception, and even marriage-is-a-death-knell Aster wipes tears from her eyes.

"Are those happy tears?" I whisper as we file out. "Because if you start with the fire and brimstone routine, I'm going to deny being the one who brought you."

"I'm fine," she whispers back. "But I'll be even more fine when I get some lunch."

"I hear you. I'm about to pass out."

The reception hall is across the street, forty frigid steps that have everyone shivering when we hustle inside. The wedding party is small, about thirty people, and we're all famished as we take our seats and wait impatiently as the serving staff come around with baskets of bread and starter salads.

If someone had told me three years ago I'd be at any event with Brix where there were starter salads, I'd have laughed in their face. Now I grab my fork and dig in.

"Ohmygodbread," Aster mumbles, slathering a piece with butter and shoving it in her mouth.

I chuckle around a mouthful of lettuce. "There's more food coming."

We'd stopped for donuts and coffee at the halfway mark, figuring lunch would ruin the wedding meal, but that was clearly the wrong call. Fortunately everyone seems to be in the same boat and they save the speeches until we've all inhaled our appetizers and calmed our raging stomachs.

Wes gives a funny and raunchy toast, then Brix's parents say a few words, then the bride's. I don't know much about Brix's new wife, but every time she looks at Brix there's love in her eyes, and I wonder if that's what Jerry lost. If Aster made him feel the way Brix looks now, and I took that away.

If that's how Jerry made Aster feel.

Maybe I've made a huge mistake. It's not that I don't want Aster, but maybe sex can't replace what I've stolen. I'm not going to love her like Jerry did; I'm not a job on Wall Street, I'm not a winning lottery ticket. I'm just a guy who wants to fuck her, not much different from every other guy who looks at her.

The food I'm chewing turns to sawdust in my mouth and I wash it down with the remnants of the champagne we'd used for our toasts. I'm driving us home later so this is the only alcohol I'll have, and when I hear the cheesy wedding songs start to play, I know it's not going to be enough to get me on the dance floor.

They introduce the bride and groom and the happy couple takes center stage for an endless slow dance that starts out romantic and goes on forever. The women in the room gaze at them adoringly, but Aster's focused on cutting her prime rib.

"Does this song ever end?" she mutters out the corner of her mouth.

"It's been at least eight minutes," I reply, chewing on a piece of steamed broccoli.

As though the deejay can hear us, the song wraps up and everyone applauds. Half the room sweeps onto the dance floor as a faster song comes on, and Aster pushes away her plate and downs the last of her champagne.

"Let's dance," she says. "We've been sitting all day."

"I don't dance."

"What?"

"I don't dance."

"Come on, Aidan. You're not going to make me go out there all alone, are you?"

"Come with us!" the bridesmaids squeal, rushing up with more champagne.

Aster takes a glass and shoots me a disapproving look. "I'd love to."

They squeeze onto the tiny dance floor, writhing like they're way drunker than they are. There are three servers carrying trays of champagne, and the girls commandeer one guy to be their personal waiter, stationing him at the edge of the floor, ready with constant refills.

This is a side of Aster I haven't seen. The one that gets tipsy and shakes her ass and shimmies in ways that should be illegal. The one that forgets it's Valentine's Day and her heart's broken.

"There's more to this story," Wes says, sliding into Aster's empty seat as T.J. takes the one opposite. "Spill."

I sip my water calmly. "There's nothing to say. She's been going through a hard time. I thought a road trip might help take her mind off things."

"Are you that hard thing?" T.J. asks shrewdly.

I watch Aster spin in a circle, hands above her head. The gold chain floats in the air and nestles back between her breasts, making me jealous. "I wish," I admit. "But not yet."

"How much not yet?" Wes demands.

"Not at all not yet."

"Is today the day?"

"Who knows?" I say, like it's no big deal and I can wait forever. "What happens, happens."

We all look at her, toasting the bridesmaids with their umpteenth glass of champagne, giggling and happy. It's Valentine's Day. Love is in the air. The alcohol is paid for. Maybe today could be the day.

But though we've talked about women before, shared sex stories and sex secrets, I don't want to talk about Aster like that. Especially when I know she's just recently been betrayed—and that I'm the one responsible, even if she doesn't know it. I started this whole ball rolling with a clear plan in mind—fuck Aster— but the more time I spend with her, the less solid the plan becomes, slowly morphing into something I can't identify and don't have a name for.

10

"I can't believe this is happening," I mutter six hours later. It's ten o'clock and we're halfway between Lawrence and home, and squarely in the middle of butt fuck nowhere. It's pitch black and freezing and the rental car has been making alarming noises for the past five miles. Aster's phone says we're just a mile from the nearest town, though I can't see any lights—or hope—on the horizon.

We sputter to a stop on the shoulder of the empty two-lane road, no street lights or signs of civilization in sight.

"Uh-oh." Aster hiccups and giggles. She swears she's just tipsy, but she's drunk. Too drunk to change out of her dress but too drunk to wear her heels, so she's sitting beside me in her party dress, sneakers, and puffy yellow jacket.

"You know anything about cars?" I ask. I know how to pop the locks, break the windows, and hot wire them. I don't know how to fix an engine.

"Nope." Another hiccup. "Did you get insurance when you rented this? Can we call AAA?"

"Yeah, but who knows how long it'll take to get someone out here. Wherever we are."

"Oh well. It's Saturday. If we get home late, who cares?"

"I care," I snap. "We can't just sit out here on the side of the road, hoping someone shows up to help." She flinches at the raised tone and I exhale. "Sorry. I just don't like being helpless."

"You're not helpless," she says calmly. "I'll help you." Her words are a little slurred, but she holds up her phone, calls AAA, and requests roadside assistance. "Okay," she says. "Okay, yes, thank you. Goodbye." She turns to me. "It'll be seven hours."

"What?"

"Just kidding. There's a town up ahead, they'll send someone to collect us."

"What about the car?"

"The town doesn't have a rental office, so they'll tow it to the garage and the mechanic will work on it tomorrow."

I grip the wheel, watching the tattoos on my knuckles darken against the blanched skin. *Ride hard.* Or not at all, apparently. "We're stuck here?"

"We'll be stuck in a hotel room," she clarifies. "With running water and lights and other people. Totally not helpless."

I force myself to relax my hands. Growing up, I lost count of the number of times we had to sleep in our car because my dad had lost our house or pissed someone off so bad it wasn't safe to sleep at home. At first I thought it was a big adventure. Then I learned the truth.

"What did your friends mean when they said you were working on me?" Aster asks abruptly. It's hard to see her face in the dim interior light, but she sounds more alert, a little less inebriated.

I don't pretend not to know what she's talking about; I

65

thought she might have overheard us when she came out of the changing room. "I told them you were having a hard time," I reply. "And I was working on cheering you up."

"Oh," she says, too trusting. "That's nice of you."

"I'm a nice guy, remember?"

"There are no nice guys, remember?"

"Uh-oh—dark and angry Aster is back."

"Not dark and angry, Aidan. Just...aware."

If Aster were as aware as she thinks she is, she'd know I've been semi-hard this whole day. She'd know that the slightest indication, a hint of permission, and I'd have her bent over the nearest flat surface, making her aware of a whole host of other things.

But she's not aware, because she's only met one real asshole in her life, and she thinks his name is Jerry.

Headlights approach and slow, and we spend the next thirty minutes in the company of a tow truck driver named Fred who drives us down the road to the tiny town of Hamlet and its even tinier motel. By now it's nearly eleven o'clock and all the residents of Hamlet have gone to bed. Businesses are closed and sidewalks are empty. There's an elderly lady stationed at the front desk of the motel and she puts down her crossword puzzle when we walk in, delighted to have company.

Aster tries to pay for the room but I push away her credit card and hand over mine, ignoring her offer to pay for half. We don't discuss if we should get two rooms, and it's only when we unlock the door to our street-facing unit that I realize we've been given a single, with just a queen bed to share.

If Aster had hesitated or looked uneasy, I swear I would have gone back up front and asked for something different, but her footsteps don't falter. She strolls into the room, parks her suitcase in the corner, and flops onto the mattress. "Oh God," she moans. "That feels good. Anything that's not in a car feels amazing."

I turn my back and spend way too long locking the door and hooking the chain. As though the real threats here are the ones outside this room. I simply can't see Aster, half-drunk, sprawled on a bed and moaning. I'm human. It's too fucking much.

I steel myself, then shrug out of my coat, holding it in front of my crotch when I turn back around. Aster sat up and dumped her coat on the floor, and now she's sitting on the edge of the bed, bent over as she unties her shoelaces. This gives me a ridiculous view of her cleavage surrounded by hanks of shiny hair, and my dick pleads with me to proposition her. To at least *try*.

But something stops me.

"I'm going to take a shower," I say, striding past her to the dingy bathroom. I shut the door and turn on the water to drown out any more moans—any Aster sounds at all—then strip out of my clothes and step under the spray. There's a bottle of complimentary shampoo and a tiny bar of soap, and I take my time with each, leaving the water ten degrees colder than is comfortable to try to forget how long it's been since I've had sex.

It doesn't help. After a while I abandon my noble intentions, warm up the water, and wrap a slippery hand around my cock. I brace my forearm against the wall and watch as I stroke myself. I think about the couple from the library, the guy's moans as his girlfriend sucked him off. I picture Aster on her knees in front of me, her hair wet, her cheeks flushed, lips stretched wide.

I turn my face into my bicep and groan into my skin as I come, spurting into my palm. Eventually my shoulders slump and I can breathe normally again. I clean up and get out, belatedly hoping Aster wasn't planning to take a shower since there's definitely no hot water left.

I dry off and pull on my boxers and the T-shirt I had on earlier, then step into the dim room. The only light comes from the ancient television, an old episode of *Gilligan's Island* playing. Aster's tucked under the striped comforter, propped against two pillows.

"Hey," she says, yawning. "Feel better?"

I toss my clothes onto a chair. "Yeah." One of my socks lands on the floor and when I bend to scoop it up I notice Aster's dress is there. On the chair. Not...on her body. My hormones immediately betray me, blood rushing south, balls tightening. Oh fuck. She can't be...

I peek in the mirror and see her shoulders and head sticking out from under the covers. And then I see she's wearing the T-shirt she had on this morning, and I can only pray she's got her jeans on, too.

The room is chilly, an antique radiator rattling away near the door, probably seeing its first action in years. It's generating noise but not heat, and when I approach the bed Aster flips back the covers for me, revealing two things: there's only a comforter and a flat sheet, and her long, bare legs.

My prayers have not been answered.

"I'll, just, um, sleep under the comforter," I say, smoothing the sheet back down against the lumpy mattress, a flimsy barricade. I slide in under the itchy old blanket, inhaling the competing smells of dust and mothballs.

"Fragrant," I mutter.

"It's called 'local flavor,'" Aster says.

I adjust my pillows so I can see the television. The fitted sheet isn't doing shit to keep me from feeling Aster beside me. She could be ten feet away and I'd still know exactly where she was and what she was doing. Her whole body shakes when she laughs, and the hairs on my arms stand on end when she yawns, a feathery, feminine sound that feels far too intimate.

She curls onto her side facing me, hugging her pillow under her cheek and laughing at Gilligan as I try to ignore the curve of her ass against the blankets.

I bend the leg that's closest to her and use my other hand to adjust my aching cock. If I take another shower, she'll get suspicious. If I lie down flat, she'll see the bulge at my crotch. I'll have to stay like this until she falls asleep, then slip back into the bathroom to jerk off again, like a fucking twelve-year-old.

"Hey, Aidan?" Aster's sleepy voice makes my fingers curl around my cock, hard enough I grit my teeth.

"What's up?"

"Do you want…?" She breaks off to yawn, muffling the sound with her fingers. "Do you want to leave a bit later tomorrow? So we can sleep in?"

I want a lot of things, but spending more time in a bed with Aster in which we are not fucking is not one of them. "Let's leave around ten. I've got stuff to do when I get home."

She props herself up on one elbow, and for a split second I think maybe my dreams are about to come true. That maybe she's going to reach over here and cover my cock with her hand and say, *You've got stuff to do right now, big boy.*

But of course my dreams don't come true. They never do.

She frowns. "Are you okay?"

"Yeah," I lie. "Just tired."

She leans past me to check the time on the alarm clock that sits on the cheap nightstand, alongside the requisite Bible and town map.

"Figures," she says. "It's after midnight and it's been a long day."

"Yep."

"Hey, you know what?"

"What's that, Aster?"

"It's Sunday."

"So?"

"That means it's not Valentine's Day anymore." She smiles at me as she lies back down and closes her eyes, the rest of her words mumbled. "I forgot all about it. Your plan worked."

My cock jerks in my hand. The plan has *not* fucking worked.

She sighs and snuggles into the bed, already drifting off, totally, blissfully, unaware. "Thank you, Aidan."

I turn off the television so the room is dark, then get out of bed and beeline it for the bathroom. "You're welcome, Aster."

11

The following Friday I'm eating a bowl of cereal on the couch when Jerry comes out of his room dressed like a park ranger. He's got the hat, the boots, and the overstuffed pack. There's even a canteen hanging from his belt. He comes closer and I can smell the *new* radiating off his clothes.

I almost choke on my cereal. "What are you doing?"

"I'm going on a camping trip," he says proudly.

"Er...now?"

I know Jerry has Fridays off because he normally spends them right here studying, but it's not even nine o'clock in the morning, and Jerry is not a seasoned camper. Jerry is, at best, a glamper. Glamorous camping. The kind where someone else pitches the tent and builds the fire and cooks you a gourmet meal.

"I signed up for a program to help at-risk youth learn real-life survival skills," he says, sounding like he's reciting lines from a brochure. "I've been reading up on it all week."

"You've been reading about survival?"

"Yep."

"What, uh, what brought this on?" I finish my cereal and do

my very best not to look incredulous.

"You know," he says, as though I should know.

"I do?"

"Aster!"

"She's forcing you to camp?"

He adjusts his canteen. "Of course not. She has no idea. But after what I did, I took stock of my life and saw that I've been very selfish. I have a lot, Aidan, and that means I have a lot to give. And a lot to give back. So I researched some local volunteer programs and this one had an opening."

"Did you tell them you had survival experience?"

He falters. "Maybe."

"*Do* you have survival experience?"

He laughs awkwardly. "I've made it this far, haven't I?"

I peer down the hall. He's made it sixteen feet.

"Jerry, if you're hoping Aster will forgive you for what happened, I'm not sure this is the best way to go about it."

"This isn't for Aster," he explains. "It's *because of* Aster. There's no way she's taking me back. You know that saying, forgive and forget?"

"Yeah?"

"Well, Aster doesn't. She either doesn't know the saying, or she doesn't know how to forgive and forget. Whichever one is irrelevant. I'm dead to her. She told me so herself."

"When?" The last time I heard them talking was the night of the break up and all Aster did was cry and tell him to shut up.

"When she gave me back the things I'd left at her place. Or, what was left of them. They were mostly just ashes."

"She—"

"Anyway, I have to get going. Wish me luck!"

He sounds like a court jester as he walks, buttons and hooks and pieces jangling on his vest.

"Good luck, Jerry," I say, thinking it might be the last time I ever see him and adding another weight to my guilty conscience.

* * *

I'm still thinking about what Jerry said during my shift at the library later that afternoon. I'm obsessing over it, actually. I can't picture Aster telling someone they're dead to her, and I really can't see her giving someone a box of ashes. That image doesn't gel with the woman in the car, the one still feeling the sad but pragmatic about the end of her relationship.

It doesn't help that I haven't seen or spoken to her since we got back on Sunday. The car was repaired, we made the rest of the trip, she thanked me for inviting her and said she had a good time, then…nothing.

When I hadn't heard from her by Wednesday I'd texted to ask what she was up to, but no reply. On Thursday I invited her to Frisbee baseball, but she said she was busy. Shamus told me he'd asked her too and had gotten the same response.

I'm trying not to stew about it. I don't want to be a guy who can't go a week without seeing a girl. I don't even know how she went from being somebody I really wanted to fuck to someone I really want to see. And still fuck.

But my efforts have failed me. Every blonde head is Aster's, every sweet laugh makes me crane my neck to find the source. Hell, every time I pass the Jewish deli and see their chicken soup, I think about her.

"Hey, Aidan."

I've been aimlessly pushing around a cart of returned books, and now I stop and see Missy smiling at me, a pink backpack slung over one shoulder. Missy's the super pretty southern queen bee-type, with curled blond hair and outfits so coordinated she must have someone help her get dressed every morning. In direct contrast with the flawless appearance is her killer ability on the Frisbee baseball field. She's the fiercest competitor I've ever seen.

"Hey, Missy. How are you?"

"Good. Just finished a mountain of reading and now I'm wiped out."

"It's good you got it done."

"I could really use a drink," she says, smiling at me. "What time does your shift end?"

"Not for a while." I've turned down Missy lots of times before, but she doesn't really seem to care. And I've never really cared, either. Except my long-neglected dick is noticing how hot she is in her red pea coat and knee-high boots and demanding to know why I'm not just taking what's on offer.

"When's a while?" she presses, like she can hear my body's plea and is willing to help out. "I can come back. I live nearby. Or…you could come over when you're done."

"Tonight's no good," I hear myself say, my brain overriding my dick for once. This is, after all, exactly what got Jerry in trouble.

"Aw." She pouts for a second, then brightens. "Well, maybe tomorrow."

"Tomorrow?"

"The makeup games? Shamus talked about them last night and you said you'd be there…?"

I shake my head. "Right, the games. Of course. I'll be there." They've been in the schedule for a while, and Shamus had reminded us of them yesterday. He'd just done it right after telling me he'd spoken to Aster and my brain had gotten so stuck on the image of the two of them together that I'd forgotten to pay attention to anything else he said.

Missy adjusts her backpack and winks at me. "Okay, I'll see you then. You can't resist me forever."

12

"What are you doing here?"

Aster glances up from where she's crouched on the gym floor, tying her laces. "I'm playing with you guys today. Shamus invited me."

She ties a double knot and stands, the blue of her eyes made more intense by her blue tank top. Something weird passes between us, a tension that's never been there before, then she blinks and it's gone.

"I've missed you," she says. "A week is a long time."

"I texted you," I blurt out. "You didn't reply."

She rubs a hand over her face. "I know. I'm sorry."

"What's going on?"

She scans the gym, players from earlier games collecting their gear and shuffling out as new people arrive. "It's so embarrassing," she mumbles.

"What is?" I drop my bag on the bench and pull off my hoodie, tugging on the team's white mesh jersey over my T-shirt. I'm desperately curious to know what's embarrassing, but I'm equally embarrassed to feel that way so I try to play it cool.

"Hang on," Aster says, zeroing in on my bicep. Normally when girls check out my arms it's to comment on any one of my stupid tattoos, but I remember too late that there's a new addition to the display. "Is that a *nicotine patch?*"

"Ah…" My face heats. It shouldn't make me blush to admit I'm trying to quit smoking, but the idea that it's so obviously for *her* makes it mortifying.

"That's great!" Aster exclaims. "Good for you."

I try to act nonchalant. "It's not a big deal, stop trying to change the subject. What's this embarrassing thing that's kept you away all week?"

She blows out a breath. "After we got home on Sunday, I went into my room and just looked at it. Like, really looked, Aidan."

"Okay…?" I've seen Aster's room. It's just a room. A little sparse, but not offensive.

"It was disgusting! That's not who I am. It's not who I want to be. Wine bottles and candy bar wrappers and dirty laundry… You were right when you called me dark and angry and depressed. It was pathetic. So I decided to clean up."

Something about this doesn't ring true. Doesn't *feel* quite right, like the image of Aster giving Jerry a box of burnt belongings. "And that took all week?"

She groans. "You have no idea. Every time I thought something would be easy, it was impossible. We only have three washing machines for the whole building, and two were out of service. I kept trying to take out the recycling when the floor was quiet so no one would see how much I'd been drinking, but the second I stepped into the hall someone would need something.

And then…" She pinches the bridge of her nose. "Then I tried to put on my favorite pair of jeans and they were *tight.*"

"Er…tight?"

"Yeah. Like, stop-subsisting-on-alcohol-and-candy-bars tight. It was awful."

I look at her from head to toe. She's wearing the mesh jersey over a tank top and the black tights from last time. She's hot, plain and simple. Except, not plain and not simple. Just hot.

"Something's wrong with the pants," I say decisively. "Because there's nothing wrong with you. Turn around, let me check."

She swats away my hand when I pretend to spin her. "Maybe I should have called you immediately after the denim debacle. I spent the whole night reading up on diet plans and the next day I went for a run."

"That's good. I mean, the running. You don't need to diet."

"No, the running was not good. I was sore for two days after. It was painful and embarrassing. Your skunk story has nothing on my week."

"Are you feeling better now, at least? Is your room clean?"

"I feel so much better, Aidan. Thank you for inviting me to the wedding. Getting away from here gave me some perspective and reminded me that there are good things in life. And good people." She smiles at me and I swear I feel it start at my toes, spreading warmth to every part of me. And not just the perverted parts, either.

"I'm glad to hear it."

"And I'm glad to report it. I owe you."

My perverted parts come back to life at the thought of Aster owing me something. Especially if she's no longer heartbroken Aster but an Aster that's ready for a rebound fling. *Fling.* Not just a fuck. I want to hang out with her some more, have fun, have sex. Nothing serious, but maybe not quite as un-serious as I'd originally intended.

"So is it hard?"

The question interrupts my thoughts. "Ah, what now?"

Aster's pulling her hair into a stubby ponytail and the way her arms are extended makes her breasts thrust out and I actually am getting kind of hard.

"Not smoking," she says. "How's it going?"

"Oh, that. It's going all right. I mostly just smoke when I'm stressed, so…"

Aster bends up one leg to stretch her hamstring, and her breasts jut out again.

I look away. "It's not hard at all," I lie.

* * *

"That was fun," Aster says, two games of Frisbee baseball and one round of beer later.

It's only six o'clock in the evening but it's dark and cold, the afternoon rain still shining on the sidewalks.

"I'm glad you came," I say. "I was starting to worry about you."

"Why? What did you think I was doing?"

"I don't know," I say, because I can't think of anything better. "I just wanted to see you."

She smiles before facing forward again. "This year has been crazy," she admits. "Two months ago I'd never even met you, and now you're practically my best friend."

"*I* am? Really?" I have friends. I don't think I've had a *best* friend since I was six years old, but the idea's not off-putting. It'd be better if Aster knew the real me, though. Then again, maybe not. Maybe then we wouldn't be friends at all.

"Well, not in a desperate, I-literally-have-no-other-alternative kind of way," she quickly clarifies. "Just in an... unexpected way."

I've never been relegated to the Friend Zone before, but I can sense we're getting close. And I'm all for waiting until her broken heart is mended and she's ready to move on, but I'm not on board with helping her recover then being the "best friend" who watches her move on with someone else. "Hey, I—"

"Oh!" she says. "I almost forgot."

"Forgot what?"

"That I owe you! I'm on chaperone duty tonight, but are you free tomorrow?"

I get that weird feeling again. I've never known a girl well enough to get a "feeling" about her, but maybe what I'm reading is Aster sensing that I was about to get a little too serious about things and she wants me to back off.

So I do. "I could be free."

"Okay, good. Meet me right here at two o'clock."

"For what?"

"It's a surprise."

"Aster, I don't like surprises."

She grins. "I think you'll like this one."

13

"I don't like this at all," I say, standing in my new swim trunks at the edge of the campus pool. I try not to shiver like an idiot, but staring at the smooth water, the tiled pool bottom deceptively close, I'm terrified. Almost as terrified as I was twenty minutes ago when I met Aster at her building and she gave me these new trunks and said we were going swimming.

The pool is enormous and we're at the shallow end in the corner. The two lanes on the far side are occupied with guys swimming laps, but otherwise the cavernous room is empty. It's just those guys, me, Aster, and my overwhelming fear of the water.

More overwhelming, however, is the sight of Aster in a bathing suit. It's just a plain black one-piece, but on her, a garbage bag would look amazing. It's cut low enough that I can see more cleavage than I ever have, and it's beautiful. The view is only improved by the droplets of water that cling to her skin, courtesy of the showers we're required to take before entering the pool area.

"Come on," Aster says, descending three steps, the water

hitting her mid-thigh. I try not to ogle her ass as it beckons me to follow, even more commanding than her voice. "You'll be fine."

"Remind me why we're here again?" I grip the metal rail like a lifeline and put my foot on the top step, resisting the urge to flee as the water slithers around my ankles.

"Because you helped me," she says, "and now I'm helping you."

"You know what would really be helpful?"

She peers at me over her shoulder and arches a brow. "Exposure therapy?"

If this were a porno, that'd be Aster's cue to peel down her swimsuit and let me see the tits I've been dreaming about for two months. But it's not a porno and this is Aster, so she's talking about actual exposure therapy and keeping all her clothes on.

"I never should have helped you," I mutter, squeezing the rail with both hands and descending another step. The lukewarm water is halfway up my calf, and I have goose bumps everywhere.

Aster pushes off, swims a few feet, then turns back around. When she stands, the water stops just below her breasts.

"One more step," she says. "You can do it."

"But why would I?"

She ignores the question. "Tell me about your tattoos."

"I don't want to." I actually don't. I started getting them when I was fifteen, just for something to do. They represent stupidity and rebellion, not art and passion. None of them have any special meaning; none are particularly lovely. They're just scars that I paid for. Now seventy percent of my arms and back are covered, the one part of my past I can't erase.

"Who's Daisy?"

I halt on the third stair. "What?"

"The tattoo on your side," she says, coming closer. She extends an arm toward me, fingers settling above my hip bone, tracing the crudely drawn daisy inked there. The white petals and yellow center are faded now, but five of the petals hold a letter, spelling out *Daisy* in capitals. I shiver when she touches me, her thumb stroking over the sensitive skin. "Who's Daisy?" she repeats.

"Um…" I hastily descend the last two steps, plunging my lower half under the water so Aster can't see the effect her touch has on me. "It was my dog," I say, something I never tell anyone. I don't tell them because I don't want to admit we lost her to pay off a debt, the way we lost everything. The way I learned that no matter how much my dad loved us, he couldn't stop hurting us. That just because you want something doesn't mean you can have it.

"You had a dog named Daisy?" The laughter in her voice eases some of the tightness in my chest, though I don't know if it's due to sadness from thinking about the dog or a heart attack from being this deep in the water.

"I used to watch *Dukes of Hazzard* reruns. I liked Daisy." That's what I told everyone when I named her. The truth is, for years I thought the cornflowers in the field behind our house were blue daisies, and because I loved them, I picked the same name for our dog.

"Of course you did." She extends a hand and I fold my fingers in hers and let her pull me in just a little bit deeper.

"Did you have a dog?" I ask, trying to think of anything but the water.

"No." She shakes her head, her damp hair sticking to her neck.

I try not to think about her neck.

"No pets," she adds. "I wanted one, but…" She cuts herself off, like she didn't mean to say that.

"But what?"

"But we're supposed to be talking about you," she says. "How are you doing?"

"I think I'm drowning."

"I read about this online," she says, ignoring me. "The best way to get over your fear is to face it. So I'm going to hold you under the water for one minute, and when you resurface, you'll be cured."

I yank my hand out of hers. "What the fuck!" My shrill voice bounces off the tiled walls.

Aster's laughing hysterically. "Just kidding."

"That is not funny."

"But you should put your head under the water."

"No."

"Your hair will still look good, Aidan. God, you're so vain."

"I wish I could pretend vanity was my biggest issue here, Aster, but it's not."

"You've been in the water for ten minutes," she says mildly.

"I—What?"

"You're doing really well."

For a long moment I don't know what to say. It seems ridiculous that being praised for standing in water should make me feel any way whatsoever, but the words make me want to keep doing better. To keep trying.

I mentally order my knees to bend, to lower me into the water, but it's not happening.

"Let's try this," Aster says, turning to face the wall. She grips the edge with both hands and lets herself rise to the surface, gently kicking her legs to stay afloat.

I get as far as putting my hands on the wall next to hers, but neither one of my feet will leave the ground.

"You okay?" she asks. She stops kicking but still floats.

"I can't do it."

"Why not?"

"I don't want my face to go in the water. And not because I'm vain. My makeup is waterproof."

She stands, smiling kindly at my lame joke. "Okay," she says. "What if we tried this?" Very carefully she reaches over and lifts my hand, stepping under it and returning my hand to the ledge so she's bracketed by my arms, our faces six inches apart.

"What are you doing?" I ask, my voice scratchy.

"Turn around."

I swallow, then exhale as I turn.

"Think of it as a trust exercise," she says, resting her hands on my hips and sliding them up, past the Daisy tattoo, fingers grazing my stomach, my pecs, coming to rest under my arms. "Do you trust me, Aidan?"

I can't speak.

"Lie back," she says, toes pressing gently into the back of my right knee. "I've got you."

My knee gives way and I wobble, leaning into Aster as I lower into the water. My other leg lifts and she holds my shoulders up until my body is floating on the surface, then adjusts her hands so her arms are linked under mine, my head resting against her breasts. I'm only half as thrilled about that particular development as I would be under other circumstances.

"You're doing it," she murmurs. "Kick your feet a little."

I kick them approximately one inch.

"Whoa. Slow down, fella."

I smile a little, realizing I have my eyes closed. When I open them, Aster's face is above me, eyes cornflower blue, just like that field. That stupid field, the thing I never knew I loved until it was gone, never knew I'd miss until I'd lost it.

"Can I lower you a bit?" she asks.

I hesitate, then say, "Yeah."

She doesn't let go, just loosens her grip until I feel my hair touch the water, the cool sensation spreading over the back of my scalp. Soon enough I'm resting there, floating, feet barely moving, the water covering everything except my face and toes, and I'm okay.

I think about Aster's breasts, so close to my face.

I'm more than okay.

"What's this tattoo?" she asks, fingernail tracing the edge of a design on my shoulder.

"It's just some silly tribal design I thought was cool when I was sixteen. None of them really have any meaning. They're just…there."

"That's a lot of ink to have no meaning. Didn't it hurt?"

I hold her stare. "Yeah. It hurt."

She's the first one to blink. "Are you still not smoking?"

"Eight days. Going strong."

"Good for you."

"Have you ever quit anything?" I ask, hoping to take the spotlight off myself.

If we weren't so close, I might have missed the uncertainty that flashed across her face, another glimpse of something she keeps trying to hide.

"Yeah," she says eventually. "Of course."

The *of course* isn't convincing. Aster doesn't seem like a girl who gives up on stuff. She's a person who has faith in people who don't deserve it.

"Like what?"

"Those diet plans I started last week," she says, smiling ruefully. "And...once I joined a book club, and they let me pick the next book. I was fifteen and trying to look brave and smart so I picked *The Shining*, and by page twenty I was too afraid to finish and I never showed up to the meeting."

"So you quit a book club?"

"Don't tell anyone."

"Shame on you, Aster. Shame."

Suddenly, I don't feel quite as bad as I did when we got here. I don't think I'm ever going to go swimming for fun, but I'm not going to drown today, either. I lower my feet and stand, running my wet hands over my face before turning.

"How are you feeling?" Aster asks.

For a second I can only smile at her. "Good."

"Ready to go under?"

My heart lurches in my chest. "I..."

She takes my hand again, and I could get used to this. I want to get used to it.

"On three," she says. "One...two...three."

On the last word she slowly sinks under, her hand floating on the surface where it's joined with mine. Tiny bubbles rise up from where she disappeared and I take a deep breath of my own and slowly lower into the water. At the last second I think about bailing on the idea, but then I think about Aster's hand and I continue to drop until I'm fully submerged. My eyes are closed and my mouth is closed and I'm doing this.

I'm in.

After a few seconds I feel my lungs tighten and I push to my feet. Aster follows right behind me, water sluicing over her face.

"Holy fuck," I mutter, using both hands to push drenched hair off my forehead. "I can't believe I did that."

"How do you feel?"

"Aster," I say, stepping toward her.

But before I can get too close, her hands come up and press against my chest, stopping me. "Wait," she says.

I freeze, too close and too far, all at the same time. Because while I may no longer be afraid, Aster is. She's just had her heart broken and she's still not ready for this. For me. I'd be pissed at Jerry if I weren't ninety percent of the reason for the heartbreak.

"I'm just saying thank you," I lie, brushing off the rejection like I wasn't hoping for more. I lean in and kiss her temple briefly, then step back, like that's all I'd intended.

Like that's all I want.

14

I see Aster often over the next week. The near-kiss in the pool doesn't seem to have bothered her, for which I'm grateful. It does bother me, however, which stings. It's not that I've never been turned down before, it's just that I've never cared. If a girl wasn't interested I'd move on to someone who was. Now I don't want to move on. The longer I know Aster, the more I want her.

On Wednesday I stroll over to Aster's dorm. We have plans to study at the library, and I walk slowly, enjoying the rare day of sunshine, feeling oddly happy for a guy who hasn't gotten laid in months.

I adjust my bag over my shoulder and squint into the sun as I see Aster step out the front door of the building with a large box in her hands. A young girl walks behind her, wheeling a suitcase, and there's a car parked at the curb, with two people, presumably parents, loading things into the trunk.

I approach just as the three get in the car. Aster leans over to say something to the girl in the backseat, then straightens as they drive away. She waves, but there's tension in her shoulders and a phoniness in her smile.

"What's going on?" I ask.

She jolts and turns to see me waiting. "You scared me."

"Sorry. Who was that?"

She runs her hand through her hair, the blond strands immediately falling back into alignment. "Sydney. One of the girls from my floor." She sounds sad. "She's leaving school."

"Permanently?"

"Yeah."

"Why? What happened?"

She waves for me to follow her inside, and in the elevator she slumps against the far wall. "She cheated on a test and got caught. When they accused her, she panicked, lied about it, lied some more, and basically made everything worse."

"And they expelled her?"

"Yep."

The elevator stops and we get out. I hold the door as Aster grabs her book bag from her room and returns seconds later, dropping it on the floor as she shrugs into a denim jacket. She studies her feet, looking miserable, as we ride back down. Even the sunshine—the first glimpse we've had in weeks—doesn't improve her mood.

We walk in silence. Aster's wearing red flats with little bows on the toes, so shiny they reflect the black of my combat boots, and I admire the contrast as we trudge along.

"Hey," I say, when we're a block away from the library. "Let's do something else."

Aster stops. "Like what?"

"I need some ice cream."

"Huh?"

"And you *definitely* need some ice cream."

"I do?" But she doesn't resist when I take her arm and steer her away from the library.

"Who knows when we'll see the sun again?" I say reasonably. "We should take advantage of it."

Her mouth quirks. "I guess any excuse to eat ice cream is a good excuse."

I hold the door to the shop and Aster passes through ahead of me. It's mid-afternoon and the place is packed with students who had the same great idea. We get in line and contemplate the flavors, and when it's time to order, Aster gets vanilla with sprinkles and I get orange-licorice swirl.

"I've got this," I say, when she reaches for her wallet.

"You don't have to."

"But I want to. Because I'm so chivalrous."

She snickers. "Oh, right. And don't forget modest."

"Screw modest. Don't forget handsome."

The cashier rolls his eyes at the exchange, but I don't care about anyone else right now, because Aster is finally smiling as she winds through the crowded room and finds us a tiny table in the corner.

"So," I say, taking the seat opposite her.

"So," she replies, licking sprinkles off the side of her cone. "Let's talk about something."

My heart stutter stops, waiting for the ax to fall. *Let's talk* never leads anywhere good.

It takes a second to find my voice. "Sure. Whatever you want."

Aster props her chin on her hand. "Have you always liked disgusting ice cream, or is this a new thing?"

I freeze stupidly. "What?" My heart feels like it's trying to beat again, but can't remember the rhythm.

"I know people like to experiment in college, but don't you think you're taking it to the extreme? I mean, orange and black licorice? Aidan, that's revolting."

I sputter. "You got the most boring option on the entire menu. I was going to be a gentleman and overlook it, but you've crossed a line."

"*I'm* boring?" she asks, fluttering her lashes as she twists the cone in her hand, tongue poking out to make a ring in the vanilla.

My cock does not think Aster is boring.

I squirm in my seat. "So boring," I manage.

She smirks. "Well, maybe a little."

A trio of girls clambers into a booth nearby, and Aster sobers as she observes them.

"Were you close?" I ask.

"With Sydney?" Her brow furrows as she thinks about it, like she really wants to get the answer right. And even before she replies I know she cares more than she wants to, and that for whatever reason, this hurts her. "Maybe not close enough," she answers.

"How close are you supposed to be? You're resident advisor to what, forty kids?"

"About that. It's just, she dug herself such a deep hole, and I can't help but feel that maybe if she'd come to me, I could have helped her out of it."

"You can't be responsible for knowing what secrets the students are keeping."

She studies her fingernails. "I bumped into her once, in the bathroom. She was crying. I didn't know it then, but she'd just been caught. She told me she was homesick and I fell for it."

"It's not your fault, Aster."

She blows a fallen sprinkle off the table. "I know. I just keep thinking that if she'd told me the truth, I could have helped her somehow."

"Maybe she was embarrassed."

"Or maybe she didn't think I was someone she could talk to." She raises those blue eyes to mine, her pain on display. "That's my whole job, Aidan. And I don't think I'm very good at it."

I scoff. "You have to be kidding. You're the sweetest person I've ever known, minus your ice cream choices. You're very easy to talk to."

"Would you tell me?" she asks. "If you'd gotten caught?"

My throat closes up for a second. "Cheating?"

"Yeah."

"I've never cheated on a test."

"Something bad, then. Would you trust me not to judge you?"

I picture her giving Jerry a box containing the ashes of his burnt belongings. "Of course," I lie.

Something flickers in her gaze, the blue darkening a shade. "Okay," she says, smiling sadly, resigned. "Then there's nothing more I could have done."

"Nope," I say. "Not a thing."

She stares out the window and eats her ice cream.

"You know what else might cheer you up?" I ask.

She glances at me warily. "What?"

"Kill Glory 5."

She makes a face. "That stupid horror movie franchise? Pass."

"It's not stupid, it's brilliant. And the new one opens on Friday. Come with me."

"I have to wash my hair."

I flick a stray sprinkle at her. "Your hair always looks dirty anyway. Just wear a hat."

She laughs, a real, reaffirming sound that makes something inside of me ease. It's a sound I didn't know I needed in my life until now. A sound I didn't know I'd been missing.

"And to think I was considering your invitation."

"What's to consider? Remember how handsome I am? We just talked about it."

She groans in mock disgust, but I know I've got her.

15

On Friday I get off work an hour early so I can hustle home, shower, shave, and even iron the shirt I picked out. Jerry's got another commitment with the volunteer program so the tiny, niggling part of my conscience that keeps reminding me I didn't take the most honorable route to this point is quiet, like it's acknowledging that I've paid my dues and have *earned* tonight.

Hell, I even have a bouquet of aster lilies sitting on the kitchen table, ready to blow Aster away with my cleverness. To further cement my position as best date ever, I pre-bought our tickets for two seats at the end of the row on the right, halfway back in the theater. Aster mentioned once that those were her favorite seats, so tonight she'll have them. Tonight she can have whatever she wants. I just hope we finally—*finally*—want the same thing.

I check myself out in the mirror. Freshly ironed black button-up? Check. Clean jeans? Check. Boots? Check. I pull on a coat and jog out to the car I borrowed for the evening.

I make the short drive to Aster's building, park at the curb, and reach the front door just as a group of students exits. I let myself in and call the elevator, counting to ten as I wait. I don't know why I'm nervous. It's not like I've never been on a date before. It's not like I haven't hung out with Aster before. Tonight just feels different.

The elevator dings when it arrives and I almost drop the flowers. "Calm down," I mutter as I step inside and press the button for her floor. "Act normal."

I step out on nine and turn left for her room, lifting my hand and knocking quickly, a strange jitteriness in my chest. I mask the nerves with a cocky smile when Aster cracks the door a couple of inches and peers out.

"Hey," I say.

She spots the flowers, a strange expression fluttering across her face. And it's not a look of flattered ecstasy, either. It's...weird. And wrong.

I chuckle nervously. "Are you going to let me in?"

She steps back, tugging the door open wider. "Aidan," she says cautiously. "What are you doing here?"

I freeze. "What am I doing here? We have a date. *Kill Glory 5*. It starts in...an...hour." The words trail off as I take her in. She's gorgeous. She's wearing a fitted gray dress with a scooped neckline that shows off her amazing figure. A pair of gold heels sits in the center of the room, waiting to be stepped into. Her hair is sleek and shiny, her eyes rimmed with dark liner that makes her look sophisticated and sexy. And her mouth... Her mouth is painted red, lips full and feminine and...frowning.

"You look beautiful," I say, knowing it's the wrong thing to say. That the dress and the heels and the lipstick are too much for a movie.

Too much for me.

"Aidan," she says, knotting her fingers together nervously. "I'm so sorry. I forgot."

She could say, "Aidan, I'm about to kill you," and I would feel less panicked.

The flowers hang limply at my side, but I don't care about them. I don't care about anything. I can barely see anything besides Aster right now, three feet away and so far out of my reach.

"What are you... What are you doing?"

She shifts uncomfortably. "I have a date."

"With someone else?"

"With Shamus." Her voice is small.

Mine is not. *"With Shamus?"*

She flinches. "Yes."

"But you... But we..."

She waits for me to finish, but I barely know where to begin.

"What the *fuck,* Aster?"

She flinches again, but this time her expression hardens and she stiffens her spine. "What the fuck, what, Aidan?"

"You're going out with Shamus?"

"Yes."

"Dressed like that?" *Dressed like that* means she wants him. *Dressed like that* means she wants him to want her.

She's never dressed like that for me.

That burns, but then an even worse idea hits me.

"How many times have you gone out with him?"

She thinks. "Four."

My jaw drops. "Four times? Are you...are you..."

"Don't you dare ask."

Of course I'm going to ask. "Are you *fucking* him?"

She looks furious. "That is none of your business."

"How is it none of my business? You know I'm crazy about you! You know I've been waiting for you to get over Jerry and you're fucking Shamus?"

"I'm not fucking Shamus!" she shouts back. "But I plan to. Is that what you wanted to hear?"

"Of course it's not!"

Her cheeks are flushed, fists balled at her side, and she's sexy and terrifying. And heartbreaking. Because she's supposed to be mine.

I'm the one who cares about her.

Not Shamus.

Me.

"You don't even know him," I mumble stupidly.

"I'm getting to know him."

"But you know me."

She stares at me for a long moment. "Do I?"

"You know you do. In the pool, you...you..."

"I *what*, Aidan? I learned that you had a dog named Daisy? Is that what it means to know someone?"

This isn't her. This isn't the sweet, shiny Aster I've known since January. Something is wrong. Very, very wrong.

"What's going on, Aster?"

She shrugs. "I have a date. I don't know what you'll be doing."

"Did you do this on purpose? You knew I was coming over here. I texted you to tell you the time."

"I texted you back," she lies. "I told you I was busy."

"You're lying."

"Everybody lies, Aidan. Or are you the only one who's allowed to?"

I toss the flowers onto the bed. "I'm not Jerry."

She blanches. "This isn't about Jerry."

"Bullshit. It's definitely not about Shamus."

"If you think it's about you, you're even more conceited than I thought."

I step toward her and she holds her ground.

"You're afraid," I say softly.

She juts out her chin defiantly. "I'm not."

"You're lying again."

"I'm not, Aidan."

I trail a finger up the side of the dress, gliding over the curve of her hip, the indent at her waist, the slope of her breast.

"Stop me," I say.

I hear her swallow.

I don't hear her say no.

I slide my hand higher, past her clavicle, her neck, her jaw. I let my fingers slip into her shiny hair, cupping her head, tilting her just slightly as I lower my lips to within a millimeter of hers.

"Do it," she says, and it sounds like a dare.

So I kiss her.

I kiss Aster.

Two months after deciding I had to have her, I'm about to.

Her lips are soft and pliant beneath mine. She doesn't resist. For a second she doesn't do anything, then I feel a tiny tug at the base of my shirt and I know she's holding on. I lift my other hand to join the first, gripping her tighter, deepening the kiss.

Her lips part and I slide my tongue into her mouth, finding hers, the wet contact making my whole body come to life.

She whimpers slightly and presses onto her toes, increasing the sensation. She tastes like mint and smells like lemons; she feels like warm cotton; she sounds like warm girl. I groan and kiss her harder, feeling her fingers curl into my chest, the shirt I ironed in anticipation of exactly this moment.

Well, not exactly this.

But close enough.

I don't know what Aster was thinking when she made this date with Shamus, but I want to show her once and for all that I'm the only guy she needs to see. That I can be everything she wants; that I can make her feel the way she makes me feel.

We break apart to breathe, our lips an inch apart. She's shaking, fine tremors racking her body as she looks up at me, her eyes troubled. Wavering. Like she's deciding something.

I lower my head to kiss her again, to help with the decision.

And then she slaps me.

Hard.

16

What.

17

The.

18

Fuck.

19

It takes me a full five seconds to comprehend what just happened, and then I leap back, gaping at Aster in shock.

"What the fuck?" I demand. Now I'm the one who's shaking. The one who's confused.

"You asshole!" she screams.

"Me? What? You're the one who slapped me!"

"You deserved it!"

"Why?"

"Because I know what you did!"

Then the shouting stops and there's an endless silence as the words settle around us.

Because I know what you did.

I swallow anxiously. "What do you mean?"

"Don't you dare lie to me," she seethes. "Not again. Not *more.*"

"But..."

"Tell me," she says. "In your own words. Explain it to me. Tell me why."

My mouth is dry.

The first time I'd been hauled into court the judge had said the same thing. Tell me why. And I'd answered truthfully. And stupidly, since it got me six months in juvie.

But I do the same thing now.

"Because I wanted to," I say quietly. Then to clarify: "Because I wanted you."

"So you hired a prostitute to blow my boyfriend?"

Hearing it out loud—hearing the words coming from Aster—is like a punch to the gut. All I can see is her mouth, her lips swollen from our kiss, the lipstick smudged, the promise of what we could have had slipping further away with each word.

"When... How...?"

I know it's the wrong thing to say, but I have to ask. She couldn't have just *guessed*.

"After the wedding," she replies.

After the wedding. When I couldn't reach her all week.

"I went to see Jerry when we got back. I thought you were amazing and I needed to know where he and I went wrong so I didn't make the same mistake. The night he told me what happened, I couldn't listen. I couldn't hear anything beyond that he'd been with someone else. But this time I made him tell me everything. And because Jerry's an idiot who's never even seen a prostitute, he didn't have a clue. But I did."

"You—"

"So I went to the bar, and I met Sindy, and she told me you gave her a bunch of twenties and told her to do whatever it took."

My stomach clenches. I did say that. I didn't say "Never tell anyone about this" because I never thought anyone would ask. I never thought *Aster* would ask.

"Is it true?" Aster presses. "Did you really do that?"

I want to deny it, but I can't lie to her. Again.

"Yes," I say quietly.

She steps forward like she's going to slap me, and I scramble back.

"I hate you," she says, face crumpling. She stops in her tracks and covers her eyes with her hands, shoulders shaking. "I hate you."

"I'm sorry," I say. "I know it—"

"You have no idea," she interrupts, lifting her head. "You have no idea, Aidan. You don't know anything. You don't know shit." The gold heels sit on the floor beside her bare feet, everything about her appearance contrasting with everything she's saying, with everything I thought I knew.

I think of those glimpses I'd had of her before. A moment in the car, an unexpected flicker at dinner or in the library or walking home. Tiny fractures in her composure, a sneak peek at what lay beneath. "What don't I know?"

"He was my chance," she says brokenly. "Jerry was my chance."

"At what?"

"At anything I wanted. At everything."

"You didn't really love him?"

"I really did," she says, tears dripping off her chin. "I loved him and he loved me. He was perfect and he was *real.*"

"I don't understand."

"How could you?" she snaps. "How could someone who pays a hooker to ruin a happy relationship understand what happy is? How could someone so fucking miserable understand anything?"

"I'm not—"

"I don't care what you're about to say," she says abruptly, swiping at her tears. "Just leave."

"Did you plan all this?" I gesture to her, the dress, the ruined makeup. "Did you really let me come here so I could see you leave with Shamus?"

She nods, the movement sharp. "Yeah. I wanted you to know how it felt. To see something you thought was wonderful fall apart in front of you."

I look at her, all the broken pieces of the stupid idea of *us*. An *us* I'd fabricated; an *us* I'd destroyed.

I reach for the door, then stop. "I didn't know," I tell her.

She scoffs. "You knew."

"When I did it," I say. "I didn't know it would ever come to this. I thought you'd fuck me for revenge, I'd get you out of my system, and we'd both move on."

She just stares at me, uncaring. Her eyes are dark, the cornflowers gone. Like the flames rushing out of a rundown house and into a dry field, destroying everything because of one stupid, selfish choice.

"I'm sorry," I say.

"No kidding," she says.

20

The next morning Jerry comes out to find me sitting in the kitchen wearing a Holsom hoodie and a pair of boxers, staring morosely into a glass of orange juice. I caught a glimpse of myself in the bathroom mirror and know I'm a mess. My skin has a sickly pallor and my hair is sticking out every which way. It's pitiful, but it's the best I can do.

"Rough night?" Jerry asks, slicing a grapefruit in half and digging in with a spoon.

"Yeah," I mutter. Not too long ago we were in this same situation, except the roles were reversed. Now I'm the miserable one. The one without Aster.

The one who doesn't deserve her.

"You want to talk about it?"

I glance up to see if Jerry's serious, and he is. He's eating his grapefruit and offering a shoulder to cry on. Except I'm moping about a fight with his ex-girlfriend, the one I paid for him to cheat on, so I can't exactly go into detail.

"No," I say, downing the orange juice. "Thanks, though."

"Want to come with me today?" he offers. "We're learning

how to tie knots."

I pause as I rinse out my glass. "Is this for the volunteer thing?"

"Yep. It's a survival skill."

"Shouldn't you have learned it before you spent a weekend camping in the woods?"

"Definitely. That trip was a disaster. But we're supposed to call it a learning experience."

"What'd you learn?"

He eats his grapefruit. "That I hate camping."

Ugh. He's just so…positive. Every mistake is an opportunity in disguise.

"I'll pass on the knots. But thanks."

I retreat to my room, throw on a pair of sweats and a T-shirt, grab my mp3 player, and go for a run. Working out is one of the few things I do at Holsom that I did growing up. Most everything else got me in trouble, and despite what happened last night, I'm trying not to get in trouble. Not to mess up. Not to be that guy.

I run for an hour, using each footstep to stomp on another memory of the fight with Aster.

The kiss.

The slap.

The kiss.

But try as I might, I can't forget anything. Not a single detail. Not the way she smelled. Not the way her tongue felt against mine. Not the way she looked in that dress and that lipstick. Not the way her eyes changed, the tiny cracks that sprung up in her armor. Out of all the things that were said last night, one theme stands out more than the rest: *You have no idea, Aidan. You don't know anything. You don't know shit.*

I know she wasn't just talking about how I'd hurt her. There was something more. It was the incongruity of those gold heels, the way they sat there, like a prop. The smudged red lipstick. The way she tried to be angry then crumpled and caved. The way she was trying to be something she wasn't.

I know what that looks like.

I see it in the mirror every day.

I was drawn to Aster because she was beautiful. Light and flawless. But last night the tarnish showed on her perfect finish, and I don't think I'm the one who put it there. I think I'm the one who bumped against that glossy shine and rubbed off the polish to reveal the secret scratches hidden underneath.

21

Aster

"What do you think? Gold or silver?"

I try to appear appropriately interested in Missy's question. She's been trying to choose a pair of earrings for the past three hours, dragging me to every store in the nearby mall in her quest for a new accessory.

"Gold," I say, when she keeps waiting for an answer. "Definitely."

"Hmm." She holds the hoops up to her ear and studies them. "Good call, Aster. Gold it is."

I try not to react to the elite black credit card she pulls out of her designer purse; the way she casually buys a pair of earrings that cost more than my groceries for a month. I do a good job looking totally happy with everything. I've been doing it for three years, after all. And it had almost started to feel normal.

Until Aidan.

Fucking Aidan.

I'd kill him, but I don't want to go back to prison.

"I'm starving," Missy says, tucking the earrings in her bag, alongside the new jeans and the dress and the forty-dollar mascara she bought on a whim. "Do you want to get some ice cream?"

"Ah…how about cupcakes?" I say, scrambling to think of anything other than ice cream. If I think about ice cream I'll think about Aidan, and if I think about Aidan I'll scream. I'll think about how incredibly stupid I am. How I'm supposed to know better.

How I do know better.

And yet.

For weeks after I'd learned what he'd done I'd tried to come up with a plan to ruin him. To build up his heart and then stomp on it the way he'd done to mine with his lie. I thought I'd bring him to the pool and let him drown, except he'd been so genuinely terrified that I hadn't had the heart. The way he'd looked, floating in the water, believing in me…no one has ever looked at me like that.

The ice cream date. Telling him about Sydney, giving him a shot to come clean. He didn't deserve a second chance, but I tried to give him one, and he hadn't taken it. It was a wasted effort, and one I won't make again.

"I could totally eat a cupcake," Missy says, navigating through the busy mall and completely failing to notice the way her bulging shopping bags bump passerby.

When I first met Missy at Aidan's Frisbee baseball game, I'd never in a million years have imagined us hanging out, but here we are. And I never would have imagined myself saying I wish I could be more like Missy Freestone, but I kind of do.

We couldn't be more different. Missy's from an old money

southern family; her mom has a brand of bourbon named after her and her father owns a plastics factory. Missy's apartment is professionally decorated and paid for by her parents; I have a dorm room in which I live for free in exchange for agreeing to listen to sobbing and STD-riddled students at all hours of the day.

"I hope they have the lemon coconut one," Missy is saying. "Ooh, or maybe the red velvet. But once they had cookies and cream and there was a whole cookie inside the cupcake—that was amazing." She stops walking. "Aster? Are you listening?"

I school my expression into its standard happy-go-lucky blandness. "Of course I am! Sorry! I'm just so hungry!"

She beams back at me and resumes walking. "I'm the one who should be apologizing. I dragged you out here on this shopping trip and then totally forgot to eat! We should get two cupcakes."

My stomach clenches. "Absolutely."

I don't want two cupcakes. I don't even want *one* cupcake, that's how bad things are. I didn't feel this miserable after the break up with Jerry, and that was honestly miserable. When Aidan asked me if I'd really loved Jerry, I wasn't lying when I said I did. I loved him. I loved everything about him. When we first met I loved the idea of him, this guy from a good family with hope and ambition and a truly huge heart. And then, with time, I loved him, too. And he loved me. He didn't look deep enough to see all the dents and dings beneath the surface, and he was totally, completely happy with the package I was selling. And I was totally, completely happy to be that package.

Until Aidan ripped it apart.

I shake my head, like that will jar loose all stray thoughts of him.

It doesn't work, of course. Somehow he'd weaseled himself in there, past all the carefully constructed walls I'd put up, making himself not just my only friend, but my best friend. I wasn't lying when I told him that, either. Finally a guy who listened to and heard me; liked me and respected me; lied to and betrayed me.

I was furious when I spoke to Sindy and she spilled the details of Aidan's little plan to have her seduce Jerry. The whole thing made sense...and then it didn't. He wanted to break us up for a reason, but what? The obvious answer is sex, but he never pushed the issue. Even when I was drunk, pants-less, and sharing a cheap motel bed with him, he didn't make a move.

"Oh, man." Missy moans as we approach the shop, their display case filled with a colorful cornucopia of cupcakes. "They have all the flavors! What are we going to do?"

I pretend to contemplate the selection, but I'm really looking at our reflections in the glass. Missy's wearing a red dress with a boat neck collar and heels so high I couldn't walk in them if my life depended on it. I'm wearing skinny jeans and flats and a tank top beneath my denim jacket. When I first got to Holsom I tried to dress fancier, tried harder to fit into this life, the life I wanted. But it was such a far stretch from the life I'd left that I couldn't do it. Instead of going from prison beige to Prada bags, I'd steered into the safer middle ground of jeans and T-shirts. At least I can afford them.

"Okay," Missy says, sighing dramatically when it's our time to order. "We're going to get four cupcakes. Lemon coconut, red velvet, cookies and cream, and vanilla. That's your favorite, right, Aster?" She reads the surprise on my face. "You mentioned it before. Said you were boring vanilla. Like anybody's buying that." She winks at me and turns to pay, waving away my money. "If I'm going to corrupt you, I'm going to pay for it," she says, steering us over to a table in the nearby food court.

Despite her regal southern belle countenance, Missy is a hardcore athlete and ruthlessly ambitious. The second time I turned up to play with the team she'd invited me to a party at her place. I'd turned her down and instead of pouting she said, "I don't blame you. Let's go for drinks instead. Do you like bourbon?"

I'd tried to get out of the invite but Missy wasn't taking no for an answer, and soon enough I'd found myself sitting across from her in a campus bar, listening to her bawdy stories of the lengths she went to in order to maintain her good girl image. "That's why I wanted to hang out with you," she'd explained. "I recognize it in you. That wild side, trying to break free. My wild side needs company. Join us."

I didn't have the nerve to tell her my wild side had been tamed after fourteen months in a women's correctional facility. I don't tell anyone about that side, keeping my past as vague and bland as my present is supposed to be.

Until Aidan.

Missy slices the cupcakes into quarters and steeples her fingers as she tries to decide where to start. "Red velvet, right?" she mutters, as though there's a wrong answer. "Or lemon coconut?"

I pick up a piece of vanilla and lick off the frosting. It's delicious, and instead of revolting, my stomach sings its praises.

When I haven't been in class I've been moping around my dorm room, pretending to be a good resident advisor, the one who'd had such a loud fight with a guy the week before that another resident advisor had been sent down to scold her.

There was no end to the moping in sight until I bumped into Missy after class this morning and she insisted I come along on her shopping trip. I couldn't think of a good excuse to get away, so here I am.

"Oh, hell," Missy says, picking up the red velvet and the lemon coconut and sandwiching them together. "I'll just eat both." Frosting smears on her upper lip as she eats, and then she beams at me, cupcake crumbs clinging to her chin. "What?" she asks, when I laugh. "Is there something in my teeth?"

I laugh harder.

All week I've been convinced I'd never feel better, never find another friend, but maybe there's hope. Maybe Missy will be my friend and I'll never seen Aidan Shaw again and everything will be just fine.

22

Aidan

"You seem better," Jerry remarks when I enter the kitchen the following Monday morning, dressed in a white button down and navy pants. "You also look better." It's a fair observation, not an insult. I've been wearing the same sweatpants and T-shirt all week, and even I had to admit I was starting to smell.

"Thanks."

"Early shift at the library?"

"Yeah," I lie. "I'm covering for someone."

"Cool. Let me know if you need to tie anything up for any reason. I have a lot of knot knowledge now."

Sure enough, the couch, ottoman, and both side tables are covered in various lengths of ropes tied up in various types of knots.

"You're really taking this seriously," I remark, pouring a bowl of cereal and watching him work on another knot as I eat.

"Well," he says, chewing on his bottom lip. "I was the worst knot-tier in the group, and it was pretty embarrassing. You don't say you're pre-med and then admit you can't tie a slip knot."

"Oh, God, no."

If he hears my sarcasm, he doesn't acknowledge it. "Anyway," he continues. "Practice makes perfect, so here I am."

The word *perfect* makes me think of Aster, and I contemplate Jerry's knots, an assortment of twisted penance for his crime of cheating. And my crime of paying for it.

I finish the cereal, down half a glass of orange juice, and grab my jacket. "I'll see you later."

"Have fun at work."

It's a rainy March day as I trudge over to the campus, passing lecture halls and coffee shops, the tempting smells of caffeine and cinnamon buns trying to lure me off my path. But I can't be late for the morning's check-in. Today is the requisite Promise & Potential Program once-a-term meeting, where, in addition to classes, jobs, and our extracurricular activity, we're assigned a task to complete to benefit the seriously under-funded program. I got lucky my first year because they had just moved offices and needed help setting up, so I spent a weekend painting walls and moving furniture and got my cooperation credits without actually having to talk to anybody. Last year I monitored the online program forum and forwarded the queries as needed. I'm hoping for something as unchallenging again this time around.

The PPP offices are located on the second floor of a nondescript gray building, its walls covered with moss and ivy. I pass a handful of people as I enter, mostly older folks dressed in cheap suits and ties.

The building is dim, the floors cheap brown linoleum, the walls a dingy off-white. I take the stairs up one level, weak light spilling in through the occasional window. My boots squeak as I make the short trip to the end of the hall and into the entrance area for the PPP. An elderly lady named Becca sits at the reception desk, and next to it is a swinging gate that leads to a cluster of small offices and meeting rooms.

"Hi, Becca," I say, signing my name on the clipboard she slides over.

"Hey, Aidan. How's everything?"

"Never better. Need anything painted today?"

She tsks. "You wish. Go straight on back."

I slip through the gate and search for the program director, a redheaded guy named Jim who's not much older than me but who possesses the enthusiasm of a ten-year-old. Not even the drab décor or the constantly dwindling budget can bring Jim down.

I pass a couple of empty offices before coming to the PPP library, a slightly larger office with two half-empty bookshelves, three small desks, and one ancient desktop computer. Today the desks have been pushed to the side, the floor space crammed with cheap metal folding chairs, arranged six across and ten deep, with a small aisle carved out in the middle.

Nearly all the seats are full, so I take one at the very back. Toward the front I spot T.J. and Wes, their heads bent together as they talk. Brix stands off to the side, having a conversation with Jim, but pretty much everyone else is sitting quietly or fiddling with something on their phones.

The room is about seventy percent male, a hundred percent diverse, and extremely confused. We've never been gathered before. Never seen this many PPP faces. But before we can worry too much, Jim moves to stand behind the makeshift podium at the front of the room.

"Good morning," he says, smiling widely. "And thank you all for coming."

A couple of people mutter some sort of greeting, but everyone else is sitting anxiously, waiting for the ax to fall. A free ride to Holsom in exchange for our promise to try our best was too good to be true, and without exchanging a word, it's obvious that everyone in here is expecting the worst.

"I know we've typically met one-on-one to discuss your cooperation credits, but this year we have a special PPP ten-year anniversary project, and we need everyone here to work together to see it succeed."

There's an expectant pause, like he's waiting for us to applaud, but no one makes a sound.

"Okay," Jim says, still smiling. "Great. The project will have a past, present, future theme, and will hopefully help to update and re-brand the program. We'll be creating new brochure materials for prospective students and donors, conducting interviews with program graduates and current participants, offering in-person campus tours, phone consults…"

"We're supposed to do tours?" Wes asks, sticking his hand in the air belatedly. "I thought we were anonymous."

"You're not anonymous to me, Wes," Jim says, but no one laughs. "Ahem. No one has to lead a tour if they don't want to. Your privacy is yours to cherish, and we respect that."

"Can I just send out donation letters like last year?" a girl in the front row asks. "I like mail."

"You did a great job with the mailings, Nikki. We'll see if

that spot is still available for you."

She cracks her gum. "Awesome."

I sigh and dig out my phone, tuning out the rest of Jim's presentation. I don't plan to lead any tours, but the cooperation credit is mandatory, and I get why it's necessary. A PPP student named Lindo greeted me on my move-in day, helping me bring my bags to my room and get settled in. I'd had an enormous chip on my shoulder, totally prepared to be the black sheep in this sea of imagined trust fund rich kids, but seeing someone who'd had a harder life than me make this place work for him gave me the confidence to believe I could have the same opportunities if I opened myself up to them.

Three years ago I never would have believed I could get a girl like Aster. Never would have had the courage to try. I might have always been destined to fail, but making the effort is its own type of progress.

"So that's that," Jim says, some time later. The sharp clap of his hands interrupts my thoughts and I put away my phone and straighten in my seat, preparing to go. "We've got the sign up sheets here, so if you have a partner in mind, add your names to the same line. I'll pair up any singles later. You can select your three preferred tasks, and jobs will be assigned shortly. I'm here if you have any questions."

A handful of people walk out, but most approach the front, picking up papers and pencils from the desks and jotting down the required information. I see T.J. and Wes chatting as they fill in their forms, and I glance around for Brix, thinking he might want to work together. And that's when I see her.

Aster.

The shiny blond hair, the sharp jut of her stubborn jaw, her denim jacket. I stop breathing for a second. My entire body misses her, desperate to close the fifteen feet between us and promise to do whatever it takes to make up for what I already did.

Then she approaches Jim, aiming that gorgeous smile right at him, and I stop breathing for another reason.

She's here to ruin me.

I think about her giving Jerry a box of burned belongings. She doesn't forgive, he said. She doesn't forget.

She's going to tell Jim what I did, that I have neither promise nor potential, that I'm a liar and an asshole and whatever else she needs to say to yank the PPP scholarship out from under me. I have no idea how she found out about it, and I don't care. I want Aster, but I want this scholarship more. I *need* it.

I elbow my way through the group of students, knocking over chairs in my haste to get to the front.

"Just one second," Jim is saying to Aster when I approach. He quickly hurries over to the sign up desks where a squabble has broken out between a couple of students.

"Hey, Aster," I say casually.

She almost jumps out of her skin, whipping around and gaping at me. "What—" She looks behind me, like answers might be lurking in my shadow. "What are you doing here?" she asks, even as realization dawns. "You're—"

Her reaction is the polar opposite of the snide *I'm going to destroy you* response I was expecting, and before the implication can completely sink in, Jim is back.

"Aidan Shaw!" he exclaims, snatching my hand in a grip I

don't return as I stare at Aster in astonishment. "Good to see you, as always. And you already know Aster Lindsey? Excellent." He beams and scribbles on the paper in his hand. "There. You're partnered up. Excellent. I couldn't have chosen better myself."

"No…" Aster tries to interject, her voice weak with shock.

He ignores the tiny protest. "Preferred assignments?"

"We're not—"

"Interviews," I say loudly, because that's one of the tasks I heard Jim mention and I can't think of anything better.

She shoots me a withering glare. "Jim, we are not—"

"—interested in mailing brochures," I finish. "We are not interested in mail."

"Sure. Nikki's got that covered, anyway." Another fight—or perhaps the same one—breaks out in the corner again, and Jim sighs. "Would you two excuse me? Who knew pencils could cause so much drama?"

He dashes off to calm things down again.

"You're in the program?" I whisper-shout as soon as he's gone.

"You're in the program?" Aster counters.

"Yes, obviously!"

She gives me a derisive look. "Yes, *obviously.*"

But now that I've seen her, witnessed those cracks in her façade, I can't un-see them. This snooty look she's trying on is like a little girl stumbling around in her mother's high heels. It's something she might aspire to, but not something that fits her.

"What'd you do?" I ask.

Aster does a double take. "That's none of your business."

"I stole cars. Did six months in juvie for fighting at school, got out, decided stealing cars was more my thing, got arrested, then got a judge who gave me a choice: Holsom or five years in prison."

Her jaw is tight. "You should have picked prison."

"Then I wouldn't have met you."

"Exactly."

That hurts, but I don't let it show. Now that I know she's not here to rat me out, I'm fucking ecstatic to have a reason to see her again.

"Seems like we're partners," I say.

"We're nothing, Aidan. I'm going to talk to Jim and find someone—anyone—else."

In the corner, the loud argument about pencils escalates into a full-on shouting match.

"Well, you have a lot of good alternatives," I observe.

Aster's nostrils flare as she exhales, frustrated and furious. "Anything would be better," she says, striding past me to the door.

I catch her arm as she leaves. She stops and stares at my fingers, then raises fulminous blue eyes to mine.

"What are you doing?" she asks in a low voice, her rage barely restrained.

"I'm sorry about what happened."

She blinks, the apology obviously unexpected. "I don't care."

"I do. I miss you."

She looks for Jim, who is taking away everybody's pencils, then pries my fingers off her arm. "You'll get over it."

"Come on, Aster," I try. "You're *here,* which means that despite appearances, you're not perfect. Give me another chance."

"*Here* is an anomaly," she says through her teeth. "Most

124

people don't get second chances. And smart people don't give them. I don't give them, and I don't waste them."

"What does that mean?"

"It means you had your chance, and you fucked it up before it ever began. And you ruined mine, and I'm never going to forget it."

I don't say anything else as she stomps away, her blond hair swinging, her body so stiff it looks like it could crack at the slightest pressure. Like the fissures in her composure are growing ever-wider, ready to burst open, and I have a crow bar.

23

Aster

I'm pacing.

I pace when I'm nervous. I picked up the habit in prison, which I guess isn't the worst thing you can pick up in an overcrowded state facility for low-risk women inmates.

I walk back and forth between two large oak trees at the side of the dorms, glancing up and down the street for Aidan. He's picking me up this morning so we can complete the first of our cooperation credit tasks. Thanks to his stupid suggestion, we've been given an interview assignment, and today we're meeting up with a former PPP student who graduated from Holsom and now runs a successful home renovation business.

I had no idea Aidan was in the program. Spend any time in prison and you learn pretty fast not to judge a person by their appearance. Nice-looking people do bad things; bad-looking people do bad things.

Everyone does bad things.

Some PPP students know each other from their work

assignments, but I've been lucky enough to steer clear. My first-year task was Nikki's dream job, working in the mail room. I dealt with Jim and Becca, and no one else. Fine by me.

Last year I was the one-person fundraising committee, calling former donors and possible donors and random donors and asking for money. Jim and Becca knew my criminal history, which made me a pretty good pick for wheedling money out of folks.

Then this year I got the resident advisor job, which no PPP student has ever gotten before. On the surface it doesn't seem like the best idea to put an ex-con in the midst of a bunch of impressionable kids who are living on their own for the first time, but dig a bit deeper and find the right person, and you've got an R.A. who recognizes someone about to make bad choices and will work her ass off to steer them in a better direction.

That's what Jim was banking on when he got me this job. He's working diligently to find new campus positions for PPP students, but like in the real world, people are reluctant to hire kids with criminal records.

It's because of Jim's bottomless kindness that I'm pacing this morning. I'd tried everything to get out of working with Aidan, but every excuse I tossed out Jim batted back like we were playing a fun game of tennis.

I hate tennis. It was my requisite extracurricular activity in year one and it was awful. Even Jim admitted that in retrospect, taking someone out of prison and sticking her on a tennis court with kids who've never even seen the inside of a police station might have been too big a jump. Fortunately the R.A. job is so time consuming that they took pity on me and said I didn't have to sign up for an extracurricular this year. Thank God for small mercies.

A car horn honks and I turn to see Aidan pulling up to the curb in a pale purple Volkswagen. It's not the kind of car you'd expect to see being driven by a guy with muscles and tattoos and sexy dirty blond hair, but I'm determined not to speak to him, so I don't make a joke when I get in.

"Morning," he says.

I gaze out the window.

"I got you a coffee."

I know. I can smell it.

"And a donut," he adds. "I hope you like chocolate."

I take my mp3 player out of my pocket and stick the buds in my ears, sifting through the music until I find a song that will drown out his voice. It's a thirty-minute drive to the interview, and the last thing I want is to hear him talk. His lame apology, the coffee and donut, they're just stupid, superficial gestures meant to make up for something he can't make up for.

I meant what I said when I told him I don't give second chances. My mother gave my father too many second chances, and by the time I was fourteen we were sleeping in bus stations because overcrowded women's shelters didn't think "financial abuse" was a big enough deal to give us a room. When I was a kid, I thought it was normal for my mom to get an allowance. A handful of bills for groceries, just enough money for gas to make the return trip but get no farther. I thought it was normal for her to ask for money to bake cookies for her book club or buy a new sweater. And I thought it was normal for my dad to say no, even though he had new sweaters and a bowling league and drinks with his friends and steadily worked his way through four packs of cigarettes a week. To this day I can't smell smoke without thinking of him and his condescending smirk, telling my mom we can't have bus fare to go to the mall.

It was only when my little brother needed an emergency root canal and my dad wouldn't loosen the purse strings that my mother finally admitted that something was wrong. She stole a credit card while my dad was sleeping and took my sobbing brother to the dentist. My dad took one look at Ramsay's puffy, numbed face and knew what she had done.

And that's when we ran.

After a few weeks we'd overstayed our welcome on friends' couches so we spent nights at the bus depot, pretending we were just early for our ride. No matter how desperate things got, my mother, who had been dependent on my father for far too long, remained totally and hopelessly unable to find a way to make ends meet.

So I figured it out.

I started small. The first thing was a bottle of vitamins. I found a receipt on the ground and read it for something to do. Then, at the bottom, I saw the words: *Receipts required for returns within fourteen days.* So I got an idea. I went to the store, I stole the vitamins, and then I returned them with my receipt. Twenty bucks. Easy.

It escalated fast, because twenty dollars won't feed and house a family of three. Neither Ramsay nor I were going to school by that point, so we had nothing but time on our hands, and soon enough we were making hundreds of dollars a day. Then it occurred to me that I could "return" things for store credit if I didn't have receipts. That meant the whole store was up for grabs.

By the time I was seventeen I'd made more than seventy thousand dollars. Enough to get us a cheap apartment and groceries, and earn myself a twenty-three month sentence at the Whitehead Women's Correctional Facility in southern Washington. I was young and terrified, but also relieved. No more stealing. No more worrying about my dad finding us. And no more watching my brother stifle his depression with heroin.

Six months after I went away, he overdosed.

Three months after that, my mother, truly alone for the first time in her life, moved in with the next man who was nice to her and stopped talking to me.

After finishing my GED, one of the prison counselors told me about the Holsom program, and with my expectations carefully low, I applied.

And got accepted.

I was released nine months early for good behavior, hopped on a bus, and started school. For the first year, I kept my head down, did my job, studied my ass off, and tried to be invisible.

In year two, I met Jerry. Never in my life would I have imagined that a guy from a nice family, with a good heart and dreams of being a doctor, would be interested in me. But Jerry saw something that had been hidden by too many rough years, a hopeful side of myself I'd forgotten existed. And the more we hung out, the more I fell for him. The more I believed in him, the more I believed in myself and believed that the life I was pretending I had could actually be mine.

Then Aidan came along.

The reminder makes my chest hurt.

It doesn't help that this interview is taking place in the town of Chester, just a few miles from where I grew up. From where my father still lives, as far as I know. From where my brother is buried. The thought makes me ill, and when we arrive at the interview site I lurch out of the car and gasp in air like I'd been under water for the past half hour. One of my ear buds falls out, making it possible to hear Aidan's concerned, "Are you okay?"

"I'm fine," I snap, jerking away from the warm feel of his hand on my back and forgetting my vow not to speak to him.

He holds up his hands defensively. "Okay, sorry. I didn't know you were sick."

I straighten and run my hands through my hair, composing myself. "I'm not. Let's just do this. Which house is it?"

We're in a brand new subdivision, the gravel-covered road lined on either side with half-finished homes, their frames and guts exposed to the elements. Construction vehicles rumble at intermittent intervals, pouring concrete and digging holes, dumping enormous loads of garbage into dumpsters.

"I think it's that one," Aidan says, pointing to the house on our left. "He said he had a yellow truck."

The driveway is just a dirt path criss-crossed with deep tire treads, and we pass a yellow pickup truck with *Lindo Construction* stenciled on the door. Through the wood frames I can see half a dozen guys in construction hats milling around, some carrying lumber, one consulting a tablet, a couple drinking coffee and chatting.

"Which one is Lindo?" I ask.

"I don't see him." At that moment, his phone beeps with an

incoming message. He pulls it out of his pocket and squints at the screen. "He's ten minutes away."

I scowl. "Awesome."

I start back to the car, hearing Aidan's footsteps follow behind me. I was planning to get in to wait, but at the last minute I lean against the hood and cross my arms, figuring it'll be easier to ignore Aidan out here than in a confined space.

"Lindo was kind of like my mentor first year," he says, copying my stance. I wish he wouldn't stand so close. I wish he didn't still look like everything I shouldn't want, but do. I wish he hadn't invited me to that wedding, slept next to me in that bed, and never tried to take advantage.

"I don't care."

"He was my only friend for a while. Then I met Wes, T.J., Brix. You."

"We're not friends."

He carries on as though I hadn't spoken. "I came to Holsom because it was an opportunity, you know? I didn't trust that it could be real. I kept waiting for the other shoe to drop. Lindo recognized it right away. He said if I did that I'd spend so much time checking over my shoulder that I'd miss seeing all the possibilities in front of me. It wasn't easy, but eventually I started believing that I could make it work at Holsom."

I take in the half-finished houses going up around us, sketches of dreams that will forever be out of reach if I lose focus. And I can't lose focus. I won't. Not for Aidan and his tattoos and his too-soft hair. Not for his apology or his donut.

My mom lost focus. Ramsay lost focus.

I won't.

"If I'd seen you that first day," Aidan continues, "I never would have looked twice. Not because you're not hot, but because I never would have expected you to look back."

I felt that way about everyone I encountered first year, too.

"I don't know how it happened, Aster, but I started believing. And when I saw you the day I moved in with Jerry, I didn't even think about it. I just wanted you, and I was willing to do anything to have you. It was like the new me and the old me, working together for the first time."

"Shut up, Aidan." It's hard to get the words out. How many times had my mother forgiven my father, made excuses for him? I tell myself to stay calm, but I don't know how much more of this I can take. Aidan's not supposed to be honest and forthcoming; he's supposed to be the smug, lying asshole who smugly lied to me.

Footsteps on gravel have us turning to see a huge mountain of a man in a straining white T-shirt approach. *Lindo Construction* is printed across his chest in huge yellow letters, and a grin stretches his face when he sees Aidan. It's hard not to laugh when he wraps Aidan in a hug that almost makes him disappear, his face crushed between the other man's pecs.

"Aidan Shannon Shaw!" the man bellows, thumping Aidan on the back so hard he grunts.

I'm grinning now, and not because Aidan sounds like he's in pain, but because his middle name is Shannon.

"Too long, man! Too long!" He releases Aidan, who staggers back, face flushed.

"Hey, Lindo. Thanks for meeting with us."

"No need to thank me."

Aidan waves in my direction. "This is, uh, Aster."

Lindo's eyebrows fly up. *"This* is Aster?"

I've got my hand halfway extended to shake, but now I freeze. He's heard of me?

"Aster!" Lindo booms, stepping forward and folding me in the same bone-crushing hug he'd used on Aidan. I feel like a cartoon witch, legs twitching as I'm pinned to his hard chest. Then he releases me and steps back, beaming down as he studies my face. "So this is the girl, huh?" he says. To me he adds, "I tried to get this kid to quit smoking every day that first year, and he wouldn't budge. Five seconds with you and he's given up the habit."

The news takes me by surprise. I knew Aidan was trying to quit; I didn't know it had anything to do with me. Not that it changes anything. I still hate him.

Lindo smiles. "Looks like he finally met his match."

24

Aidan

Oh. My. God.

If I thought Aster was red in the face after Lindo's breath-stealing bear hug, I was mistaken. Her cheeks are flaming right now, and I don't know if it's rage or embarrassment, but I don't want to find out.

"So where should we do the interview?" I interject loudly. "Right here? Maybe in your truck? Or on another day?"

Lindo grins at me. The asshole knows what he's doing. I'd failed to mention to Aster that he's kind of remained my mentor, albeit infrequently, even after graduating and getting on with his life, so he's fully aware of the situation. When I called to set up this interview I made him swear not to do anything to humiliate me, and ten seconds in he's already broken his promise.

"Let's go over there," he says, indicating a half-finished house with no construction going on. "That one's quiet."

We trudge across the street and up the dirt driveway, trailing after Lindo through the non-existent doorway. The ground level is poured concrete and exposed wooden beams, construction supplies scattered around. He gathers up empty buckets and turns them over to use as stools, and soon enough the three of us are sitting in a weird triangle formation.

I'm expecting this to be awkward and strained, but to my surprise Aster pulls a notepad and pen out of her denim jacket and smiles at Lindo. He actually blinks at the brightness of her smile, the novelty of it, considering the story I'd told him about our fight and her enrollment in the program.

"Thanks for meeting with us," Aster begins. "We really appreciate you taking the time." She tucks her hair behind her ear and scribbles on her notepad, looking every bit the super keen academic I thought I'd met when I moved in with Jerry. I listen, perplexed, as she gathers Lindo's background information, the year he started at Holsom, the year he graduated, his major, his work assignment, extracurricular activity.

Her ability to transform is astounding. This is not the woman I lost nine minutes talking to in the car before realizing she'd put in ear buds and wasn't merely ignoring me. I've spent the past week thinking I might have broken her with my lie, shattered the perfect image she'd made for herself and sent her reeling. But that's not the case at all. She's either not affected, or she's really good at hiding things.

I'm pretty sure it's the latter.

It's what I do every day, after all.

"So now you own Lindo Construction," Aster is saying. "Did you always want to have your own business?"

"Oh, yeah," Lindo says. He props his huge arms on his huge knees and twists his wedding ring around his meaty finger. Last year he'd married his longtime boyfriend, Tony, and I'd gone to the wedding. Maybe the PPP makes you marriage material.

I glance at Aster.

But maybe not.

"I've never been good at following orders," Lindo continues. "But I loved giving them. More than that, however, I loved making something out of nothing." He touches his chest. "Case in point." Then he looks at me. "Another case."

Aster nods politely. "So you—"

"Did you know that when Shaw first showed up, I thought he was a girl?"

Oh shit.

Lindo pulls out his phone. "I took a picture, showed all my friends."

"Lindo, no," I say, reaching for the phone he's passing to Aster. But she's already snatched it out of his hand and is holding it away so I can't touch it.

She laughs then, so loudly it bounces off the concrete and makes me freeze, arm extended. I'm not thrilled she's guffawing at my move-in day picture, my scrappy concert T-shirt and tight jeans and hair halfway down my back, but it's nice to hear the sound. I never thought I'd hear it again.

"You're so skinny!" she exclaims, wiping tears from her eyes as she studies the phone and compares that me to this me, briefly forgetting she hates both of us.

"Well," I mutter. "I was…young."

"I got him to work out with me," Lindo says. "First he was my water boy, then I bench pressed him…"

"Would you shut up?" I interject.

"Then he started realizing the guys at the gym were watching him like he was something they might like to take a bite out of, so he cut off his beautiful hair and got serious about bulking up. Don't worry, Shaw. You're still pretty."

Aster returns the phone. "Thanks, Lindo. This has been worth the trip."

* * *

An eternity later, we're back in the car, Aster waving an enthusiastic goodbye to Lindo as I glare at him in the side mirror and pull away. He'd spent the entire interview half-answering Aster's questions and half-exposing any embarrassing details he could drum up about yours truly. When he wasn't embarrassing me he was praising me, which was more embarrassing than the outright humiliation. *Do you know Shaw's got a 3.6 GPA? Do you know Shaw helped cook thirty-seven turkeys to feed homeless people at Thanksgiving? Do you know Shaw fell down the stairs in the Student Union Building in front of hundreds of students and limped away, crying?*

"Fuck," I mumble, sipping the last of my cold coffee and wincing. "That was horrible."

"It was awesome," Aster replies distractedly. She's jotting down more things in her notebook, back in her junior reporter role.

I turn left out of the subdivision, toward the main road that cuts through the center of town and leads to the highway. It feels supremely unfair that I was the one who was stoked about this errand, and Aster's the only one who enjoyed it.

"Drop me off up here," she says abruptly. The click of her pen punctuates the statement.

"Where up here?" I ask. The street is lined with fast food restaurants and gas stations; there's nothing here she can't find at Holsom.

"Never mind. Just drop me off. I'll find my own way back."

"To Holsom? It's twenty-five miles from here!"

"I'll be fine. Stop at the gas station."

"What are you doing?"

"I said never mind."

"Well, I don't want to just abandon you somewhere. I'll drive you back after you do whatever it is you need to do at the gas station."

"I'm not going to the gas station, Aidan. Just stop."

I pull into the next parking lot and idle in front of a laundromat. "What's going on?"

"I have to run an errand."

"How long will it take? I can wait."

"No, thanks."

"Well, how will you get home?" Holsom is in another town; there are no city buses or trains that run between them, just a long stretch of highway.

"I'll hitchhike."

My jaw drops. Sure, I've hitchhiked in my day and the mysterious new Aster probably has too, but it just seems so… unnecessary.

"Aster, that's ridiculous. You don't need to hitchhike with a stranger when you can ride with me. I'm already here. I can take you exactly where you need to go."

She looks ready to argue, then picks up the donut still waiting for her in the cup holder and breaks off a piece. "Don't ask me any questions."

"Okay…"

"And don't get out of the car."

"Is this a drug deal? That's against the PPP rules."

She rolls her eyes. "That's against all the rules. It's not a drug deal."

"Okay, last question. Is it prostitution?"

"No, you ass," she snaps, tossing the remaining donut back into the cup holder. "Now drive."

She directs me through town, which, like my hometown, has its good parts and bad parts, until we come to a quieter section with official green signs pointing the way to a cemetery. I'm hoping we'll cruise past it, but when we come to the entrance for the parking lot Aster says, "Turn here. Stop and stay in the car."

"Aye aye." I shouldn't have agreed not to ask anymore questions. I have so many questions. But I know what happens when people lie to Aster, so I keep my mouth shut and watch her ass as she strides across the empty lot and disappears behind the wrought iron gate to the plots.

I don't know this girl at all, I think. I thought I did, but I had no idea. The first day I saw her I judged her the way I assumed so many people judged me when I arrived. They saw the hair and the tattoos and the scowl and figured they knew me. I looked at Aster and saw how perfect she was and thought she had a charmed life. I thought I was dark and she was light.

I know I'm lucky to have been selected for the PPP, and every day I do just enough to qualify. I go to class, I study, I pass. I show up for work, I stack books, I go home. I play Frisbee baseball, laugh at their jokes, bail on drinks.

My promise and potential is something the judge saw, that

Jim sees, but for me it's always been a pile of kindling, waiting to be lit.

When I met Aster, I thought she was the light I'd been waiting for.

But I was wrong.

She was the spark.

25

Aster

When I step back through the wrought iron gates of Chester Cemetery, Aidan is still in the car, seat reclined, playing a game on his phone. I'd only been inside for fifteen minutes, just enough time to wind my way through the tombstones to find Ramsay's plaque, lying flat against the grass in the west corner. There was a tiny bouquet of tulips sitting on it, still fresh enough to let me know my mom had been by recently.

I don't come here often. When Ramsay died I wasn't allowed to come to the funeral, and after that I swore I'd never come at all, but the prison counselors and Jim recommended that I visit when I can. When I learned where we'd be meeting Lindo, I decided to drop by. It's my fourth time here in the three years I've been at Holsom, but I still haven't figured out what to say. Mostly I just kneel on the grass and wait for inspiration that never comes, then give up and go home.

The only thing different about today is that I'm not alone. Aidan's here, like it or not. Aidan, who I thought for sure would trail me through the cemetery, hiding behind headstones, trying to spy. But he didn't. I'd tripped over my own feet three times looking over my shoulder, but here he is, waiting in the car like I'd asked him to.

I try to muster up some of the righteous anger I'm supposed to have, but I just feel tired. Ever since the night he came over and I planned to lie and tell him I was fucking Shamus and stomp on his heart until it was a bloody mess on the ground, I've been tired. I totally failed that night. I'd burst into tears like a nitwit, absolutely not the picture of cold defiance I'd intended. It's exhausting trying to be angry when you're supposed to be trying to be happy.

I get in the car and fasten my seatbelt. I can hear Aidan next to me, faint beeps as he wraps up whatever game he'd been playing, the slight groan of the chair as he straightens the seat. Then I can feel him. Feel him watching me, feel him waiting.

"You okay?" he asks after a moment.

"Fine."

In the handful of times I'd visited this place, there has never been anyone to ask me how I felt about it. If I was okay.

I'm not okay.

Aidan backs out of the parking space and retraces our route through town until we find the highway and pick up speed. The pressure in my chest eases as we leave Chester in the rearview, the past in the past.

"So what'd you do?" he asks.

I have my forehead pressed against the window, and I see my eyes narrow at my reflection. "I said no questions."

"Not at the cemetery," he says. "What'd you do to get into

the program? Come on. I told you my crime. You tell me yours."

When I exhale, my breath fogs the window, hiding my face. "Retail fraud," I say eventually.

"Retail fraud? What's that?"

"In my case, stealing stuff and returning it for cash or credit."

"Huh," he muses. "I never figured you for a klepto."

"There's a lot of stuff you never figured about me."

"You can tell me now, if you want."

"I'll pass."

We make it another mile in blissful silence, then Aidan ruins it.

"So you just like shiny things?" he guesses.

"No, Aidan."

"The thrill of the hunt?"

"No."

"Sticking it to the man?"

I turn and glare at him. "I was broke. We needed money. I found a way to get some."

"Is that why you were with Jerry?"

"I told you it wasn't. I loved him. He was...nice." I know *nice* is a damning word to some people, but I like it. It's comfortable. It's rare.

Aidan drums his fingers on the steering wheel. "Does he know you're in the program?"

"No."

"About the fraud?"

"No."

"Did you go to juvie?"

"No. Too old."

He hesitates, then ventures, "Prison?"

I shrug, like it was no big deal. Like I wasn't terrified every day. "Yeah."

Now he looks gratifyingly stunned. "Holy shit, Aster."

"That's what I said."

"So how do you do it?"

I sigh. "You just find a receipt, go in, steal the item—"

"Not steal stuff, genius. How do you do this Jekyll and Hyde thing you've got going on? It's like flicking a light switch. You ignore me for half an hour in the car, then you smile at Lindo and all of a sudden you're perfect little Aster again. What's the secret?"

"There is no secret. I'm just tired. Perfect little Aster is who I really am."

"Right."

I huff. "It's a work in progress."

"So if Jerry didn't know anything about you, how could he love you?"

I flinch. The same fear had circled my brain for the duration of our relationship, but my version was slightly reworded. *If Jerry knew anything about me, how could he love me?*

"He just did," I say lamely.

"I see."

"Well, what about you?" I counter. "You didn't tell me you were in the program. Do you tell the girls you date that you used to steal cars?"

"I don't date a lot. And when I do, we don't do a lot of talking."

I mock gag. "Spare me."

"Except you," he adds. "I talked to you."

I scoff. "You lied to me."

"Not technically," he replies. "I mean, if you think about it."

"If I think about it I'll stab you with my pen."

"Okay, don't think about it."

"Who's Daisy?" I ask. "For real. Don't tell me it's your dog."

"It's my dog," he answers. "Was my dog." He keeps his eyes on the road, even as I stare at him suspiciously. "My dad has a gambling problem. Everything we got, he lost to pay off whatever new debt he'd accumulated. One day I came home from school and Daisy was gone. He'd given her away to cover his ass. Sometimes I'd see her around town with her new family. She didn't remember me."

"For real?"

"For real."

I sit with that story for a second. He seems sincere. "That's the opposite problem I had," I say eventually. "My dad wouldn't give anything away. He held the purse strings so tight we couldn't get groceries some weeks."

"Is that who you were visiting? At the cemetery?"

"That was my brother. Drug overdose." I've never told anyone about Ramsay. I didn't even tell my bunkmate when I got the news in prison.

"I'm sorry."

"Whatever. My mom must have been there recently. When I went to jail she found a new man to take care of her and we lost touch. But I think he's probably okay. Gives her gas money."

"You lost touch with your mom?"

"Do you talk to your parents?"

146

"Yeah, of course. They're fucked up, but they're my parents. I can't tell them where I'm staying or my dad will show up and find a way to get in trouble, but I love them anyway."

"Your mom's still with him? Even though he lost your dog?"

"She's an enabler. Helping him is her addiction."

"That sucks."

He runs his hands through his messy hair. "I think that's why I don't date a lot of Holsom girls. They see me and they want to fix me. I don't want someone who sees a project."

"What do you want them to see?"

"I don't know. What did you see?"

I look away. "Not a project. You were my friend when I didn't have any. At least, I thought you were."

He slumps a little. "I was, Aster. I still could be."

"No. You can't."

"Why not? Because of that kiss? It was totally mediocre. There's no chemistry. Friends only."

I scoff, offended and amused all at once. With everything that had happened before and after the kiss, I hadn't given it much thought, which is probably for the best. Thinking about kissing Aidan is a huge mistake.

Kissing him was a huge mistake.

I thought it would be empowering and condescending to kiss him and push him away, but instead it stuck with me, reminding me what I'd been missing.

Because Jerry never kissed me like that.

No one has.

"You're right." I sniff. "It was disgusting."

"Revolting," he agrees.

147

I turn back to the window, feeling a little less tired, like the weight of my anger has been lifted, replaced with the relief of having someone learn the truth about me and not run screaming in the opposite direction.

I catch a glimpse of my reflection again. I'm smiling this time. Just a little.

26

Aidan

I drop off Aster, grab a sandwich for lunch, then make my way to the library for the afternoon shift. The library might not seem like the most natural environment for a guy like me, but I like it. It's quiet, and we're allowed to work on our homework during any lulls.

It's a slow day and I get a bunch of course reading done, and by the time I clock out at eight, I'm yawning non-stop. I'd tossed and turned all night in anxious anticipation of spending the morning with Aster, and now it's catching up with me.

I wasn't lying when I told her I never really dated. That also means I'm not good at dealing with women who are angry at me, and I'm definitely not good at making things right. My hopes for reconciliation had dwindled the longer we'd driven and the more she'd ignored me, but Lindo's embarrassing stories seem to have made her a little more forgiving. I could have done without the humiliation, but his strategy got Aster talking, and that's what I wanted. I hadn't expected her to tell me she'd spent time in prison—and I'm still trying to reconcile the idea of Aster in prison orange with the Aster I thought I knew and the Aster I'm trying to know—but it was kind of a relief, in its own way. Maybe if she's got her own scars she won't be afraid of the parts of me I'm always trying to keep hidden.

I return the rented car to the lot on campus and walk the rest of the way home. The day's sunshine was great, but it means that without the clouds to trap in the heat, the night is freezing. I jog back, my breath puffing in the air, and I'm breathing hard when I step through the front door. Hard enough that I've removed my coat and shoes and poured half a glass of water before I hear it.

Laughter.

Coming from Jerry's room.

I stop pouring and listen carefully.

There it is again.

A pretty, feminine laugh.

I ease into the living room and peer down the hallway, but his door is closed.

Jerry has a new girl.

At least, I assume she's new. What if Aster forgave him?

I listen for more laughter but none comes, and without acting like a creep and pressing my ear to his door, I can't make out anything beyond muffled voices.

It's not Aster, I tell myself as I rinse my glass and head down the hall to my room. It couldn't be. She'd only take him back to get revenge on me, and today we'd made some progress mending fences, so…it's not her.

Our bedrooms share a wall and the voices are slightly louder in here, making it impossible to concentrate on the essay I'm supposed to be writing. All I'm really doing is glaring at the laptop screen like that will help me hear better, and it's not working.

I try to listen to music, but I can't concentrate when I do, so I just lie on the bed, staring at the ceiling, picturing Aster and Jerry in there, going at it. Again.

I get up and retreat to the living room, turning on the television and increasing the volume until I can't hear anything over the corny jokes. Just when I think I'm safe, a female squeal pierces the air, immediately followed by Jerry's loud moan. I cover my face with a throw pillow as the rhythmic squeak of mattress springs starts a steadily intensifying march toward orgasm.

I'm not a voyeur. I'd much rather be the one participating than eavesdropping. But all these sex noises are reminding me that I haven't been with anyone in forever, and my body hates me for it. So does karma, because my shallow little plan to bang Aster has backfired in spectacular fashion: traditionally I've had sex without many feelings. Now I have tons of complicated feelings and no sex.

Life sucks.

"Jerry!"

Grunt.

Okay, now it really sucks.

"Jerry!"

Louder grunt.

"Yes!"

Squeak.

"Yes!"

Grunt.

"Yes!"

Squeak.

"Yes!"

There's no way Jerry's that good, is he?

"You're killing me!" she shouts.

Is he?

An impassioned female cry answers that question, joined by Jerry's deeper moan, then the slow creaking of the mattress springs as they finally settle down.

I exhale and take the pillow off my face. I'm jealous. I'm horny. And I don't know what to do about anything. Before I can dwell on it, I hear soft footsteps pad across the hall, then the click of the bathroom fan turning on. Moments later the fan clicks off, but instead of retreating to the bedroom, the footsteps grow louder.

She's coming down the hall.

Distracted humming joins the giggling of the studio audience and I sit up abruptly when a blonde in a rumpled white shirt stumbles into the kitchen, failing to notice me on the couch. Her hair is tangled on one side, her long legs bare and gleaming as they disappear behind the counter. She opens the fridge door, silhouetted by the interior light, like a sex goddess out of a movie.

I barely manage to pick my jaw off the ground before she turns and spots me, pitcher of water in hand.

"Oh!" she exclaims, fingers flying up to cover her mouth, cheeks flushing pink. "Aidan. My goodness. I didn't realize you were here." After a second those fingers fall, her sex-soft lips curving as her eyes rake me over. "How nice to see you again."

I hold the pillow in my lap like a shield, trying to hide my horror.

My roommate's new girl…is Missy.

27

Aster

A knock at my door at ten o'clock at night is nothing out of the ordinary. Students requesting emergency condoms, students reporting someone throwing up in the bathroom—and all over the bathroom—and students asking for more condoms because they "lost" the last ones are pretty standard fare.

What's not so standard is seeing Aidan Shaw framed in my doorway when I yank it open after the sixth urgent knock.

For a second I just stare at him. He hasn't been back since our fight, and this time I'm not dressed to kill in a borrowed dress and heels. This time I'm wearing hot pink sweatpants and a clashing orange Holsom T-shirt, my hair still wet from the shower.

"Did you know Jerry is banging Missy?" he blurts out, then barges into my room without waiting for an invitation. "Missy from Frisbee baseball?" he adds. "The blonde who plays second base?"

I take my time closing the door, keeping my back to him.

I may know a little something about this.

I may have…introduced them.

"Maybe?" I offer.

I turn just in time to see him gape at me. "Maybe?" he repeats. "You maybe know about this?"

"Just a little."

"What did you do? And why did you do it? And how? And why?"

"What's the big deal? Jerry and I broke up. He's allowed to move on. He can never truly be happy again, but he can try."

"I can't tell if you're joking."

"Fifty-fifty."

Aidan scrubs his hands over his face, genuinely pained. I expect him to continue ranting about Missy, but then he surprises me. "I thought it was you," he mutters through his fingers.

"What was me?"

"Tonight," he says. "I got home and I could hear them through the wall, going at it."

I wince. I may have introduced them, but I don't want to *think about it.*

"I thought maybe you'd taken him back or something."

"Never," I say firmly.

Aidan looks a bit sheepish, and I try not to notice how hot he is. His jeans and combat boots are fine, but when Aidan gets dressed for work, the contrast of the crisp white shirt and dress pants with his tattoos and hair…

It's not fair.

I tip my head, like I can pour out the dirty thoughts. "Why are you here?"

"I had to get away," he says. "And I didn't know where else to go."

I raise a doubtful brow. I know he has friends because I met them at the wedding. And I saw T.J. and Wes and Brix at the PPP meeting, so I know they're still alive.

"Fine," he mumbles. "I just wanted to come here."

He pulls out the chair from my desk and straddles it, resting his arms on the back and his chin on his hands like a petulant kid in detention.

"You seem pretty upset," I comment, sitting on the edge of my bed. I close my laptop—I'd been playing games instead of studying, anyway—and use the heel of my foot to push some dirty laundry out of sight.

"I'm not upset," he says. "I'm...confused."

"About your feelings for Jerry?"

He lifts his head enough to glower at me.

"About Missy?" My heart does a tiny, alarmed flip in my chest. Of course I'd seen Missy's aggressive brand of flirtation during the Frisbee baseball games, but I'd never once seen Aidan reciprocate. I figured she was exactly the type of project-seeking girl he wanted to avoid. But now that I know her, I also know she's beautiful and smart and funny and down-to-earth.

I didn't think this through.

In my defense, it's not like I planned it. We were walking across campus a couple of weeks ago when she spotted a hot guy and dragged me over to "bump into" him. Bump into...Jerry. It could have been awkward—and it was—but I was still angry at Aidan, so what better way to punish him than to invite more Missy into his life? I knew if Missy and Jerry went out that Jerry would immediately confess his sins, so once we were alone I'd confessed for him, telling Missy how he'd cheated on me, the first and only time in his life he'd ever done such a thing, and he felt so bad that he'd absolutely never do it again to anyone else. His cheating was actually kind of...a good thing.

I used to make a living selling lies.

And apparently, Missy bought them.

"I'm very clear on my feelings for Missy," Aidan says. Then he clarifies: "She terrifies me."

I hide a smile.

"And she's super loud during sex."

I cringe. "Don't tell me this stuff."

"Why not? Misery loves company."

"You're miserable knowing that Missy is having orgasms?"

"No, I'm miserable because I'm not."

The words hang between us for an incredibly long time.

"Are you?" he asks softly. "Having...?"

I should tell him that it's none of his business and never will be, but I can't seem to blink and he's watching me so, so closely.

I move my head slightly from side to side, a reluctantly admitted *no*.

"Why not?" I ask after a moment.

"Why not what?"

"Why aren't you...with someone?"

He rubs a hand over his jaw, palm rasping against the stubble. "Well..." he says cautiously. "I was waiting for you."

My heart squeezes. "You were waiting for something that doesn't exist."

"You exist," he says, holding my stare. "Not in the way I

thought you did. But in this way. A real way."

I was fourteen when we fled from my dad, and I'd never had a boyfriend before then. When I was stealing and lying and figuring my life was fucked so why not, I'd hooked up with a few guys. Sometimes it was a bed for a night or sometimes it was a meal, and sometimes it was just someone to tell me I was pretty and be nice to me for a while, even if it wasn't true. It didn't matter. It's not like I told them the truth about my life. Never showed them the real me. Then I went to prison, and never had to.

My first year at Holsom was self-imposed isolation. A couple of guys asked me out, but I felt like such a freak I turned them down. I stayed on campus during the summer and worked at one of the language schools, and it was the combination of extreme loneliness and seeing those students come to a new country, learn a new language, and make new friends, that inspired me to do the same. I'd learn the language of college students and figure out this new world, go through the motions like I belonged, and pray that I eventually convinced myself it was home.

Then I met Jerry and he made the illusion feel real. Like, if he bought it, so could everybody else. And maybe I could, too.

Until Aidan.

Unlike before, I don't feel a flash of rage when I remember what he did. I'm never going to be grateful for it, but maybe Aidan's involvement was just a catalyst, a way to speed up the end of a relationship that had always had an expiration date.

Aidan's the only guy in my life to see all of me. The person I was and the person I want to be and the person I am now. And for whatever reason, he's still looking.

It's terrifying.

As though he can read all this on my face, he stands, stretching his arms over his head, revealing a tan strip of skin above the waistband of his pants. I'd seen way more skin than this that day at the pool, but I'd been thinking about drowning him then, not dreaming up ways to see more.

Now my long-dead forgiveness reflex is rushing back in and dragging my hormones with it, and they're all saying, *Let's do this thang.*

"I should go," he says quietly.

His eyes are darker, like he's fighting some inner battle, saying the words not because he means them, but because he has to.

"Yes," I agree, because I have to, not because I mean it.

28

Aidan

"I'm open!" Wes calls. I pass the basketball across the court. He snags it with one hand and makes his shot.

"That's game!" I shout, high-fiving my teammate.

Brix grabs the ball, circles the net, and dunks it. He's been racing around the outdoor basketball court the whole game. At first I thought it was a new strategy he and T.J. were trying out, attempting to make me and Wes dizzy, but now I think it's something else. It's like he's a tiger that's been let out of his cage, doing his best to burn off all the excess energy he stored while locked up.

We grab water bottles from our bags at the edge of the court and watch Brix practice his lay-ups. "He knows the game's over, right?" T.J. mutters, joining us.

"Hey!" I snatch up Brix's water and toss it to him when he turns. "Take a break!"

He catches the water and tosses it through the net, grabbing it before it hits the ground. Then he bounces the ball back to

Wes and takes a seat in the middle of the court.

"What's going on?" T.J. asks. "You on something?"

Brix flops onto his back and contemplates the sky. "High on life, man."

We exchange dubious glances and join him on the concrete.

"How's the wife?" Wes inquires. "We haven't seen you too much since you got married."

"Just busy," Brix replies. "Gotta paint the house, repaint the house, pick out a couch, find the right coffee table, visit nine dozen galleries hunting for the right piece of art to hang over the fireplace…"

"You have a fireplace?" T.J. exclaims.

"You have art?" I add.

"Now I do."

"You like it?" Wes asks.

"The fireplace is okay. The art's horrible."

"How about being married? Is that okay?"

He props himself up on one elbow and wipes his face with the hem of his sweaty T-shirt. "It's awesome," he says eventually. "I know everyone says we're too young…"

"You are," T.J. interrupts.

Brix ignores him. "…but when it's right, it's right. And it feels right. Stupid art gecko and all."

Wes scratches his ear. "Do you mean art deco?"

"Nope. The artwork is a three-foot bead sculpture of a gecko."

"Why?"

"No idea, man."

We ponder this for a moment.

"What about you?" Brix asks, kicking my foot. "You brought a date to my wedding. What's the story there?"

I concentrate on trying to spin the ball on one finger. "No story. We're friends."

"She's too hot to be your friend," Wes points out. "She might think of you as a friend, but that can't be all you want. What was it you said at the wedding? *Not yet?*"

I hesitate. It's one thing to discuss a one-night stand that meant nothing; it's quite another to discuss someone who means a whole lot. Fortunately, Brix jumps in and saves me.

"It's better when you're friends first," he says. "There's more on the line when you cross it, but if it works out, it's awesome. You get a friend *and* you get sex."

T.J. snorts. "I've got friends. I'm just looking for sex."

They crack up and I tune them out as I think about what Brix said, about crossing the line. I've been friends with Aster for nearly three months. We've kissed, traveled together, conquered fears, played sports, eaten ice cream, had a big fight, made up... We've basically had an entire relationship, minus the hooking up. It's more than I've ever had with anyone, but I still want more.

I like Aster.

I care about her.

And I want her.

I need a new plan.

29

Aster

I can count on one hand the number of pieces of paper mail I've received this year, so as I walk past the row of mailboxes on my way to the elevator, I do an exaggerated double-take when I spot the edge of a white envelope peeking through the glass on my box.

I dig out my keys from my pocket and retrieve the envelope, staring at the handwritten address in confusion. It's made out to Aster Lindsey at Holsom College, then the town name and state. No zip code. No building name or room number. But there's a stamp, and it couldn't have gotten into the mailbox without following the official channels.

I don't know why I feel nervous, but as I unseal the flap during the ride up in the elevator, my heart starts to pound. Who would write me a letter? I don't have any prison penpals. I don't have anybody.

Once in my room, I lock the door and sit on the edge of the bed, staring at the opened envelope. Then, with trembling fingers, I pull out the single sheet of lined paper waiting inside.

Aster, I read. *It's me.*

I fold the paper in half, and in half again, then cram it back into the envelope and drop it on the floor, like it's possessed and folding it up a bunch of times will help.

It's from my father.

He knows I'm at Holsom because when I got accepted to the school, they wouldn't send the enrollment documents to the prison and I had to give them a home address. I didn't know where my mother was living so I gave them my dad's address and he passed along the papers. No message, no note, just a forwarding stamp on the front of the envelope, followed by the prison address.

I have no idea why he would be trying to contact me now, and if the sweat pooling in the small of my back and my shallow breathing and my tiny heart attack are any indication, I don't want to know.

I've only seen him once since the night I fled with my mom and Ramsay. We didn't have enough money to go far, so we just lived on the opposite side of town and stuck to the sketchier corners we knew he didn't visit. About a year after we'd left I was leaving a drug store with a two hundred dollar store credit to my name, when I almost walked into him in the parking lot.

He'd steadied me with a hand on each shoulder, holding my gaze as I stared up at him in terror. "Watch it," he said, then let go of me and continued walking, like he hadn't recognized me at all.

I crumple the envelope and toss it toward the trash can near the desk. It bounces off the rim and rolls under the radiator, lurking in the shadows, a trite metaphor for my tragic back story.

I grab my textbooks out of my bag and try to read. This is my life now. Everything is different. Everything is better.

I live in the present, not the past.

* * *

"No responses," Jim says a couple of days later. Aidan and I sit across from him in the PPP office as he scans his email. Our next assignment is to interview a present day PPP student about their experience, but so far we haven't managed to find anyone willing to talk to us. Jim even sent out a mass email asking for volunteers, bribing them with the promise of counting the interview as one of their credits, but no takers.

Not even Aidan's friends were willing to help.

I, of course, have no friends.

Being accepted into the program is a source of pride, but there's also a strong stigma attached to it. Holsom is a nice school with nice kids, and nice kids don't steal cars or go to prison or do whatever it is everyone in this program has done. It's no mystery why no one wants to cooperate—I certainly wouldn't agree to sit in front of someone and field questions about my life. Not that I have any answers.

"What if we just interview a recent grad?" I try. "Someone from the last year. We can talk about how they're doing… presently."

Jim smiles kindly at my lame effort, but doesn't relent. "You've already spoken to Lindo, that's the past component. But we want kids coming into the program next year to see the same names and faces from the campaign around campus. They need to see being here as a tangible source of pride and accomplishment, not just an idea. They show up with a chip on their shoulder and it's our job to help whittle that down until it's no longer an obstacle that holds them back."

Aidan shifts in his seat beside me.

"Obviously everyone still has too big a chip if they're not even willing to do the interview in exchange for the cooperation credit," I argue. "And if the program is supposed to be anonymous, we can't force anyone to help."

"You're right," Jim says. "No one can be forced." Then he looks between us meaningfully.

"What are you getting at?"

"You have plans for after you graduate, right, Aster? You'd like to go to law school?"

"Uh-huh."

"And Aidan? Any plans for you?"

He shrugs, the ever-sullen kid in the principal's office. "I don't know yet."

Jim folds his hands on the desk. "As you're aware, so long as you continue to meet the enrollment requirements, the Promise & Potential Program will cover the cost of your four-year degree. Any education beyond that is up to you to fund."

"Right."

"But."

I sit up a bit straighter in my seat. I've been squirreling away whatever spare change I can in a weak effort to finance the upcoming three years of law school, but it's not adding up fast. Combined with the fact that I have no real possessions to speak of and no one to co-sign a loan, I don't have a whole lot of options.

But could be an option.

"There are grants," Jim says. "For people who excel in the program. For people whose promise and potential would be limited by a four-year degree. We're sometimes able to wrangle grants for those students, but they're hard to come by, and so are the people willing to put themselves on the line for the opportunity."

Aidan fidgets in his seat.

I already know what Jim's getting at, but still I check. "What are you saying, exactly?"

"I'm saying we're not allowed to force you to give an interview, but perhaps I can entice you. Knock this one out of the park, and I'll put in a good word."

"And by knock it out of the park you mean…"

"Be the interviewee," Jim says. "You'd be a great spokesperson for the program, Aster. You're smart, you're friendly—"

Aidan shifts again, increasingly uncomfortable.

"—you're the kind of hope these kids need. The light at the end of the tunnel. The promise and potential they want to see in themselves. I know it's asking a lot of you. I know everyone has a past and sometimes that history isn't the ideal fit with the life we're trying to lead. But you don't have anything to be ashamed of—none of you do. You're here for a reason."

Aidan's staring at his tattooed knuckles.

Ride hard.

I close my eyes and summon my courage.

"Okay," I hear Aidan say before I can. "I'll do it."

My eyes fly open.

Jim's face mirrors my surprise. "You?" he says. "Aidan?"

"Yeah." Aidan flicks a look at me, then stands, signaling the end of the meeting. "We'll do the interview. No problem. Thanks for your time."

I quickly say goodbye to Jim and hurry after Aidan out of the offices and down the empty hall to the stairs.

"Hey," I say, snagging his arm when I catch up. "What are you doing?"

"Just getting the interview done. No big deal."

"Why are you walking so fast if it's no big deal?"

"Because I've got plans for us."

I stop walking. "For us?"

His mouth quirks and he runs his hand through his messy hair, *HARD* stamped across the knuckles.

"Yeah," he says. "Did you think I was doing this because I'm a nice guy? I'll do it, but you've gotta give me something in return."

30

Aidan

"A movie?" Aster says as we approach the theater. "That's your big something?"

"Why?" I hold the door. "Were you expecting something perverted?"

She purses her mouth primly. "No."

"Get your mind out of the gutter, you perv. I told you. We're just friends."

She tries to hide it, but I see her smile and it still gets me.

I wave her in. "Come on. *Kill Glory 5* starts in twenty minutes. I want to see the previews."

I haven't been to a matinee since my dad took me to see *Ice Age*. I don't remember anything about the movie, just how excited I was to be there. I didn't know until later that he'd brought me to the movie to get me out of the house while some guys showed up to take our living room furniture.

"I haven't seen *Kill Glory* one, two, three or four," Aster frets. "I hope I can follow along."

"I'll explain all the complicated parts."

I buy both tickets, ignoring her attempts to give me money. I'm forcing her to be here, after all. The least I can do is pay. It's not like chivalry's completely dead.

We order snacks at the concession, and Aster jabs me in the gut with her elbow when she thrusts money at the cashier before I can pay again. Okay, now it's dead.

"Fuck," I wheeze, half hunched over as I carry my popcorn and drink down the hall to the theater. "You're a mean date."

She fastens her lips around the straw and sucks, cheeks hollowing. "Who me?" she asks, tongue peeking out to lick a stray drop of soda off her lip.

I pick up the pace.

Because it's a matinee and the movie is several weeks old, the theater is mostly empty, just a few people scattered throughout. We snag seats on the end, the same ones I'd reserved for our first failed date night, the ones we'd never managed to fill.

As soon as we sit there's a shrill ring, and Aster jolts. "Shit," she mutters, shoving her popcorn into my arms as she fumbles to get her phone out of her bag.

I start to make a joke about who might be calling her, but stop when I see her face, lit by the dim glow from her phone. I can't see the screen to check the number, but the tense set of her jaw and the sudden strain on her face tells me it's not good.

"What is it?" I ask as she shuts off the phone and crams it back into her bag.

"Nothing," she mumbles, taking back her food and sinking into her seat. She stuffs a handful of popcorn into her mouth and focuses her attention on the car ad playing up front.

"It kind of seems like something," I say, treading lightly. Learning that Aster's bright and shiny façade covers up seven years' worth of dings and dents has shown me we're more alike than I thought. Most of the cars I stole got stripped down for parts, but there was the occasional car they re-outfitted and sold to some buyer who was fine not asking questions. Whenever I saw the transformed cars I'd look past the new paint and the rims and the upgrades and see the original. No matter how good the cover up, you can never completely erase the past.

"Nope. Nothing."

"Are you in trouble?"

She meets my eye. "No."

We sit silently for a few minutes, absorbing ads for credit cards, phone plans, and more soft drinks, then Aster asks, "Why'd you volunteer for the interview?"

I did it for her, obviously. I did it so she didn't have to. So she could be as bright and shiny as she wants to be, without ever admitting to the scars she keeps hidden. But of course I can't say that. "To get out of the meeting. I hate meetings."

"You could have said that before the meeting. Then there would have been no meeting at all."

"I was hoping Jim could find us another victim."

"Are you worried?"

"That your questions will be perverted? Yes, of course."

She smirks.

"Promise me you'll keep it clean," I say. "At least while—"

"Have you ever been with that…woman?" she asks abruptly. "From the bar? Sindy?"

The ellipsis means "prostitute," a gap in the question that's as dangerous as a huge hole in the ground, a nest of vipers writhing at the bottom.

"I didn't know the interview was going to start now," I hedge.

Aster just stares, waiting me out.

"No," I say finally, cautiously circling around the gaping hole. "Of course not."

"She knew you," Aster says. "You weren't just some guy who showed up that day and paid her. She said you went way back."

Turns out there's another big hole right beside the last one, and I topple in headfirst.

"Three years way back," I admit, scrubbing my hand over my chin uncomfortably. "I met her when I first got here. I didn't know anybody, was convinced I'd never have any friends, and I went to the bar with my fake ID, intending to get drunk and forget my problems."

"But you didn't?"

"Well, partly." No one besides Sindy knows this story; I'd begged her never to repeat it. "I got very drunk and fell off my stool and knocked myself unconscious. When I woke up I was on the floor in the back room, covered in a blanket. I heard Sindy having sex with some guy—I didn't know he was a client at the time—so I stayed still until he left, then she said, 'You can come out now.'"

Aster's cringing. "Okay, I thought my prison cavity search was a low moment, but you may have just topped it."

"It gets worse. She made me pay her for the time she'd wasted convincing the manager not to call the police—or an ambulance—and as I handed over the only cash in my wallet, I realized that while I may have thought I'd hit rock bottom before,

I'd just uncovered new depths. So I turned things around."

"And became friends with a prostitute."

"She's more like a really mean aunt. That's why I prefer to drink at Bender instead of any of the places on campus. If I'm there, I've got someone to make sure I stay in line."

"Have you ever paid for it?"

"I'll answer your question if you answer one of mine."

"I've never hired a gigolo."

"Are you sure? Because this date is costing you three hundred dollars."

"What a rip-off. I should have been allowed to pick the movie."

"I've never paid for it," I say. "Lindo may have mocked my long hair, but it was a hit with the ladies."

Aster snickers and eats another fistful of popcorn. "I should ask him to send me that photo."

"Too late. I already bribed him not to."

"Dammit."

"Anyway. My question."

She lifts a brow and waits.

"How come I never heard you wailing the way Missy does when she comes? If Jerry's such a superstar in bed, how'd you stay so quiet?"

Aster's mouth falls open, a piece of popcorn held between her fingers, just a millimeter away from its destination. "Aidan!" she exclaims, swiveling around as though any of the four people in the theater might be eavesdropping. "That's none of your business."

"It's because he's bad in bed, right? And Missy's faking it? For my benefit?"

173

"God, you're conceited."

"Or was it so good your screams were so high, so loud, the human ear couldn't hear them?"

"Yes, that's why there were so many dogs in the parking lot," she says dryly. "Every. Single. Night. *Multiple* times."

I know she's lying, but it still affects me. Still makes me picture Aster's face when she comes, the sounds she might make, the things she might like.

"Why didn't you bring anyone over?" she counters. "Jerry said you never had company."

"Because I wanted you," I reply. "And nobody else."

"You didn't know me," she says. She'd said that before, too. Like she doesn't trust that the image she's presenting could possibly be real. It may be a work in progress, but it's still her. Part of her, anyway. The superficial part, the one that hides the deeper, more interesting parts. The ones she's still convinced have to be hidden.

"I know you now."

She rolls her lips, and I know the next question. I know she wants to ask if I still want her, if discovering those depths changes how I feel.

"And?" she asks softly, fiddling with her straw.

The movie starts then, jolting us in our seats with the terrifyingly loud thud of Glory, the film's hero, crashing to earth in a bloody heap, the way each film in the series begins.

"Fuck," Glory mumbles, holding a hand to the brains oozing out of the crack in her skull. She sits up and glares around Times Square. "Not this again."

From the corner of my eye I see Aster grimacing in horror.

I reach over the armrest, finding her hand on her thigh and sliding my fingers through hers.

"What are you doing?" she whispers, staring at our joined hands.

"Holding on," I whisper back.

31

Aster

I decide we'll do the interview in the far corner of my dorm room, the interview chair facing the rest of the suite, the curtains drawn behind it so the background is nothing more distracting than pale green linen. I set up a second chair six feet away from the first, arranging a notepad and pen on the seat in preparation. Being this close to Aidan, alone in my room, is going to be difficult. Maybe I should open the curtains so I can focus on something instead of his face, his shoulders, his tattoos...

My phone rings, scaring the crap out of me. I'd taken to keeping it turned to silent recently, and the piercing sound makes me curse as I snatch the phone off the desk and glare at the screen. Another blocked number.

I decline the call, and they don't leave a voice message.

They never do.

A sudden knock at the door makes me jump again. "Jesus," I mutter, tossing the phone down and hurrying over to twist the lock.

Aidan's waiting in the hall. It's not a surprise; he's supposed to be coming over. I've been waiting for him. But it still somehow manages to feel like a surprise, like every time I see him I find something I didn't expect.

Today that something is ice cream.

"Get in here with that," I say, stepping back to usher him in.

"Good day to you too," he replies. He's wearing jeans and a black Henley that clings to his broad shoulders and trim waist, his hair a little too long and a little too messy, reminding everybody that he just doesn't care. But he does.

I reach for one of the two pints in his hand, but he holds them out of reach.

Okay, maybe he doesn't care.

"What's happening?" I ask, hands on hips, eyes on ice cream.

"I've been thinking," he begins.

"Uh-oh."

"You don't even know what I thought about."

"Your hair?"

He pauses. "I just thought about my hair for a minute. The real focus of my thoughts was you."

"I'm going to need that ice cream now."

"You have the same expression on your face you had at the theater when your phone rang. What's going on, Aster? Is someone bothering you?"

"Just you. I'll get spoons."

"I was also thinking," he adds as I retrieve spoons from the bookshelf and pass him one in exchange for a pint, "about how much better I felt after our talk about Sindy."

"You did?"

"Yeah. That was a really embarrassing story and I thought I'd feel humiliated after I told you, but I didn't. Instead it was like saying it out loud brought it into the light and made me see that it wasn't as bad as I thought."

"It wasn't great, Aidan."

He ignores that. "And at the pool, when I ducked under the water, it was the scariest thing I'd ever done. But you were there for me."

"I brought you there to drown you."

"But you didn't, that's the important part. Also, duly noted, you psycho."

I eat some ice cream. It's the expensive stuff, the kind I never buy.

"Anyway," he continues, "I just figured that you were there for me, and if you want, I could be here for you."

"You are here."

"You know what I'm saying. *More* here."

We're standing in the middle of my room, eating from separate pints of ice cream. Mine is plain vanilla, my favorite, while the name on the side of Aidan's carton is three lines long. It's got brownies, cookie dough, and even cherry pie.

When I met Jerry, I thought he was the nicest guy I'd ever known. To be fair, I hadn't exactly surrounded myself with a lot of nice people in the previous years, but he was so remarkably kind and sincere that I convinced myself he was what I needed. But he wasn't.

This is.

"I think my dad's trying to get in touch," I hear myself say.

Aidan raises a brow. "Did you talk to him?"

"I don't pick up. He doesn't leave a message. The number's blocked, so I can't trace it."

"So why do you think it's him?"

"Because he wrote me a letter." I sit on the edge of the bed and balance the ice cream on my knees.

Aidan rests against the desk. "And?"

"I didn't read the whole thing. It didn't have a return address so I opened it, and when I saw, *Aster, it's me,* I stopped."

"Where's the letter?"

"Aidan, I'm *afraid.*"

He pauses to consider that, then takes another bite of ice cream. "Of what?"

"Of... Of..."

I keep seeing the spoon slide in and out of his mouth and fall off my train of thought.

I shake my head.

"Of feeling that way again. Of letting the past back into my life. The letter is like a portal... I escaped all that. It's behind me. I can't have it here. I can't. Maybe one day I'll be ready for it, but not yet."

He studies his boots. "I know what you mean," he says, licking the back of his spoon. "Three years at this place and sometimes I see a car and I know exactly how to pop the lock, start it up, what its parts are worth. Sometimes it's tempting."

"Did you really love stealing cars?"

"No. Stupid, right? I just loved doing something. Feeling like I was doing something. Something important."

"You're doing something important now."

"Please don't remind me of my promise and potential."

"I meant giving me ice cream."

His cheeks turn pink. "Oh." Then he spoons up a heaping mountain of whatever concoction he chose for himself and extends it to me. "Want to face your fear?"

"I'm not afraid of ice cream."

"Prove it."

"That's stupid."

He just arches a brow in challenge.

I'd really rather not prove it, but I can't back down now, so I place my carton on the nightstand and rise, crossing the short space as confidently as I can. With just a foot between us, the spoon hovering mid-air in front of my mouth, I look at Aidan. His dark eyes, intent on mine. The messy hair falling onto his forehead. The tattooed knuckles wrapped around the handle. *Ride.*

My gaze flickers up to his. He's still watching me. Waiting for me to take the ice cream, maybe.

But maybe not.

He reaches back and places the pint on the desk behind him, freeing one hand to rest on my hip. He's so warm I feel the heat of his palm through my jeans and T-shirt, feel it spread, reminding me I like that feeling. I like this.

I *miss* this.

A drop of ice cream falls to the floor, landing in the tiny space between our feet.

"Uh-oh," Aidan says. "You'd better eat it."

I glance at his mouth.

"Or I can eat it," he offers. "If you want."

32

Aidan

I kiss her.

I don't even think about it, I'm just acting on instinct. The hand on her hip slips around to the outside of her arm, up to her shoulder, her neck, fingers curling into her nape. She doesn't move, doesn't look away from my mouth, and the soft flutter of her lashes is the last thing I see before my lips touch hers.

She makes a tiny sound when our mouths meet, and I feel a tremor roll through her, like a frisson of energy arcing from her body into mine. I fumble behind me to stick the spoonful of melting ice cream back into the carton, only fifty percent sure I manage the task, a hundred percent sure I don't care.

I cup her face with both hands, feel her silky hair teasing my fingers, the softness of her mouth, her breasts pressed against my chest. The tip of her tongue touches my bottom lip at the same moment her hand comes up to stroke my cheek, and I leap away like I've been electrocuted.

Aster yelps in alarm. "What—what happened?" she demands,

one hand clutching her chest. "Was it a mouse? They said they got them all—"

"I—" I bury my face in my hands. I'm so fucking mortified.

There was no mouse, of course.

It was Aster.

"Aidan?" she asks, coming forward. She reaches out tentatively, touching my wrist. "Are you all right? Did I...do something?"

I peer between my fingers, but she's not mocking me, not being judgmental or duplicitous. She genuinely doesn't know.

"I thought you were going to slap me," I admit.

Her jaw drops, and for a long second she just gapes at me.

Then she starts to laugh.

"What? Why?" She sobers. "Did you lie about something else? What is it? Tell me."

"No!" I exclaim. "I haven't done anything. I just..." The truth is, the second I let my guard down last time, she Trojan horsed her way in and tried to destroy me. I may have deserved it, but that doesn't mean it didn't hurt.

"I wasn't going to slap you," she says. "Honest."

"Last time..."

"Last time you'd paid a prostitute to blow my boyfriend. Have you done that this time?"

"Of course not."

"Anything comparable?"

"No. Fuck." I rub a hand over my face. "I'm embarrassed."

"Yeah, well, that was really embarrassing for you."

"You hit me really hard."

Her face softens. Maybe it's compassion. Maybe it's guilt.

"I'm sorry I hit you," she says. "I still think you deserved to suffer for what you did, but I should have just stepped on your foot or kneed you in the balls or something."

I wince. "Don't joke about that."

"Okay."

"And I'm really sorry about Jerry," I say. "I'd like to tell you my motives were pure, but they were not."

Her mouth quirks. "I know."

I clear my throat. "They're still not."

The words are a warning shot, a last ditch opportunity for Aster to say she's changed her mind, on second thought, let's just do the interview, but she doesn't move an inch. Doesn't even blink when I step forward, backing her into the desk, stepping too close so she has to boost herself up, legs parting to make room for me between them.

I touch my forehead to hers and rest my hands on the desk on either side of her hips, the position forcing her to lean back on her arms. It arches her spine, her breasts flush against my chest, and cranes her neck, putting her mouth in just the right spot.

"You want this?" I ask, my voice rough. I know she can feel my hard-on through my jeans, pressing against the inside of her thigh. I want to be sure this time. I want to know we're on the same, honest page. Having learned a little about her family, I understand why Aster doesn't forgive and forget. She has a fucked up past; a semi-fucked up present. Well, so did I. But unlike Aster, I have two parents who love each other despite the drama, and unlike Aster, I think there's a way to make things work.

If we want them to.

She watches me for a long second, the cornflower blue back in her eyes, hiding nothing, seeing everything. And then she nods.

It'd be great if she cried, "Yes, Aidan, give me everything!" but I'll take the nod.

I kiss her. The second our lips touch it's like a match being dropped into a pile of kindling. Forget the fucking spark—it's like tossing the kindling into a raging inferno. Everything around us vanishes, consumed by heat. I forget the room, the ice cream, the interview. All I can taste, touch, feel, smell, is Aster. She whimpers against my mouth, tongues too tangled to say anything, and pushes herself up straighter so she can wrap her arms around my neck. I press my hands against the small of her back, drawing her into me, lodging my cock between her legs and nearly dying from the sensation of being so close but still too far away.

Her fingers are twisted in my hair, short nails scraping my scalp in a way that feels better than it should. I slide a hand over her hip and under her T-shirt, finding soft, warm skin and the scratchy lace of her bra. When she doesn't stop me, I seek out the clasp between her shoulder blades and work it open. She smiles against my mouth and I can't help but smile back.

"Shirt off," I murmur, snagging the hem and tugging it up.

"You too," she replies, lifting her arms.

I pull the T-shirt over her head and she lets the bra fall to the floor at our feet. For an endless moment I just admire the view. Aster Lindsey, topless and willing and right in front of me.

Finally.

"C'mon," she mutters, yanking on my shirt. "Your turn."

She strips away the Henley, and if I thought I was hard looking at her, seeing the way she bites her lip as she studies me, the sexy way her cheeks flush, I nearly come on the spot.

All this time I'd been thinking about how much I wanted Aster.

I never realized how much I wanted her to want *me.*

I tug her onto her feet and get to work on her jeans. She shimmies out of them, leaving her in a scrap of black lace that's supposed to be panties and is far sexier than anything I'd expect her to own.

"What the...?" I murmur, stroking my thumb over the front of the lace. "These are fancy."

"Look around," she says, gesturing to the sparse room. "I'm a fancy girl. Plus, I got tired of prison panties."

I growl. "Stop trying to turn me on."

She laughs as I bear her back onto the bed, shucking my pants as we go. Then we're skin to skin and mouth to mouth, and I feel like a kid at a carnival, trying to figure out where to start and how to never stop.

She fumbles with one hand to retrieve a box of condoms from the nightstand, never breaking our kiss. The box falls and a colorful array of shiny packages spills across the floor, a buffet of possibility.

I nip her lower lip and trail kisses over her jaw, down her throat, across her chest. When I reach her breasts it's like the culmination of a three-month hike, finally reaching the pinnacle. I want to take a selfie and plant a flag with my name on it.

Aster clenches my hair as I cover her nipples with my mouth, my tongue, my hands. Everything I've got, I'm giving her. I work her panties down her thighs with a free hand and she lets her legs part. I feel the heat from her center against my belly, and I tell myself to take my time, make every second count.

I've never invested so much in a girl. Never needed to.

Never *wanted* to.

I trail my fingers up the inside of one smooth thigh, feeling her tremble beneath the touch. When I find the damp folds of her pussy I gauge the expressions rolling across her face as I stroke her, closer and closer, thumb finding and seeking her clit, rubbing carefully.

Her lashes flutter in an effort to keep her eyes open, losing the battle altogether when I work one, then two fingers inside.

Inside Aster Lindsey.

She flops back onto the mattress, hips arching, and I stop watching her face and start watching my fingers. I place damp kisses on the straining skin of her inner thigh, see the flesh turn pink where I suck, moving closer and closer to my pistoning fingers. I can hear her harsh breathing, feel the fumbling hand that clasps my head and tries to drag me to where she wants me, then I acknowledge her unspoken request and fasten my lips over her clit.

"Argh… Gah… Ohmywhaaat…" She mumbles incoherently, agony and ecstasy, pleasure and surprise in the sounds. I wonder if Jerry ever did this for her. If he—

"Aster?"

A sharp knock at the door makes me freeze. Aster bolts upright on the bed, elbows digging into her pillow.

Another rap. "Aster? Are you in there?"

It's a male voice, young-sounding.

Do you need to get that? I mouth.

"Um… Aster… I need a condom," the kid whispers anxiously.

Aster sighs, exasperated.

"Ignore him," I murmur, preparing to resume my work.

A louder knock.

"Aster, it's really urgent!"

"He'll go away."

"Aster, I know you're in there! Please help me!"

I scramble off the bed, scoop up a handful of condoms from the mess on the floor, and thrust them through the gap at the bottom of the door. "Do not fucking knock again!" I snap.

I hear a rustling on the other side as the condoms are collected. "Got it!" the interrupter replies. "Thanks, man!"

I turn back to the bed where Aster has now covered herself with a sheet.

"You need to get another job," I tell her.

"Is the library hiring?"

"I'll put in a good word for you."

I shuck my boxers and crawl under the sheet, on top of her. She opens her legs for me, her arms, her mouth. She gives me everything.

I nod back down her body. "Do you want me to…?"

"Nuh-uh. I'm ready. Do you want me to…?"

"Nuh-uh. I've been ready since January."

From this close up, her smile nearly blinds me. I scoop up a packet from the floor and roll on the condom. Aster doesn't even blink as I nudge my cock against her center, pushing gently, feeling her body give way. I hear her breath hitch and I stop breathing too, not daring to inhale until I'm buried all the way inside.

My chin bumps her shoulder, and I try to hold myself up on my elbows but it feels too good. I've never done it like this before. Never done it when it wasn't fucking, when it wasn't just a means to an end, a three-act play, beginning-middle-orgasm.

Aster moans and my body starts to move instinctively, hips retreating then forging back in, tentatively at first, then more aggressively. She kisses me, nails scoring my back, heels digging into my ass, spurring me on.

"Aidan," she mutters, more yearning words lost against my mouth.

I don't know how much time has passed, but it feels like forever. I'm sweating, I'm gasping, I'm trying so fucking hard not to come first.

"Aidan," she moans again.

"What...do...you...need?" I grunt out. Sensation is rocketing up and down my body, from the top of my head to the tips of my toes, things I've never felt before and don't know what to do with.

When I first saw Aster, first thought of fucking her, I didn't think it would be like this. I thought she'd be prim and proper, maybe ride me like a dainty cowgirl. I thought I'd dirty her up, scandalize her a bit.

Now I don't think I could scandalize Aster if I tried. She fucks like it's the most natural thing in the world, like my hands pulling her hair is the thing she likes most. Like my mouth on her nipples and my cock plowing into her is something she lives for. I want to earn those responses. I want to hear them. I want to taste them.

I pull out and shift down the bed, splaying her legs wide and opening her pussy with my fingers. My mouth finds her clit again, sucking hard. I lash at her with my tongue, pressing two fingers inside and stroking until I find the spot I'm seeking.

She comes with a muffled cry, and a quick glance up confirms she's got a pillow clutched to her face. I lick her until she's spent but still squirming and trembling, then I pull myself up and press into her again. Her pussy clenches around me, drawing me in deeper. I start to fuck her when her eyes focus, when she knows what I'm doing, when I'm all she can see and she's all I can feel. It only takes a minute before I'm coming, neck arched and teeth gritted, the orgasm so intense I collapse on top of her, a shuddering mess, my hips driving into her welcoming body over and over again until I have nothing left to give.

I shift to the side so she's not bearing too much of my weight, our legs still tangled together. For a long time the only sound is our exhausted breathing, like we've finished a marathon and are bent over at the finish line, gasping for air. Our skin is slick with sweat, my body weak from the exertion.

Three months without sex is two months and three weeks and six days too long. I've forgotten how good sex feels. Or maybe it's just never been this good.

"Wow," Aster says eventually.

She's staring at the ceiling.

"Wow good?"

Her mouth twitches. "Wow great. Wow you didn't even need to soften me up with ice cream."

"Seriously? That was the expensive stuff."

"Total waste of money, pal."

I smile into the pillow, then groan and push myself up. I stand and deal with the condom, keeping my back to Aster as I pull on my boxers. I hear the rustle of clothing behind me and when I turn she's got her panties and T-shirt back on. I yank on my Henley, too, but ignore my pants, my greedy hormones whispering that there could still be a second round. There is, after all, half a box of condoms spilled over the floor. Someone has to clean them up.

Aster yawns and stretches, T-shirt riding up to expose her stomach. I just saw it—kissed it, touched it—but my opportunistic cock is ready to go again, right away.

Then Aster ruins it.

"Okay," she says, looking at me seriously. "We need to talk."

33

Aster

Aidan's face falls so fast you'd think I'd said *I love you.*

Jerry said it, the first time we had sex. And he wasn't even lying. Wasn't saying it to get my clothes off, wasn't saying it in the heat of the moment.

He meant it.

I'd been a little surprised, but it hadn't scared me away. We'd been dating for nearly two months at the time, and it was my goal to find a nice guy, someone who matched up with the new life I'd envisioned for myself. I didn't say it back, because it wasn't true then. Jerry wasn't offended. He never took offense to anything. And when I told him I loved him a couple of months later, he wasn't relieved, he just beamed at me, happy to hear it.

Then he cheated and tore down all the walls of the new life I thought I'd been building, and forced me to admit that they were just flimsy constructions made up of silly dreams and fantasies with no foundation.

Aidan is not perfect, and he doesn't pretend to be. He's not going to tell me he loves me or bring me flowers or introduce me to his parents. I don't even know that I want him to. I just know that he was a friend when I needed one, and he's really good in bed.

I mean, Jesus. I just almost died.

Not that I'll tell him that, or he'll get even more conceited.

But seriously.

"The interview," I clarify, reading his terror and speaking before he can bolt out of the room, pants in hand. "We have to get it done so we can submit something to Jim by Friday."

He grips the side of the desk like it's a lifeline. "The interview," he says, swallowing. "Right. Yeah. Of course."

I point toward the far corner. "I set up some chairs. You're by the window."

He retreats to the interview area, his relief obvious. I collect my things and take the second seat, curling my legs beneath me and pretending to skim the brief list of questions I'd come up with. It's nice to see Aidan off-kilter. Nice to know I'm not alone.

"Ready?" I ask.

"As I'll ever be."

"Question number one: do you always conduct interviews with your pants off?"

His mouth curves, looking sexy and tired. "Always."

"During the viewing of the horror film *Kill Glory 5*, how many times did you squeal in terror?"

He gasps. "Traitor."

"I'll answer that. You squealed six times."

He snatches a discarded sock from the floor and throws it at me. "This interview is over!"

I catch the sock, tossing it over my shoulder. "Okay, we'll come back to that one once you've calmed down. You're in your third year at Holsom, correct?"

"Yes."

"And how do you feel your promise and potential have progressed since you first arrived?"

"Since I knocked myself unconscious on a bar floor and was saved by a prostitute? Um…"

I hold up a hand. "Hang on. I'm writing this down. *Saved… by…a…prostitute…*"

"That was off the record. The on-the-record answer is, Holsom has been a once-in-a-lifetime learning experience and every day I'm grateful for my time here and determined to make the most of it."

I mock gag. "That's on the welcome sheet they hand out each year."

"You read that?"

"Come on. Answer for real."

He sighs and studies the ceiling. "Okay. When I first came to Holsom, I knew I had an opportunity. But it's one thing to give someone an opportunity and quite another for them to know what to do with it. Hence the unconscious-in-a-dirty-bar part."

"Okay."

"So I just started emulating the things I saw around me. Go to class, take notes, speak up once in a while, do the readings, pass the tests. I got the job in the library and I showed up, did my work, and went home. I did all the right things to stay out of trouble."

"Uh-huh…" I scribble this down as fast as I can.

"And I thought I was doing okay. I thought enough time away from temptation would mean it wasn't tempting anymore. I stole cars for money, but it also made me feel something. Feel...powerful, maybe. Like I could have those things, if I wanted them."

"Mm hmm."

He exhales and studies his tattooed knuckles. "Then I saw you and it dawned on me that the temptation wasn't stealing the car, it was having something that was out of my reach. And I wasn't immune to it at all. No amount of promise or potential could override the feeling of being willing to do whatever it took to have you."

I stop writing.

"But then..." He keeps examining his hands. "Then you were so sad, and that was the first time in my life that I'd had to deal with someone my actions had hurt. It's not like I ever saw those car owners again. But you were right there in front of me and seeing you made me want to do better. Be better."

My chest feels tight. My sinuses sting. It's one thing to know how his deception hurt me; it's another to learn that it hurt him, too.

"So to answer your question, how have my promise and potential been developed here at Holsom?" He strums the armrest. "I guess I've learned that having the opportunity to do more with my life isn't everything. It's important to have a reason to want to do better. Finding the reason shows you how lucky you are to be here, and you see that the promise and potential isn't just you, it's everything around you, if you're willing to see it. And willing to let it see you."

A heavy silence falls over the room when he finishes speaking.

I haven't written any of this down. I didn't want to record it on my phone in case the conversation veered into inappropriate territory, but now I wish I had, because there's no way I can paraphrase what he just said.

"Wow," I say inanely.

He lifts his eyes and shrugs, trying to appear nonchalant but not succeeding. He's more embarrassed than he was when he thought I was going to slap him. Veering back into less vulnerable territory, he echoes our conversation in bed. "Wow good?"

"Wow—"

A pounding at the door interrupts. "Aster?"

"Is she in there?" another voice asks. "I need—"

"I was here first. Get in line."

More pounding. "Aster?"

Aidan drags his hands over his face, then gets up, stalks over to the condoms still on the floor, and jams more under the door.

"Go away!" he orders.

"Um, thank you, but I just need a corkscrew," a small voice calls. "I can't drink my wine."

"And do you have change for a dollar?" the first voice asks. "I need quarters for laundry. Why do you have so many condoms? Are these flavored?"

Aidan rests his forehead against the wall, shoulders slumping in defeat.

I pull on my pants, grab quarters from the jar on my desk and the corkscrew from the drawer, then push Aidan out of sight and open the door to reveal the needy faces of my residents.

"Who's here?" one asks, trying to peek inside. "Is it Jerry?"

"I thought they broke up."

"They did? Why?"

"Not sure. Why did you—"

"None of your business. Here's the corkscrew. Return it tomorrow. Here are the quarters. Give me the dollar."

"How do you use a corkscrew? Are there instructions?"

"Google it."

"When you do laundry, is it important to use laundry detergent, or will dish detergent suffice?"

"How do you not know the answer to that?"

"Well, I—"

"If it's not Jerry, who is it?"

"Goodbye, guys." I use my foot to pull the stray condoms back into my room while fending off the interlopers with my hands. "See you tomorrow."

"Can we—"

"No."

I close and lock the door, turning to see Aidan now sitting on the bed, elbows resting on his knees.

"You need a new job, and you need a new place to live," he says. "If we're going to do this properly, the interruptions need to stop."

"All right," I say. "I'll give up everything for you. What does *properly* entail?"

He sticks his finger through the belt loop on my jeans, pulling me close. "Take off these pants and I'll show you."

34

Aidan

I stumble out of my room around noon the next day. I snuck out of Aster's building at four a.m., hoping to avoid both her residents *and* Jerry. There's no way for him to know I'd just crawled out of his ex-girlfriend's bed, but I'd rather he not ponder the question in any context. And while my feelings about all the sex we had yesterday are predominantly positive, I still feel a bit…guilty about how things came to be.

Jerry's standing at the sink when I enter the kitchen, rubbing my blurry eyes.

"Hey," he says.

"Hey," I mutter, pouring a glass of orange juice and downing it in two swallows. I pour another one. Aster and I didn't get much sleep last night and I'm in desperate need of refueling.

"Want some aspirin?"

"Ah, no. I'll be okay." I grab a couple of frozen waffles from the freezer and stick them in the toaster, then plop a frying pan on the stove and turn on the heat, adding three eggs when it's hot. There are bananas on the counter, so I eat one while I wait for everything to cook.

A rhythmic clicking sound has me paying closer attention to Jerry, and I see he's trying to use a flint to start a fire in the sink.

"What, uh, what are you doing?" I ask, flipping over the eggs.

"Practicing my survival skills," he replies, blowing on a tiny spark that quickly peters out.

"You're still doing that? The volunteer stuff?"

"Of course. It's been a real learning experience."

"You can't learn to bring matches?"

He hits the flint again. "It's a progression. The first few trips we stay in a cabin and work on basic outdoor survival skills. Then we move to the real outdoors, using tents, matches, fishing rods. Then we start working with less – flint, etcetera. It's about getting back to basics."

A spark flies up, lands on his polo shirt, and promptly burns a tiny hole through the cotton.

"Dammit," he mumbles, patting it out with his hand, then sighing. "Okay, I admit, the learning curve has been steep. I miss the cabin. A lot. You got the sense of being out in the wilderness, alone, uninterrupted, but you didn't actually have to be in the wilderness. That might be more my style."

The only word I'm hearing right now is *uninterrupted.*

Aster and I worked our way through a generous helping of condoms yesterday—and today—but there were non-stop visitors at all hours of the day and night, interrupting the very dirty proceedings.

"Where is this cabin?" I ask, sliding the fried eggs onto a plate, then adding the waffles and a squeeze of maple syrup. "Nearby?"

"About an hour drive," he says, naming a popular state park. "Maybe a bit more. Once you leave town you travel north on the highway until…"

He chats merrily as he fails to start a fire, and I eat and make a mental note of the directions. State park. Dirt road. Large rock. Forked tree. Another large rock. Drive straight for three hundred yards.

Empty cabin.

* * *

"What?" Aster says the next day once I've pitched her the idea.

She'd met me at the library after her class, and now that my shift has ended we're walking back to her place, presumably to continue our "interview." We're taking the long way around, navigating a quiet, tree-lined pathway that's more popular with cyclists and joggers than students going to and from class. It's also more private.

"What's not to understand?" I say. "We can't go to my place because of Jerry, and your place gets too many visitors. This way we can…" I trail off when I see the expression on her face. I know she enjoyed the other night as much as I did, but maybe she's not liking the idea that I might only want to spend time with her to bang. I mean, that was my initial goal when I started this whole ball rolling back in January, but it's different now. I want the sex *and* I want more.

I clear my throat. "…finish the interview without the interruptions."

She arches a brow. "The interview?"

"Yes, Aster. Why, what were you thinking?" I gasp. "Were

you thinking about sex? God, you're obsessed!"

She laughs. "Shut up."

"I knew you'd become addicted. This is my fault. I'm too good."

She laughs harder. "Seriously. Shut up. There's no way to be alone in the woods if your giant ego's there. Plus we have exams. I need to study. Promise and potential and blah blah blah."

"Well, if you can keep your hands off me for a minute, we can study at the cabin. At least, I can study. I'll exhaust you sexually, then get some reading done when you're passed out."

"You've really thought this through."

I check that we're alone, then back her into a tree. "I haven't thought about a whole lot else," I say, dipping my head.

She presses onto her toes and kisses me back, curling her fingers into the neck of my shirt and holding on. I step into her even more, aligning our bodies, grateful that the warmer weather means thinner clothing, which means I can feel more of her.

"Have you ever done it outside?" I mumble against the soft skin beneath her ear. "Because we can do it right here and—"

Ding! Ding! "Get a room!" a jerk on a bike shouts as he whistles past, bell ringing righteously.

Aster snickers as I curse.

"I think we'll have to discuss your...potential...back in my room," she says, pushing away from the tree and resuming the walk.

I drag my hands through my hair. "I hate that guy."

"Yeah, he's the worst."

"But seriously," I say, snagging her hand. "Have you ever?"

"Ever what?"

"Done it outside?"

"Is that why you want to go to the cabin?"

"No, I just want to talk about sex."

"Oh, shoot!" she exclaims, darting behind a tree near the end of the path. Her residence is about twenty yards away across a short field, and Missy is pacing in front of the doors of the building, typing something into her phone.

I join Aster behind the tree. "Why is Missy here?"

She groans. "Because we have plans."

"What? You and Missy?"

"Yes. We're...friends."

"Even though she's banging your ex?"

"I'm banging his roommate!"

"That's different. It's not gross. Also, what's this about you two being friends?"

"It just happened," she mutters, peering past the tree. "She's very persistent."

"I know. She's been trying to fuck me for three years."

"You have to leave."

"Well, now that I've seen Missy, I want to leave," I say tersely. "But it's awfully convenient that my worst nightmare spends her nights wailing away on the other side of the wall from my bed, isn't it?"

Aster looks exceptionally guilty. "No?"

"Aster, did you introduce Missy to Jerry?"

"Yes, but not on purpose," she says quickly. "We just bumped into him."

"Did you tell her he cheated on you? With a prostitute?"

"Yes!"

"And that didn't scare her away?"

"I mean…you kind of deserve it, Aidan."

My mouth falls open. "What?"

"I still really hated you then, and I know you're afraid of Missy—"

"*Afraid* is a strong word—"

"So I told her he'd learned his lesson from the break up and probably wouldn't do it again."

"I sleep three hours a night because of her!"

"Well—"

"I can't believe you."

"Are you really mad?"

I'm about to assure her that I am indeed furious, then consider my priorities and redirect my efforts accordingly. "I guess that depends…" I curl a finger into the collar of her shirt and pull her close. "Are you coming to the cabin or not?"

She arches a brow, not at all oblivious to my intentions, and failing to lose sight of her own. "Do you promise to finish the interview when we're there?"

I try to be angry, but can't muster up the required righteousness. Hooking up Missy and Jerry is a brilliantly devious plan, and I'm kind of proud of Aster for coming up with it. Plus, if she's agreeing to come to the cabin, I'm willing to let bygones be bygones.

"Yeah," I say, leaning in to kiss her again. "Come to the cabin and I promise to give you whatever you want."

35

Aster

This time they leave a voice message.

"I'm hoping to speak with Aster Lindsey," says an unfamiliar male, his voice terse and formal. "Please call me back at your earliest convenience." He leaves a number and hangs up without saying goodbye.

I sit on the edge of my bed and frown at the darkening screen display. I've already listened to the message six times. There's no hidden meaning, nothing I'm missing. It's not my father's voice and I don't recognize the number, though it's a Washington area code.

I stand abruptly, nearly tripping over the duffel bag I've packed for two nights away at this mysterious cabin in the woods with Aidan. He's due to arrive any minute, so I grab my laptop and quickly Google the phone number. Because whoever this is— assuming it's been the same person all along—has been so vague, I'm not expecting any search results, so it's a huge surprise when the first hit brings me to the website of a small law firm in Chester.

We had no money to hire a lawyer when I was arrested, so I'd been assigned an eager but ineffective public defender. I click the link for staff profiles at the top of the website, but there are only four people at the firm, two lawyers, one paralegal and a secretary, and I don't recognize any of them.

My phone beeps and I jump in alarm, irrationally paranoid that they might somehow know I'm visiting their site, but it's just Aidan texting to say he's downstairs. I close the laptop and step out, locking the door behind me. I'm hoping to keep this recent development a secret until I figure out what to do about it, but Aidan takes one look at my face when I get in the car and says, "What happened?"

"I got another phone call."

"Did he leave a message?" He pulls away from the curb, probably expecting the same "No" I've given him every other time he's asked.

"Yes."

He twists in his seat. "What?"

"Yes. Watch the road."

He turns back. "What'd he say?"

"It wasn't my dad. It was a law firm. They just asked me to call them. Didn't say why."

"Did you call?"

"No. I got the message five minutes ago."

He drums his fingers on the wheel. "Do you think you're in trouble? Something about your parole?"

"No. I've been a model citizen. It has to be about my dad. It's too much of a coincidence not to be."

We drive in silence for a moment, then Aidan asks "Did you bring it?"

I sigh. "Yes."

He's talking about the unread letter from my father. Until today, I still hadn't moved it from its position beneath the radiator, but with the redoubled efforts of the mysterious caller and the matching increase in my stress levels, Aidan insisted I read it. When I balked, he told me to bring it on the trip and, if need be, he'd read it. He calls it the monster under the bed. If I shine a light on it, I'll see there's nothing to be afraid of.

But I know better.

Still, opening it far away from Holsom seems like a good idea. Like whatever bad karma the note brings with it will be restricted to that cabin and won't infect the life I'm building for myself. Our plan is basically the plot of a horror movie.

"Do you know anyone who's been kicked out of the PPP?" Aidan asks abruptly.

Now I twist in my seat, happy to ignore my own issues and dwell on his. "Why? Are you in trouble?"

"No. Wes."

"I don't personally know anyone who's been kicked out," I say, considering. "But I remember one time in my first year I was working in the mail room and I heard Jim and Becca talking about someone who'd been dismissed. What did Wes do?"

"Turns out, he hasn't been doing much of anything," Aidan replies. "His mom got sick and he's been traveling back and forth to Portland to take care of her whenever he can. He's failing a class, missing shifts at the daycare, skipping his extracurricular, and hasn't even started his cooperation credit."

"That's terrible."

"He's in his third year," he adds. "He can't afford Holsom—

205

he can't afford anything—without the PPP. And until all this happened, he was on track to graduate. He has promise and potential, but there's no wiggle room with the program."

"What's he going to do? Talk to Jim?"

"I don't know. He's afraid that if he comes clean about how behind he is, they'll kick him out sooner. He's trying to fix it."

"I'm sorry," I say. "That's a lot worse than getting a few hang-ups and a letter from your dad."

"Past, present, future," Aidan says, eyes on the road. "I guess it's all hard."

* * *

It's noon when we reach the cabin. I'd been expecting something dark and dreary, but the structure is quaint and cozy, with peeling gray paint and yellow shutters. Aidan told me he has a friend who camps out here as part of a volunteer activity, and the group must have been by recently because there are plants growing in window boxes and the small porch is clear of debris.

"Wow," I say, climbing out of the car. "The cabin is real."

"Yeah," Aidan says, popping the trunk before getting out. "And you know the best part?"

"You brought stuff for s'mores?"

He throws me a rolled up sleeping bag. "No interruptions."

"No s'mores?"

"C'mon, Aster," he says, exasperated. "Of course there are s'mores."

I smile and follow him to the cabin. Two stairs lead up to the porch, tiny herb gardens starting to grow on either side. Aidan crouches and lifts up a few rocks, shaking them next to his ear until he finds what he's looking for.

"I thought people only hid things in rocks on television," I say as he proudly holds up a tarnished brass key.

"Me too," he admits. "Maybe volunteers are more trusting."

He twists the key in the lock and the cabin door swings open easily. The hinges are shiny with fresh oil, and when we step inside it smells like lemon furniture polish and bleach. Even the fireplace is swept, logs arranged neatly behind the grate and stacked thigh-high in a box in the corner. A small couch sits beneath the front window, covered in a white sheet, and two chairs are tucked against the far wall. The center of the room has been cleared, as though making room for a dance floor.

"This is great," I say, turning in a circle to take it all in. We never went on family vacations when I was growing up, and the one time I was supposed to go camping with a friend's family I got chicken pox and was uninvited.

On the far side of a narrow counter is a tiny kitchen with a single sink stationed in front of a window that overlooks the woods behind the cabin. A bathroom sits off to one side, and next to that is the lone bedroom, the queen bed unmade, garbage bags of what I assume are linens stacked neatly on top.

"Home sweet home," Aidan says, tossing his duffel on the bed and slinging an arm around my shoulders. "Want to break it in?"

"Interview first," I remind him, though I do want to break it in, quite badly.

"We can talk outside. Let's go for a walk. My legs are cramped after sitting in the car so long."

"It only took so long because you got lost."

"The directions were vague!"

We exit and round the side of the cabin, passing a fire pit, neatly rimmed with stones, a dark pile of ashes at its center. Aidan locates a narrow trail in the woods and soon we're surrounded by looming old growth trees, the smell of moss and earth and clean air filling my lungs. We walk for a bit, then I remember my task.

"Okay," I call. Aidan's about six feet in front of me, tromping through the woods like a little kid on an adventure. The usual tense set of his shoulders has relaxed, and in his white T-shirt and cargo pants he looks natural and happy. "Question one. What would you suggest new PPP students do to ease the transition from their home life into Holsom life?"

He glances over his shoulder. "Really?"

"Yeah. What's wrong with that?"

"I don't think there's anything we can do to 'ease the transition.' It just takes time. You adapt. Evolve." He gives me a pointed look. "You pretend."

"I'm not going to tell new students to fake it."

"Fine. Tell them to make friends. Whether it's other kids in the program or just other kids at school, it's important to have a support system. You get lonely, you get bored, and trouble finds you. Tell them to keep up with their extracurricular, even if Jim makes them play Frisbee baseball. It helps to have structure."

"Okay. Good answer."

"I aim to please."

"Next question. Most PPP students come from a troubled background. Issues at home, run-ins with the law. Their previous coping mechanisms won't work at Holsom. How would you recommend they approach the challenges they face at school?"

He glances back at me again. "Seriously? How do they solve all their problems?"

"Not solve. Approach."

"What's the difference?"

"*Solve* is a big picture issue. It's huge and overwhelming. Approaching an issue can make it seem more manageable, like approaching a mountain. You don't start climbing from the top. You find a handhold and work your way up." At least, that's what Jim said.

"Seems like you have all the answers already."

"Aidan."

"Let's take a break," he suggests. "I'll ponder your question as we enjoy the scenery."

"What? We just started…" The words trail off when we come to a break in the woods, the trees parting to reveal a crystal clear lake, the water so smooth it reflects the cloudless sky above. And even though I know he's just avoiding the interview—again—I can't help but fall for it as I take in the pristine view. "Whoa," I whisper. It's so crisp and quiet that speaking any louder would feel like sacrilege.

The lake abuts a tiny shore, the beach maybe six feet wide, a couple of large logs lying across the rocky sand. A few cabins dot the perimeter of the lake, but none close enough to spoil the isolated effect.

"I found this online," Aidan says, stepping in behind me and linking his hands over my stomach, resting his chin on my shoulder. "I thought about you trying to drown me in the pool and figured you might like it."

"I love it." I crouch to dip my fingers into the freezing water. "Perfect drowning depth."

"You're so sweet."

I look over my shoulder and smile, and when he smiles back, I know that no matter how many coping mechanisms I've developed, I'm in trouble.

When I first arrived at Holsom, I was terrified. It was new and strange and even among thousands of students, I felt hopelessly alone. Meeting Jerry helped, but I never truly relaxed. Never felt like I belonged. I thought I might, one day, but even after a year of dating I knew that deep down, he never really knew me because I never really let him.

Aidan knows me. I only let him know me because I thought I'd never see him again, but here we are, out in the middle of nowhere, and I don't feel alone at all. I feel like he sees me and he's totally okay with what he sees. Scars and all.

I stand and close the short distance between us, lifting my hands to cup his jaw, then pressing onto my tiptoes to kiss him. He's startled but pleased, lips curling as our mouths meet. I kiss him the way I wanted to kiss him even when I knew he'd been lying to me. I kiss him without any of the walls up, nothing separating the kiss from the truth.

He wraps his arms around the small of my back and just holds me, letting me touch him, feel him. His broad shoulders and strong back, his biceps, the dip of his waist, the curve of his spine. He stiffens when I squeeze his ass, so I do it again, grinning when I feel his growing hardness against my stomach.

"Don't start something you can't finish," he warns, his voice laced with arousal and banked intentions.

"Who says I can't finish it?"

"I didn't bring anything."

"You're a terrible boy scout. Luckily one of us came prepared." I retrieve a condom from my back pocket and hold it up.

"Were you a girl scout?"

"No. But I wanted to be."

I kiss him again and he kisses me harder, without restraint now that he knows there's no need for it. We fumble our way to the ground, knees in the damp sand, and Aidan sits with his legs extended, pants unzipped, back resting against one of the fallen birch logs.

He strokes his cock as I stand and work my jeans and panties over my thighs, stepping out with one foot and straddling him. I watch the way his cock thickens and hardens in his hand, the way he rolls his thumb over the head, a muscle in his jaw twitching from the pleasure. I make mental notes for later.

"Get down here," he orders, eyes dark. He reaches for me as I lower myself, positioning my body over his cock, kissing him as I inch my way on, the process eased by the lube on the condom.

He doesn't rush me, just strokes my back and my ass, the rough pads of his fingers scraping my skin in hot contrast to the softness of his lips. His tongue finds mine and we battle for dominance, laughing at the futility of the fight since we want the same thing.

At long last I'm seated, his cock buried inside, taking a moment to adjust to the aching fullness. I grind my forehead into his shoulder, feeling him, feeling everything, and he lets me take my time, no pressure, no hurry.

I shift so my lips find his neck, his racing pulse betraying his laidback demeanor. I flex my thighs and lift up slightly, then slide back down, finding an easy, unhurried rhythm that makes everything inside me go soft and molten.

I've never felt like this before, not even the last time we did it. Not even all the times we did it that night. Sex with Jerry was good, but nothing like this. Jerry called it *lovemaking*, and though the term was supposed to imply some sort of wondrous closeness, I always found it off-putting. I never complained, though, figuring it was my issue, not his. And while I loved Jerry and I know he loved me, there was a distance between us that was wholly my issue. It was the gap between who I was and who I hoped to be, and it wasn't closing nearly fast enough.

There's no gap at all now. There's not a single inch of space between me and Aidan, my hips moving instinctively, up and down, taking him in deeper and deeper, the only sounds our rough breathing and the quiet slap of skin. He drops his hands from my hair and I see him digging his fingers into the sand at his sides, trying to hold on. Trying to wait for me.

That's what sends me over. The sight of this man, weak but still so strong. Hard, solid, tough, sweet. A study in contradictions.

I come with a soft cry, stifling the sound in the curve of his neck, tasting his sweat on my tongue. My body spasms in long, slow waves for what feels like an eternity, and when the orgasm ebbs away Aidan jerks beneath me, hips pushing into mine as he anchors me with his hands on my waist, holding me in place while he takes what he needs.

My limbs feel like jelly, like there's no earthly way I can stand, no possible way I'll be able to hike back. I lift my head and absorb the quiet forest, the pristine lake, the boundless sky. This is the farthest from civilization I've ever been, but out here, with just me and Aidan, I've never felt closer to home.

36

Aidan

We stumble out of the trees some time later, sex-tired and happy. The knees of our jeans are stained with lake water and dirt, and my ass bears two chilly damp patches that chafe my cheeks but are totally worth it. We don't talk much on the way back, but there isn't anything that needs saying. Aster just blew my fucking mind.

I was joking when I told her I'd have to exhaust her sexually in order to get any reading done, but now I think the joke's on me. As soon as we get inside, I'm going to pass out on that unmade bed and she'll get some quality study time after all.

We circle around the front of the cabin, our fingers linked, our tousled hair and flushed cheeks signs of more than just a great hike. And that's what Jerry and Missy see when we stumble to a halt, six feet away from the steps where they sit, waiting for us.

Well, waiting for somebody.

Because the shock on Jerry's face confirms he was not expecting anybody he knew.

He was not expecting me.

He was not expecting *Aster*.

Shock isn't even the right word to describe him. He's...gobsmacked. Completely and totally blindsided.

Because of our schedules, Jerry and I often go several days without seeing each other, so I never thought to tell him I was leaving town for a couple of nights. As a result, I had no idea he was planning a trip of his own.

Missy's doing her damnedest not to burst into hysterical laughter. She shares Jerry's surprise, but unlike his horror, hers is pure delight.

Jerry is the first to speak. "Aster?" he utters, the word breaking in the middle. "You... You're...here?"

Beside me, Aster is frozen, stuck in panicked deer mode, not quite sure how to react. Three years of good behavior have dulled her deceiving instincts to the point that she's not doing anything at all.

I scuff my boot on the ground. "Hey, Jerry."

Slowly, he turns his attention to me. If this were a fifties movie, Jerry would be the golden boy prom king, stepping up to fight the kid from the wrong side of the tracks who dared steal his girl.

But this isn't a movie, this is real life, and Jerry just looks... crushed.

I shouldn't feel bad. He cheated on her, after all. Their relationship was more than over before we got together. But because I live with Jerry and I saw how he'd beaten himself up, because I know he punished himself for what he'd done, this feels like overkill. Like kicking someone when he's down...then fucking his girlfriend.

Now I don't know what to say either.

Missy stands. "How'd you two know about this place?" She doesn't seem disappointed that Aster got what she's been after for three years; she still looks hilariously entertained.

"I told him," Jerry says quietly. Then to me he says, "I told you."

"I know."

"And now you two are...are..." He takes in our disheveled clothing, no way to pretend we weren't doing what he thinks we were doing.

"Yeah," I say.

"Is it serious?" Missy inquires.

Jerry makes a pained sound, like that answer will only add to his suffering.

And maybe it will, but I don't get to answer because Aster finds her voice.

"We broke up," she reminds Jerry reasonably, but not unsympathetically. "And we moved on."

His tone is incredulous. "To this place?"

"Well..." She shoots me a peevish look. "I didn't know you were the friend he was talking about."

His expression darkens. "We're not friends, obviously."

I sigh. That's probably the best Jerry can do. The meanest thing he can think of to say.

"Okay," Aster says, making a move for the stairs. "We put some stuff inside. We'll get it and go."

"Great idea," Jerry replies. Then he turns to me. "And when you get back to Holsom, grab the rest of your stuff from the apartment. You're evicted."

* * *

"Well," Aster says, twenty-five minutes later. It's the first thing either of us has said since our premature cabin departure, and its woeful inadequacy makes it the perfect word for the situation.

"That was brutal," she adds, when I don't reply.

I want to say something, but I don't know what. Here she is, gorgeous and bright and smart, a fucking *ex-con* who's working hard to stop repeating past mistakes and actually succeeding. And here I am, falling off bar stools and paying for other people's prostitutes and getting evicted. Three years of college and I'm still an idiot.

It's humiliating. Just like when I got sprayed by that skunk, all I want to do is hole up in my room and be alone until it passes. Except I no longer have a room. Or a home.

"We still have the s'more stuff," Aster says. "Why don't we stop at one of these campgrounds we keep passing and start a fire? I'm starving."

"Let's just drive back," I mutter. "I have to pack." I reach over to flip through the radio stations, hunting for one that's coming in clear.

"We have some boxes at the dorm," she tries. "We can grab them and—"

"I'll call Wes. He can help." I tried not to show it at the cabin, but I'm reeling from the encounter. Somehow over the course of my plan to steal Aster, I hadn't actually bothered to consider the consequences. I thought when she slapped me I'd paid the price for my lies; turns out I still had debts outstanding.

When people asked me if I felt bad for the people I'd hurt

217

when I was stealing cars, I lied and said of course I did, but I didn't. They had money, they had insurance, they had other cars. Jerry doesn't. Jerry's just someone who trusted the wrong guy.

Who trusted me.

"Resident advisors aren't allowed to have roommates," Aster adds, "but obviously you can stay with me for a couple of nights while you find a new place."

Her voice, her sympathy, her pity—it's making me grit my teeth. "I don't want to live in a dorm, Aster. Being there makes me fucking antsy. There's always someone who wants something from you. I'm obviously not the right person to set an example. I'm not even close to that person."

She blinks. "What kind of person?"

"Someone that should…" I wave a hand in her general direction. "Be there."

"Be at the dorm or be with me?"

I pinch the bridge of my nose, willing away the headache that started when we got in the car and is now reaching critical levels. I can't look at her right now. I can't talk to her. "I just need to think."

I hear her pained inhale, but she doesn't say anything else. From the corner of my eye I see her fold her hands in her lap, knuckles turning white from where she's squeezing them.

I need space right now, and this fucking compact rental car puts approximately eighteen inches between me and Aster. Any other day, I'd be thinking of ways to erase those inches, but not now.

That sex in the woods is the best thing that ever happened to me. It lowered all my defenses, gave me a glimpse of the real promise and potential in the world, and in the process, it revealed all the weak spots in my armor, making the subsequent eviction sting all the more. I need some time to repair all those dents and dings, cover them up the way Aster does hers, and put my old, stoic mask back on. Then I can deal with shit. I can't do it while I've got embarrassment burning a hole in my gut.

The mask is barely in place when we pull up in front of Aster's residence an hour later. She hasn't said a single word, hasn't even breathed in my direction since I snapped at her.

I sigh. "Hey," I say. "I'm sorry—"

But she just climbs out of the car, grabs her bag, and strides into the building without a look back.

37

Aster

I tell myself I'm not going to cry, but the second I'm in my room, I collapse against the door and slide down to the floor, burying my face in my hands as the tears start to fall. I acted like I was letting Aidan cajole me into this trip, but I really wanted to go. I wanted a romantic cabin. I wanted peace and quiet and nature and s'mores and sex in front of a fireplace.

The sex. Ugh. God. I can't even.

It was too much. Too good. We couldn't have gotten any closer physically, but in other ways, we'd gotten closer than I've ever been with anyone, even Jerry. But just like the night I confronted Aidan about his deception, I'd once again I'd convinced myself I was strong enough to handle something, only to have the theory tested and proven untrue.

Before seeing my dad in the parking lot that night, if anyone had asked me what I'd do if I saw him again, I'd have said I'd do absolutely nothing. I'd hold my head high and stroll right past like he didn't even exist. But the reality was nothing like that. His calm dismissal had shattered me, snapped any hope I had that our current circumstances were only temporary, a misunderstanding, fixable.

But some things you can't fix.

I fumble for my duffel bag and stick my hand in the zippered compartment at the side until I find the wrinkled edges of an envelope. I pull it out, holding the corner between my fingertips and letting it dangle there like a talisman.

"You ruined my trip," I murmur, but the envelope doesn't burst into flames or do anything to show it's possessed. It's just an envelope.

I swipe the back of my hand across my cheeks, wiping away my tears, and pull out the single piece of lined paper, neatly folded into thirds. The first thing I see as it unfurls is my name at the top in my father's terse handwriting, each letter written with as much economy as possible.

Aster, I read. *It's me.*

I'm unwell. I don't have long, and I don't have anyone else. There is a lawyer who will handle the details, but I need someone to act as executor. I am leaving the house to you; perhaps you can sell it. There are some local groups to whom I would like to leave a few items. Please see to it that they receive them.

Goodbye,

Phillip Lindsey

I read the last words a dozen times. *Goodbye, Phillip Lindsey.* Not, *I love you.* Not, *I'm sorry.* Not, *how is school?* Just…goodbye. The word we'd been running too fast to say when we left.

Phillip Lindsey. Like he was never my father. Like in all the years we'd been apart, he hadn't learned a single thing. Still as stingy with his kindness as he'd always been. Maybe that's why I fell for Jerry. He was so generous. With his time, his encouragement, his love. He was so completely and utterly open, drawing me in with his sheer newness and unfamiliarity.

I grab my phone and replay the lawyer's voice message, then call back before I can talk myself out of it. The ringtone sounds ominous, like a time warp or a warning. After the third ring, a woman's voice answers.

"Good afternoon, Goldman Hartshorne Law," she says.

"Hi," I say, the word coming out scratchy. I try again. "Hi. My name is Aster Lindsey. I'm returning a call from Mitch Goldman."

"Oh!" she trills, as though she's been waiting to hear from me. "Just one moment, I'll tell him you're on the line."

Tinned hold music starts to play, and before I can convince myself to hang up, the same male voice from the message comes on the line. "Ms. Lindsey," he booms, managing to sound both stern and pleased to speak to me.

"Yes," I say, trying to pretend I'm an adult and not a drama queen slumped on the floor of her dorm, tear-streaked and hungry. "I got your message."

"We've been attempting to get in touch with you for some time," he says. "We don't have your exact mailing address— you're at school, correct? Holsom College?"

"Yes."

"Right, that's what your father thought. Unfortunately the school registrar wouldn't confirm or deny your enrollment, and our attempts to locate you were largely unsuccessful."

PPP students are strongly encouraged to avoid all forms of

social media. They're possible links between our past and our present, a way for people we wish to avoid—or simply should avoid—to contact or to tempt us. And likewise, the school registrar has even more stringent procedures to follow before releasing the names of any of its students, like gatekeepers determined to keep out the past.

I consider the letter, now resting against my knees. It's dated January 20. He sent it nearly two months ago, but because of the unspecific address it likely took a while to arrive, and even longer for me to open. Two months. Two months ago when I was in love with Jerry and Aidan was just his hot roommate. Two months ago when my days were an endless repeat cycle of going to class and coming home and seeing Jerry and going to class and coming home again. Two months ago when I didn't make a road trip to a wedding or slap a man or kiss that man or have sex next to a picture perfect lake, icy water chilling my knees. Two months ago when I thought I'd fallen in love for the first and only time.

"Why have you been calling?" I ask, not sure if I want to hear what I'm expecting or not. Do I want him to be dead or do I want him to have found me?

Goldman takes a deep breath, and I know the answer.

38

Aidan

"Too bad," Wes remarks, scanning my apartment—my former apartment—as he carries the last box of my paltry belongings to the door. "This place is nice."

"I know."

He pauses in the hall as I twist the key in the lock, then crouch down to slide it back under the door. "You think he'll get another roommate?" he asks. "My place just went from cramped to crowded."

"It's only temporary," I remind him. "Another six weeks of school, then you guys take off and I move back on campus to work for the summer."

"Six weeks," he says as we get in the elevator. "Time flies."

"How's your mom?"

He squints into the box as we ride down, and I don't know if he's scrutinizing my toiletries or avoiding the question. "All right," he says eventually. "Hanging in there."

"You hang in there, too," I tell him as we step outside.

"You'll have me and T.J. around now. We can help out when you need it. You just do what you need to do to pass this year."

He exhales as we stuff the items into his battered old car. "I'm trying not to add to people's problems," he says. "You've got enough going on."

"I'll be fine," I lie. It's been four hours since I dropped off Aster and called Wes to weasel myself a room. He and T.J. live in an older house on the opposite side of town where they rent out the two top levels from an elderly lady and get a break on rent for helping out with yard work and minor repairs. I've been there before, so I know they've got space. Problem is, neither one of them is quite as committed to the program as they should be—as I'm trying to be—which is why I didn't room with them when I needed a place before.

"You picked a good day to move in," Wes says as he starts the short drive. "T.J.'s throwing a birthday party for his cousin tonight, and her hot friends are coming."

"You can just admit the party's for me," I tell him. "No need to make stuff up."

"Ha," he scoffs, parking at the curb in front of the ancient Victorian. It's got pitched roofs and gingerbread trim, a recent paint job leaving it even greener than the new grass on the lawn. "You can hook up with anyone you want, but steer clear of Shawna. I've been laying the groundwork, and tonight's the night."

"If you say so."

"Also, I know you have a thing for your roommates' ladies, but stay away from Pearl," he adds. "She's a wonderful landlord, and still quite a looker for eighty-three. You might have a hard time keeping your hands off."

I sock him in the arm. "Shut up."

* * *

T.J. and Wes's parties are legendary, and by midnight the place is vibrating with pounding bass, dancing bodies, and at least a hundred voices. Wes told me Pearl sleeps with ear plugs and doesn't hear a thing, which is how they get away with it.

When I met Wes and T.J. first year, I came to their parties pretty frequently, but quickly learned that they're a cesspool of temptation I can't afford to get sucked into. Again.

I'd spent the past hour doing my best to be sociable, but I'm in no mood for it. The drugs and alcohol and half-naked girls and too-macho guys are a one-way trip to the past, a place I can't afford to revisit, no matter how easy it would be to slip into that role.

And maybe three months ago, if I'd had a day like today, I'd have given in to all those vices, offering myself whatever justification I needed to throw away everything I've worked so hard for. But tonight things are different.

Tonight I'm in my new "room," a miniscule space beneath one of the dormer windows. Everything I own can fit in the trunk of a compact car, so I don't have any furniture. My new "bed" is an over-stuffed red *chesterfield*—Pearl's word—that's approximately four feet long and two hundred years old. The crushed velvet upholstery makes my skin itch, and the smell of dust and mold makes me feel like I'm suffocating.

Tonight, for the first time since laying eyes on her, I don't know what's going to happen with Aster. The day we met, I knew I'd have her. The day she slapped me, I knew I'd get her back. But there was nothing at stake those times. I liked her more and more each time we met, but nobody's heart was on the line. There weren't feelings involved.

But that fucking lake sex changed everything.

Aster changed everything.

Now I'm lying on a chesterfield, ninety-six different springs digging into my spinal chord, my head pounding with the unrelenting bass from downstairs, and she's...alone.

I sit up abruptly.

I just did to myself what I did to Jerry. Made a mistake, left the door open a crack like a fucking welcome sign for the next guy who comes along. I'm not blind. I see the way the guys on this campus look at Aster. They look at her the way I first looked at her, and that's a problem.

A huge problem.

And my problem solving skills are shit.

I stand and grab my jacket from the pile of belongings on the floor, then hurry out of the room and down the stairs. Someone calls my name but I ignore it and weave through the crowd to the front door, jogging down the steps and pausing for a moment to orient myself before starting the twenty-minute run to campus.

By the time I get to Aster's building it's nearly one o'clock in the morning, the chilly air cooling the sweat on my skin as I try to contemplate a way in. I'm spared the effort when a guy comes out to smoke and holds the door for me. I pace around inside the elevator for the twenty-second ride up, feeling like a caged animal, and on the ninth floor I stride down the hall to Aster's corner suite, taking a minute to gather myself before raising a hand to knock.

No answer.

No light under the door.

I knock again.

Then, after a second, weak light spills through the gap at the bottom. My shoulders slump in relief, but when I hear her twist the deadbolt, I straighten, trying for some semblance of composed and reasonable.

And forgivable.

Another second passes, then Aster squints into the hall, face soft from sleep. Her blond hair sticks out on one side from where she'd slept on it, the same shade as her rumpled yellow T-shirt and plaid pajama pants.

She looks adorable.

And then she recognizes me and her expression turns to one of annoyance. She must have been expecting a student pleading for condoms or coins or corkscrews. All better options than me.

"Question three," I say, thrusting out a hand to block the door when she would have closed it. I add my foot to the mix when she pushes harder. "You asked how I'd recommend new students deal with the obstacles they face at Holsom, how they'd handle things differently than they did before."

She doesn't invite me in, but she does stop trying to shut me out. My heart, barely calm after the run over here, starts pounding again, a rapid patter against my rib cage.

"I'd tell them to do everything differently," I continue. "If they would have started fighting before, they should walk away and think about things now. And if they would have run away, they should stay and face the problem. PPP says the past is the past, but it's only the past if you deal with it. If you don't, it sticks with you and stays a problem."

My hands are shaking so hard I have to stuff them in my pockets to hide them.

"In the past, I would have let what happened today be an excuse to make a whole bunch more mistakes. But I'm not going to do that now. I moved in with Wes and T.J. I returned the apartment key to Jerry. I finished my reading for tomorrow's class. And I'm here to tell you I'm sorry."

Aster curls her fingers in the hem of her T-shirt, watching the fabric stretch. She's still trying to be angry, but it's not working. I can barely take a full breath, but I plow on, seizing my advantage.

"I'm sorry I wasn't honest about the cabin. I'm sorry you didn't get your s'mores. I'm sorry about the car ride back. I was…" Fuck. I just said a hundred words and now I can't manage the one that matters. "I was embarrassed," I say quietly, scuffing my sneaker on the worn carpet. "I want to be better than I am, sometimes."

Aster sniffles and slowly looks at me, her eyes shiny with tears. But they're blue again, not dark and stormy. It's that sea of cornflowers, blooming through the ashes. After a moment she steps back and holds the door, letting me in.

Again.

When she locks the door behind me, all the tension I'd been holding onto eases away, making room for something else. Something better.

I extend my arms and she steps into them, hugging me back, her cheek pressed to my chest, my chin resting on top of her head. I don't even think about how she smells like lemons or her breasts are soft or am I going to get laid tonight. I think about how some people, like Jerry, do good because that's just who they are. But some people, like me, do good when they have a reason.

And I have a reason.

39

Aster

I wake up early the next morning, a razor beam of sunlight lasering straight into my brain through the gap in the college-issue green curtains. I wince and cover my face with my forearm, moving carefully so I don't disturb Aidan. He doesn't budge. I'm starting to learn that the guy sleeps like the dead.

I shouldn't be awake right now; we barely slept last night. We had hours of sex, slow, dark sex, under the covers, everything hidden and everything bared. It was intense and exhausting, and I feel the twinge between my legs that reminds me this isn't something I normally do. Jerry and I never did it that much, never that long, never that...*good.*

Aidan snuffles in his sleep and I spy on him from the corner of my eye. Mouth parted, lips fluttering with each little snore. He's on his stomach, arms extended above his head, fingers linked like a makeshift halo. The tattoos that span his biceps and shoulder blades are a random hodgepodge of ink that manages to say both nothing and everything at the same time.

These are my mistakes.

Don't look.

Look closer.

Don't judge.

Much like the last time we fought, I'd come away thinking it was over, we were done. For three years I've told myself I can't repeat past mistakes; I can't make any mistakes.

But mistakes are unavoidable.

Hearing his response to my unanswered question made me forget my determination to slam the door in his face and spend the rest of my life avoiding him. His advice to new PPP students can apply to older PPP students as well. All students.

Do things differently.

Running is my *modus operandi,* and it worked when I was a teenager. But then I went to prison and my brother died and I haven't spoken to my mother in three years, so the plan is not without its flaws.

After hanging up with Mitch Goldman yesterday, I'd been determined to continue running and ignore the situation with my dad's will. Goldman himself had given me the out: they had companies they could use to pack up and sell the house and send me a check when all was said and done. I didn't have to do a thing, if I didn't want to. Didn't have to return to the place I swore I'd never return to, didn't need to bear witness to the remnants of a life I needed to forget.

I told him I'd think about it and get back to him, though I had no intention of calling. But Aidan saying that you couldn't forget the past until you'd dealt with it struck a chord, and my past is an open wound that's healing much too slowly. I wasn't ready to deal with it before, choosing to let it fester while I tried to move on with my life. But it's still there, haunting me, hurting me, so just like Aidan knocking on my door and confronting the issue, I have to deal with it.

No more running.

Aidan snorts and I feel him shift on the mattress as he comes awake.

"You up?" he mumbles sleepily.

"Yeah."

He groans. "Why?"

"My dad died," I say, concentrating on the stucco ceiling.

He stills. "What?"

"I read the letter and called the lawyer. Yesterday."

He takes a second to absorb the news. "So what happens now?"

"He left me his house. I can go back and deal with the stuff he left behind, or the lawyer can hire someone to handle it. Sell it. Whatever."

"That's bullshit," Aidan says. "You've got your own life to deal with."

"That was my first reaction."

"You've already had a second one? In less than twenty-four hours?"

"Your speech inspired me."

"Well, I'm a pretty inspiring guy."

I roll onto my side to face him, fingers trailing over the old tattoos. Some mistakes, some maybe just memories. Or reminders. "You are, sometimes. When you want to be."

His cockiness fades as a private battle of emotion wages war across his face. Discomfort. Pleasure. Uncertainty. Hesitation. Like he's still on the fence about who he's going to be. But I don't care. We're all straddling one line or another. We don't have to pick a side yet.

"You inspire me," he says softly, rolling the ends of my hair between his fingers, concentrating on the task and dodging my compliment.

I'd be irked by the obvious evasive maneuver, but I'm glad he's not looking at me because I'm pretty sure the same smorgasbord of discomfiting emotions washes over my face. Turns out, it's embarrassing to be called inspiring.

But it's kind of amazing, too.

* * *

The knock on my door later that afternoon sounds too fierce and determined to be Aidan. An eye pressed to the peephole confirms the worst.

"I know you're in there!" Missy hollers, mouth close to the peephole, big and small at the same time. "Let me in. You have some explaining to do."

I do a quick scan of the room, grateful I'd tidied up a bit when Aidan left for class. I pull open the door. "Hey, Missy."

She arches a brow. "Aster." She strides in without invitation, thrusting a small box into my hands as she passes. "I brought you a vanilla cupcake as a bribe."

I wait warily as she takes a seat at my desk, crosses her legs, bites into a red velvet cupcake, and fixes me with a serious stare. She chews, swallows, and without missing a beat, asks, "What's sex with Aidan Shaw like?"

I almost drop the cupcake. "Missy!"

"What? I've been wondering for years."

"I can't—I can't—"

"I think you can," she says, shooting a pointed glance at the box of condoms on the bedside table. "And I think you have. Just spill."

"No!"

She sets down the cupcake and holds her hands about two inches apart, slowly widening them. "Just stop me when I'm close."

I press the back of my hand to my heated cheeks. I don't think I'm a prude, but my experience with girl talk extends no further than listening to my prison bunkmates boast about their illicit sexual encounters.

"Stop," I protest, when her hands are about fourteen inches apart.

She pauses and peers between her palms. "Wow."

I laugh in spite of myself. "Shut up. I meant, stop asking."

"But I brought you a cupcake."

I think about Aidan bringing me ice cream. Maybe I'm easy.

Missy sighs. "Fine. Did you at least take pictures?"

I throw a pillow at her and sit on the bed, cross-legged, as I fish out my cupcake. "No."

"Dammit. I was hoping I could live vicariously through your romantic getaway since mine got ruined."

"I didn't have a romantic getaway either, remember?"

"I bet you didn't spend the afternoon listening to Aidan cry."

"Jerry *cried?*"

"Yep. He'd never evicted anyone before. Said he felt like a monster."

Oh, Jerry.

I'm seeing now that we were never meant to be.

"I'm sorry we ruined your trip."

She waves a hand dismissively. "Ruined it, improved it. I'm not exactly the outdoorsy type, Aster. I just went along to be nice. Jerry's so proud of his newfound survival skills, I felt like I had to agree. Surviving the sight of you and Aidan, however, is not something he was prepared for."

"It wasn't really that bad, was it?"

"How could that be anything but bad? He's convinced you cheated on him."

Even though Jerry's the one who cheated on me, the accusation still stings. "I didn't start seeing Aidan until after we'd broken up. Long after. It was…innocent." It's hard to say *innocent* with a straight face, but I'm not about to admit Aidan started this whole thing by paying a prostitute.

Missy pulls another cupcake box out of her oversized purse and bites in. "Is it serious?"

"Serious?" I concentrate on folding my wrapper into a tiny square. "What does that even mean?"

She lifts a shoulder. "It means is this relationship going somewhere or is it just for fun? Because when I saw Aidan, I saw hot and temporary. But when the two of you came out of the woods yesterday, I saw hot and…" Her eyes wander the room as she looks for the right word. "Happy," she decides. "You looked hot and happy. Sex happy. Hand-holding happy. Got-a-great-deal-on-these-Manolos happy." She studies her designer shoes. "Like, I got a *really* great deal. And you were even happier than that."

"That's pretty happy."

"So it's serious? You see a future with him?"

"A future? Missy, it's only been… I mean, we're just…" I can feel my cheeks burning. "I'm just thinking about the present right now. The future will come…later."

She licks frosting off her thumb. "Okay," she says. "Suit yourself. Be vague. But are we talking, like, six inches vague? Eight? Ten?"

"Missy!"

She sniffs. "Goodness, Aster. You're so well-behaved. You should try doing something bad once in a while, just to keep life interesting."

I bite into my cupcake and try not to laugh.

40

Aidan

I see Aster before she sees me.

I'm parked in front of her building in Wes's beat up old car, watching as she turns in a small circle, shielding her eyes against the spring sunlight. She's wearing skinny jeans with a hole in the knee and a black tank top, a messenger bag slung over one shoulder. She's the picture of all-natural college perfection, and she's waiting for me.

I honk the horn and wave to her through the rolled down passenger window, and when she spots me she comes over, slinging the bag into the footwell as she slides in.

"What are you doing behind the wheel?" she asks. "I thought this was my driving lesson."

"It is. We'll go to Carters and practice there. They've got a huge parking lot and the far corner's always empty." Plus I kind of lied to Wes about why I wanted to borrow his car, telling him I needed to buy a number of things in bulk from the grocery store.

"Shouldn't I, y'know, drive?" she wheedles as I pull away from the curb. "Out of the frying pan, into the fire?"

"I don't think you're using that phrase correctly. In your case it'd be more like, out of the frying pan, into the passenger seat."

She smiles and sits back. During our failed trip to the cabin, I'd learned two new things about Aster: one, she's never had a s'more; and two, she doesn't have a driver's license. Being homeless and then imprisoned had deferred that rite of passage.

"Whose car is this?" she asks, stroking the torn leather on the inside of the door.

"I borrowed it from Wes. I told him I needed some bulk items from Carters."

"Yeah? Like what?"

"Like…toilet paper. What else comes in bulk? Cereal?"

"Tomato sauce?"

"Yeah, I need those three things."

She laughs. "When the apocalypse comes, you'll be ready."

I turn into the Carters parking lot, steering away from the large green building and its bustle of Saturday afternoon shoppers and driving us to the far corner where our only company is a three-wheeled shopping cart and a flattened diaper box.

Aster claps her hands together. "I'm so excited. The only way this could get better is if I had a s'more in one hand."

"You're going to need to keep both hands on the wheel," I inform her sternly. "At ten and two o'clock. That's lesson one."

"Okay." She pushes open her door. "I think I got it. Let's do this."

I plant my feet on the asphalt, but don't get out of the car as she rounds the front and waits for me to stand.

"What?" She plants her hands on her hips. "Is there a second lesson? How hard can this be?"

I take the keys from the ignition and get up. "Lesson number two," I say, tilting her chin so she's looking at me. "When we haven't seen each other for three days, you're supposed to jump my bones. At the very least, make out with me passionately and let me get to second base."

She rises onto her toes to kiss me. "Maybe that should be lesson one."

The whole reason for keeping our relationship under wraps was so Jerry wouldn't find out, but we still haven't quite shaken off the cloak and dagger routine, even though there's no longer any need for it. Keeping things close to the vest is force of habit for some PPP students, and knowing what I do about Aster's history, I think it's second nature for her.

Still, she kisses me in the deserted corner of the Carters parking lot like she really is going to jump my bones, and I'm totally on board with the idea. I squeeze her ass with both hands, filling my palms, and she squirms against me, tongues tangling until she breaks the kiss and steps away.

I try not to ogle her tits as they rise and fall with each ragged inhalation, her raspy breathing matching mine. "Are you going to do something about this?" I ask, gesturing to the erection tenting the front of my cargo pants.

"No, I can't. I'm still on parole. If I get arrested for public indecency, I'm in a shitload of trouble."

I purse my lips. "You Holsom girls. Can't take you anywhere."

Aster laughs as a gust of wind sends the diaper box pinwheeling past. "Nowhere nice, anyway. Now give me the keys."

I do and we switch spots, Aster sliding behind the wheel as I take the passenger seat, nudging her bag aside with my feet.

"All right," she says. "Where do I begin?"

I guide her through starting up the car, which pedal does what, pointing out park, drive, and reverse on the gear shift. Like a toddler, she presses every button she can reach, turning on the windshield wipers, spraying wiper fluid, and popping the trunk and the hood, giggling foolishly as she gets out to slam them shut.

Soon enough she's driving in painfully slow circles around the lopsided shopping cart, smiling like a pageant winner. It's impossible to watch her and not feel happy, maybe the first time I've had a girl who's made me feel that way. I've been with women I liked and respected, but it's never been like this. It's never been just...good.

"Okay," I say, when she comes to a stop. "You've mastered driving in circles. Want to try parking?"

"Yep."

"All right. Try to park in..." I lean forward to read the yellow numbers painted on the spaces. "Sixty-eight."

"Okay." She bites her lip as she eases forward, like she might scare the spot away. "Bonus points for not picking sixty-nine."

"I'm a gentleman."

"Tell me about stealing cars," she says. "When did you start? What was it like?"

I lean back in my seat. "Well, for me, the gentlemanly art of stealing cars began at age fifteen."

"Whoa, really?"

"Yes. I was a young gentleman."

She snickers. "Stop saying gentleman."

"Much like you, we needed money. My dad had—has—a gambling problem, and there weren't a lot of jobs in our town. Plus, there was this group of guys—not a gang, but as close as you could get, basically—that I really wanted to be a part of. Just something...stable, I guess."

Aster doesn't comment as she straddles the line between sixty-seven and sixty-eight, then drives through the spots and starts a slow circle back.

"Remember that story about getting sprayed by a skunk?"

"Yeah."

"Well, I lied. I told you I didn't get the job, but I did. It was my first assignment."

"So how'd you do it?"

I narrow my eyes suspiciously. "You're not going to steal yourself a car, are you?"

"I don't steal anything anymore," she replies. "A few months ago I bought a candy bar from a vending machine and two came out, and I left the second one there and only took the one I paid for."

"You're so lame."

"Boring and free."

I smile. "Anyway, how it worked was they'd locate the car they wanted—I never knew where they got their orders from—and text me the details of where to find it. A photo, make and model, address, whatever. Then I'd wait until the middle of the night and just go take it. It was pretty easy, mostly. I mean, they weren't million dollar cars or anything, they were just cars. A paycheck."

"So how'd you get caught?"

"Have you ever heard of a bait car?"

"No."

"Well, it's exactly what it sounds like. The police plant a bait car with GPS and cameras and stuff, and when you steal it, they find you and arrest you."

"Yikes."

"Yeah. I was a week away from turning eighteen. I could have gone to jail. But the judge looked at my records from juvie, saw I'd behaved myself while I was in there, got good grades, participated in the group sessions, and said I had potential and promise. Asked me did I think I had the same."

"What'd you say?"

"Well, a dozen of the guys I worked with were there and I didn't want them to think I was a pussy, but the guy was basically offering me a way out, so I stared at my feet and mumbled, 'Yeah,' and soon enough later, here I was."

"Did you go to juvie for stealing cars?"

"No. I went to juvie for fighting. My dad used to give our stuff away to pay off our debts. When I was thirteen he gave away all my birthday presents, the stuff my mom had been collecting, wrapping, writing stupid cards for. The kid whose dad took them rubbed it in my face at school, reading those cards out loud to everyone. I beat the crap out of him. It wasn't my first fight, but it was my worst. So off I went."

"Wow. We're just two prime specimens, huh?"

Because we lived in a relatively small town, every girl there knew my story. It scared some, turned on others. Wes is the only friend at Holsom who knows what I did, thanks to a night of drunken confessions I regretted in the morning. But telling Aster feels natural. It's just information for her, it doesn't tip the scales one way or the other. She understands that people make mistakes.

"Oh!" she exclaims, stomping on the brakes and nearly giving me whiplash. "I did it!" She puts the car in park and leaps out, running in a circle around it to admire her parking job. It only took nine tries.

"I'm the best at this," she says, dropping back into her seat. "I knew I would be."

I rub my neck. "So great."

"What's next?" she asks. "Parallel parking? Highway driving?"

I check the time on the display. "Lesson's over. I need to buy sixty rolls of toilet paper, then we have to meet Jim in half an hour."

Aster consults her watch, in case I'm lying about the time. "Dammit," she mutters, reaching for the gear stick. "Okay, let's go shopping."

I reach over to pull out the keys. "You're not driving near real people."

"What? Why not?"

"Because even though you're so great at this, it's only been one lesson."

She thrusts out her lower lip and bats her lashes at me, but I'm not buying it.

"Get out," I order. "Time to trade places."

She harrumphs but does so, and when she tries to pass me in front of the car, I loop an arm around her waist and pull her close.

"Don't forget to thank me for the lesson."

She's trying to look angry, but her mouth twitches. "I'll thank Wes when I see him."

"No! Don't mention this to him. He doesn't know I let my girlfriend drive his car."

Aster freezes and an endlessly long silence grows…and grows.

"Also," I say awkwardly, face flaming, "I…kind of…think of you as my girlfriend."

I see her gnawing on the inside of her cheek.

"But do you think of me as a good driver?"

Something inside of me softens and warms as I look at her. As I fall just a little bit more. "Am I going to get laid later?"

"Oh, yeah. Absolutely." Her eyes sparkle. "Since you're my boyfriend now."

I've never been anybody's boyfriend; never wanted to. And never, in my plan to make Aster mine, did I ever imagine I would be.

As a kid I'd wished on every star in the sky that my dad would stop gambling and we'd get our house back and our dog back and our things back. By the time I was twelve I knew wishes didn't come true. I thought good things only happened to other people, people in the movies, make believe stories with a preordained happy ending. I didn't think happiness was real, and I definitely didn't think it was tangible, something you could hold, touch, feel. But now, as I slide my fingers through Aster's hair and press my lips to hers, I see that I was the best kind of wrong.

41

Aster

"Aster, you're the best," Jim says, not for the first time.

I preen in my seat, but beside me I can practically hear Aidan scoffing at the praise. Today's meeting has been to show Jim the work we've done for our cooperation credits, and I'd typed up the interview with Lindo—our past component—and the questions for Aidan and myself—our present component—and organized them neatly inside a folder with color coded tabs and photographs.

I'd spent way more time on the project than I should have, staying up too late, waking too early, working when I should be studying for finals. But it's worth it. Every minute is a step toward the grants I'll need to help pay for law school, and since Aidan doesn't care about the money, it's fine that he's not doing as much work.

"You too, Aidan," Jim adds as an afterthought. He turns the page to a color photo of a cross section of a model house I used to show how the building blocks of the program paralleled

Lindo's success as a renovator, transforming homes as he'd transformed his life.

Aidan grunts and I try to avoid his accusing glare. I hadn't exactly shown him the finished project before we arrived today, but it's not like I'm taking all the credit for the work, just half. I put both our names on the laminated cover page.

"Okay," Jim says, sighing happily as he sets the bound booklet on his desk. "This is really excellent. When I saw you two speaking at the meeting, I knew you'd be the perfect pair."

"Yeah," Aidan says, tone bland. "Perfect."

I stiffen in my seat. Every time he's in here he reverts to that old "I'm a badass" personality, and I lose sight of the guy I'm falling hard for. The guy who calls himself my boyfriend.

If Jim notices Aidan's attitude, he ignores it. "So," he says, leaning forward to brace his arms on the desk. "What are your plans for part three, the future component?"

"We haven't quite gotten that far," I admit. I'd lost more than a few hours' sleep racking my brain for some brilliant idea to complete the project. But how can we talk about the future when we don't even know who the new students will be or what the hell the future holds? "We're still brainstorming."

"Sure," Jim says, running his thumb over the spiral cord that binds the booklet. "You have two weeks until the deadline. Think you'll get it done by then?"

"Yes, absolutely. Do you think…" I trail off.

"Do I think you're well on your way to a glowing recommendation letter for every grant the school has to offer? Absolutely, Aster." Jim glances at Aidan. "You too."

Aidan shoves himself to a standing position, boots clomping

on the floor. "Awesome. Thanks. See you next time."

He strides out of the room, his heavy footsteps retreating at too fast a pace to be anything other than pissed.

I thank Jim and hustle out of the office, following the sound of Aidan's stomps to the stairwell at the far end of the hall.

"Aidan," I call, hurrying down the steps just in time to see him banging through the front doors, out into the sunlight. "Aidan!"

He stops at the edge of the grass. "What the fuck, Aster?"

"Why are you so mad? We did a good job."

He glares down at me, shoulders bunched, hands fisted at his side. "No," he says through his teeth. "You did a good job. Where the hell did those answers come from? You only asked me three questions!"

"I asked you a bunch of questions," I retort, "you only *answered* three. And I answered some myself. You're not the only voice in the equation."

"I thought we were going in there to talk about our progress, not win a fucking Nobel prize."

I picture him slouched and scowling in the office. "There's nothing wrong with doing a good job, Aidan. With trying to be...better. I just want the grants."

I see his nostrils flare as he inhales, calming himself. "You should have told me."

"I'm sorry. I didn't think you'd care so much."

He scratches his chin. "Maybe I wouldn't have," he admits. "A few months ago, I wouldn't have cared at all. But I do now. You pretended when you were with Jerry. You pretended with me when we first started hanging out. Don't pretend now."

"I'm not. I promise."

"All right, fine." He turns to resume walking, his pace slower. His tattooed knuckles bump against mine, and after a second he snags my fingers in his and holds my hand. If any of the people we pass notice or care, it doesn't show. But to me it feels like a giant neon arrow lowering from the sky and pointing between us, telling everyone we're together. We're a couple.

And we're okay.

42

Aidan

When my phone buzzes for the sixth time in thirty minutes, Aster makes a point of slamming shut her Poly Sci text and glaring at me, then the phone, then me again. The message is clear: one of us needs to die.

"I'm sorry," I say in a hushed voice. I scan the library, but none of the other students seem to care about the interruptions. "Wes's mom got worse and she's back in the hospital. I told him I'd be available if he needed me. I can't turn it off."

She sighs, irritated, and runs her hand through her hair. Normally sleek and shiny, today it looks tangled and greasy. The dark circles under her eyes and the ever-present coffee cup in her hand tell me what she won't: she's working too hard. She refuses to admit it, but she's overwhelmed by everything she's got going on, and the fact that this afternoon's brainstorming session generated zero ideas for the future component of our cooperation credit hasn't helped. The program is great and it's what allows us to attend school for free, but it's basically an additional class on top of an already full workload, and for someone like Aster, who's actually acing her classes, it's critical mass.

"Who is it?" she demands. "I don't even care if you're cheating on me. Just answer her."

"It's not a girl. It's Shamus."

"Tell him you'll be at the tournament."

Our season-ending Frisbee baseball tournament is two weeks from now, right in the middle of finals, and Shamus is going crazy trying to wrangle enough players.

"I did."

"Then what does he want?"

I sigh. "He graduates this year. He wants me to run the team when he's gone."

Her brows raise. "Really? You? Does he know you hate everybody?"

"I thought he did. Maybe I haven't been trying hard enough."

She snorts. "Just tell him you're not interested."

"I did. He's not convinced. He keeps sending me examples of why other teammates would do an even worse job." I call up the most recent message. *"Remember the time Missy called our volunteer umpire a little dick because he called her out on that double play?"* I read. *"It wasn't as bad as the time she charged the third basewoman like a crazed rhinoceros and head-butted her into the stands."*

Aster snickers. "I like Missy."

"Then you and Jerry have something in common."

"Look." She presses her hands flat on the table. "Just tell him you'll think about it. Then after the tournament, say you're not up to it. He'll graduate and be out of your hair. And maybe next year you can find a new extracurricular."

"I can't find a new extracurricular. I tried four in my first year and got kicked out of all of them. They were all stupid."

"They didn't like your positive attitude?"

"I'm not a leader."

"You're not exactly a follower, Aidan."

"I'm a lone wolf," I say. "Like you. I do what I want, and I like to be left alone by everyone except you."

"Maybe that's precisely why you're the best person for the job," she says, totally missing my point. "You're not trying to sell anyone a bunch of bullshit. You show up, do your thing, it's impersonal and effective, and then you go home. Aidan, I think you might be a..." She lowers her voice conspiratorially. "...good example."

"Aster Lindsey, you take that back."

"No. Never."

"You know, if you hadn't given me the blow job to end all blow jobs this morning, I'd break up with you right now."

"Don't talk about blow jobs in the library."

"All right, let's go outside."

She points a stern finger in my face. "I need to concentrate so I can get good grades and have my law school paid for. That's my reason for being here. You may have a different reason for being—"

"My reason is blow jobs."

She kicks me under the table, even as she tries to stifle a laugh. "You need a reason you can expect more than once every three months."

My jaw drops. "Every three months? Are you insane?"

Her shoulders shake with laughter as she pointedly ignores me and reopens her textbook, good and evil and everything in between.

And as I watch her work, it hits me.

* * *

The next day I drop by the PPP office without an appointment. The building is quiet, and when Becca glances up from her perch, she looks surprised to see me.

"Hey, Becca," I say. "Is Jim in?"

She checks her computer, confirms the visit is unscheduled, then slowly stands. "One second. Let me see what he's up to."

Moments later Jim comes out from the back. "Aidan! Nice to see you."

I cram my hands in my pockets. "Do you have a minute?"

"Of course. Come on through."

"Thanks."

I follow him to his office and take the same seat I'd sat in last time. This time, however, I make an effort not to be grumpy or resentful.

"It's about the cooperation credit," I begin. "The future component."

"Mm hmm."

"I don't think…" I scrutinize my tattooed hands, clutching my knees like a lifeline. "I don't think it's something just Aster and I can do."

Jim's face falls.

"It's something everyone can do," I venture cautiously. "I think we would all agree that this program is a wonderful opportunity, but not everyone knows what to do when something this great falls into their lap. It can be overwhelming."

"Okay…"

"So I was thinking that the future component could be, like, a mentorship program. Where current students meet with new students on a recurring basis—maybe monthly—to check in with them. I know you try to meet with us, but there's a lot of us and just one of you."

He looks interested. "Right."

"And instead of the mentorship meetings being just a basic meeting, maybe they could be, like, excursions or experiences. Something where we explore things a bit further. Not everyone declares a major first year, so this could be a chance to find a goal. Something to work toward." I think of Aster. "Inspiration."

Jim nods, mouth turned down at the corners as he thinks, no doubt wishing Aster were here beside me, making everything better.

"Well," he says. "I think that's a wonderful idea, Aidan."

It takes me a second to comprehend that he's agreeing with me. "You do?"

"Yes. Of course. As you're no doubt aware, the program is always short on funding, and I've been trying to fulfill the mentorship role myself, but there are only so many hours in the day. I love that your idea involves using resources we already have, and makes the idea of a 'future' something visual or even tangible for students, depending on the excursion."

"Ah, yeah." I make a mental note of those words. *Visual. Tangible. Resources.*

"Okay, wonderful. Can you put that in writing for me? You

still have…" He consults the tiny flip calendar on his desk, pictures of cats in hats celebrating each month. "Four days," he says. "Will you be able to submit a proposal in that amount of time?"

"Yeah, definitely." If I start now and do nothing else until it's done.

"Excellent. Thanks for coming in, Aidan. Please let me know if there's anything I can do to help."

"Okay. Will do. Bye."

I stand and hurry out of there, just as fast as I always leave, only this time I'm not fleeing, I'm running toward something. I'm running like there's a fire lit under my ass, one that's motivating me for the first time in forever.

A spark, if you will.

43

Aidan

I spend the rest of the day at the library, leaving only when they kick me out. It's late when I get home, yawning into the crook of my arm as I hang my jacket over the banister. I have one foot on the bottom stair when I spot Wes and T.J. a few feet away in the living room, sitting on the over-stuffed chairs on either side of the coffee table, counting bags of white powder. Neatly bundled stacks of cash dot the floor and the unholy contrast between Pearl's antique furniture, the two bulked up guys sitting on it, and the thousands of dollars in drugs almost manages to convince me I'm dreaming.

But I'm not.

I close my eyes, but when I open them they're still right there, staring at me. Not even trying to hide it. I should go upstairs to my room, gather my measly belongings, and walk right back out. Except I have nowhere to go. Aster's got her hands full with R.A. duties and school pressures and I don't want to add to her stress, and I already paid this month's rent and don't have enough for another place. My last exam is in twelve days—if I can hold out until then, they'll be gone and I'll be living somewhere else.

For weeks I've known they've been up to something, but I convinced myself it was just the situation with Wes's mom and did my best to keep my head down and ignore it. And until now, they've done their best to let me. I made it clear I was in the program and intended to take advantage of the opportunity, and though I could see them silently mocking my sudden change of heart, they kept their contrary opinions—and their activities—to themselves.

Until now.

"What's going on?" I ask, in spite of my better judgment.

Wes rubs his hands across his face, his stress evident. "I'm in trouble, bro."

I jerk my chin at the table. "You sure?"

"I'm short ten grand. I was short forty and I've been working my ass off to make up for it, but I got nothing left. I need help."

I shrug helplessly. "Dude. I sleep on an antique *chesterfield*. I own two pairs of pants and one pair of boots. Do you really think I have ten thousand dollars lying around?"

Wes and T.J. exchange a look.

"No," I say, before they can speak. "Drugs aren't my thing. Don't involve me in this."

"I wouldn't if I weren't desperate," Wes says, desperately. "I must have gotten robbed at one of the parties, didn't know until I started counting the cash and saw that I was out. I have ten days left to make up the deficit or…or…"

"Why did you even start up again?" I shout. "We had everything fucking handed to us—all you had to do was take it!"

Wes flinches. "I know," he mumbles. "I just... I fucked up. I didn't fit in here, all these kids with their clothes and their cars and stuff. I just...wanted more."

I think about how I felt when I first saw Aster. How badly I wanted her. What I was willing to do to get it.

"Shaw," T.J. says, when Wes can't continue. "You've gotta help us."

"I can't," I hear myself say. "Drugs...that's not my scene."

"I know," Wes says. "But you steal cars, right?"

"No." My voice is adamant. "Past tense. I *stole* cars. I don't anymore. I don't steal anything anymore."

Well. Mostly.

"Please," Wes says, voice breaking. "I've done everything I can think of. Just call your old crew—"

"Is your mother even sick?" I interrupt. "Was any of that true?"

He hesitates, the answer obvious.

"No? So all those trips out of town? The missed classes, extracurriculars—that's all because of this?"

He tips his chin, the barest acknowledgment of his lies.

I scrub my hands over my face. "Oh my God."

"They know where we live," T.J. ventures. "They said we have ten days, then they'll come and they'll..."

I know how that sentence ends. Hell, I know how this whole story ends. I heard it every day of my life growing up. My dad and the ever-present threats lurking over his shoulder. The promises. The broken promises.

The repeat cycle.

"Please. Just make a phone call," Wes says. "I've got a couple things lined up here, but it won't be enough. We can go with you, back home. One weekend—one night—we lift a few cars and—"

"Have you ever stolen a car before?" I demand.

It's clear from his expression that he hasn't.

I glare at T.J. "You?"

"No."

"What about Brix? Does he know about this?"

They shake their heads. "We didn't want to involve him," T.J. mumbles. "He's married, they have a house, a life. He's different now. He's different from us."

"That's because he's trying!" I snap. "He's *trying* to be different." I want to add that I'm trying too, that I'm not married, but I have Aster. And I don't have a house, but I could, one day, if I don't fuck everything up. It sounds so trite and stupid, so fucking naïve, so…hopeful. And I know just as I believed my dad when he said he'd get Daisy back, that we'd get more birthday presents, that they'd rebuild our fucking burned down house, that no matter how much Wes and T.J. believe what they're saying, it doesn't make it true.

Until I met Aster, I'd been living firmly in Holsom's gray area, not doing too great, not doing too bad. I'd done well to ignore the familiar temptations of the dark side, never seeing any reason to move toward the light. Then Aster came along, and without even realizing it, I'd been sidling closer to that bright side, to the promise and potential I'm supposed to have. That we're all supposed to have.

"We're trying, too," Wes insists. "If you help us out, we can do this. We'll pay back the money and we'll get out and we'll never do it again. I've learned my lesson. I knew it was a mistake, I was just stupid. Haven't you ever made a mistake?"

"We all have," I snap. "But three years in, we're supposed to have learned something from them."

"You know us," T.J. insists. "We've been friends a long time. That whole first year, when you wanted to walk away from all this, we kept you here. We helped you. Now we need you to help us."

"Just this once," Wes adds. "It'll be the last time. I promise."

The words sound achingly familiar, my instinct to help them as ingrained as it is wrong. But even as I shake my head, trying to say no, trying to do the right thing, I feel myself stepping away from the light and wading back into the murky gray.

* * *

I feel guilty when Aster smiles at me. The same smile that hooked me the day we met, the one I've lived for every day since, makes me lower my eyes in shame as I step into her room. I take off my boots and put my bag on the desk, scanning the small space, everything sparse and tidy and upfront. No lies here. Not until I showed up.

"You okay?" she asks.

"Totally fine."

She looks doubtful, and she should. She'd called me an hour ago to invite me over to hang out, and while I've always jumped at her invitations, today I didn't. I didn't want to see Aster, but I couldn't turn her down, either, and I know she heard the reluctance in my voice.

"You sounded pretty upset on the phone," she comments. "I

was just kidding about the vegetarian pizza. I ordered the one with all the meat." To prove her point she lifts the lid of the large orange box sitting on the table, and I know it's bad when not even the smell of fresh pizza improves my mood. Not even when she makes a comical show of wafting the aroma in my direction to lure me over.

"This is great," I say, taking a seat and trying to sound enthusiastic. "Thanks."

She grabs two beers from her tiny fridge and sets them on the table before sitting down, her knees bumping mine. She eats straight out of the box, a string of cheese refusing to relinquish its hold on the pizza until she twirls it in her finger to snap it. "So today," she begins, chewing thoughtfully, "one of the kids on my floor called to say she was hearing weird noises from another student's room and thought he might need help."

"Oh yeah?" I take a bite of my pizza, but it tastes like dust.

"Yeah, so I went down there to check on him, and he's acting really weird. Won't come to the door until I threaten to get the master key and unlock it myself. Finally he lets me in, barely opening the door wide enough for me to fit through, then slams it closed."

I remember the last time she told me a story like this, that day at the ice cream parlor. How she was opening the door for me to confess, and I'd walked right by it and into an ambush instead. But how could she know about the problem with T.J. and Wes?

"Was it drugs?" I ask warily.

"A squirrel," she says around a mouthful of pizza.

I stop chewing. "What?"

"He'd been raising a squirrel in his room since November.

And now it wants to go outside, except it doesn't know how to go outside, and it's making lots of anxious little squirrel noises."

"You're kidding."

"Nope. He's probably the only guy in here whose browsing history includes 'how to feed a baby squirrel' and not lesbian porn."

"He probably has the porn, too."

She sips her beer. "Yeah. Probably."

"So what'd you do? Confiscate the squirrel?"

"Well, technically we're not allowed to have pets. Not even a goldfish. But I thought, what the hell? There are only a couple of weeks left until everyone's exams finish. Move-out day is the end of the month. I'll just let him keep the squirrel."

"So it's still in there?"

"Yep. Our little secret."

"I don't know if you're a good R.A. or a terrible one."

"What I am is a great secret keeper," she says. "Totally trustworthy."

My stomach clenches. Turns out this is *exactly* like the ice cream parlor, except this time she doesn't know what the problem is, only that there is one.

"Aster," I lie, feeling horrible, "I don't have a secret."

"Then what's bothering you?" she presses. "You've taken two bites of pizza. Zero beer. You didn't even kiss me when you walked in. Didn't even try. And look how low-cut my shirt is! Not even a grope? Something is obviously *very* wrong."

She's trying to make light of it, but I can tell she's hurt and concerned.

I give myself a mental kick. I thought I'd helped with some

of her stress by talking to Jim about the mentorship project, but all I'd done was replace one issue with an even bigger one.

This is the second time Aster's given me an opportunity to come clean, essentially promising to forgive me if I tell her the truth. But I don't think she will forgive me this time; I don't think she can. Aster may be part of the program, but she knew her promise and potential before she ever set foot on this campus. She's done making mistakes, and she's done with people who make them.

It's hard to know I'm sitting a foot away from her, lying to her face. It's hard knowing my friends are in a bad place, and it's hard knowing I'm slipping back into that precarious gray area to help them out. But the hardest thing of all would be watching Aster walk away, slamming the same door she'd opened for me, hearing the lock click as she turned the deadbolt and gave up on me forever.

If I tell her, I'll lose her. And that's the one thing I'm not willing to risk.

44

Aster

I've never been dumped before. Jerry's my only proper boyfriend, and I dumped him when he confessed to cheating on me. But that whole evening he'd been acting strange, not making eye contact, fidgeting, being distracted. When I pressed him for answers I thought he was going to say he'd gotten a bad grade on an essay or had a fight with his mom; I never expected him to say he'd gotten a blow job at a bar.

Now, as Aidan picks at the toppings on his meat lover's pizza—his favorite kind—I'm waiting for the same bad news and remembering my stupid joke at the library: *I don't care if you're cheating on me.* That's not true at all. I would care. I would be devastated.

I try to keep my hand from shaking as I reach for my beer and take a fortifying sip. As bad as the news was about my father's death, what was worse was the build up. Finding the letter, hiding the letter, ignoring the phone calls. I'd peeled back the bandage with agonizing slowness when I could have saved myself a lot of pain if I'd just mustered up the nerve to yank it off and admit there was a wound.

"Is it about Sindy?" I ask abruptly. I watch Aidan for any sign of guilt but the only emotions that cross his handsome face are confusion and surprise.

"What?" he exclaims, sounding sincere. "From the bar? The pros—What? No. No. God. No."

"Someone else?" I push. I know there's a secret, I just don't know what the hell it is.

"No! Aster, I'm not cheating on you. I wouldn't."

"Then what's going on?"

He drops the pizza and runs a hand through his hair, frustrated. "Nothing. Jesus. I'm just tired. Work. School. You know the drill."

"The squirrel story is true," I say quietly. "You can trust me. With anything."

He studies the table for a second, hands flat on the surface, the ink on his knuckles stark against his skin. *Ride hard.* He looks like he's working up to something, but instead of a confession he gives me a small smile. "I know I can," he says, reaching out to stroke my jaw with his thumb. "It's just stress. End of year stuff and all that. You're the only reason it's bearable. Don't let me mess up."

I cover his hand with mine. "I won't."

"Good." He leans in to kiss me, soft and sweet, just his lips on mine, his fingertips on my cheek. He takes his time, almost too much time, and finally I'm the one to touch my tongue to his bottom lip, nudge him open, deepen the kiss.

He makes a soft sound in his throat and lets me in, the

intimacy sweet and reassuring. I shift to the edge of my chair and he slides his hands around my waist, pulling me onto his lap, my thighs straddling his. I curl my fingers in his hair, press my breasts against his chest, my nipples tight, an ache growing between my legs. What I don't feel, however, is him.

And not just because there's still some sort of emotional distance, but because he's not hard. I tell myself it's stress, stop being so impatient, but after several long minutes of kissing and groping and hips grinding, there's just…nothing. I try to slip a hand between us to make sure I'm not missing anything, but he tenses and snags my wrist before my fingers can locate his waistband.

"Aster," he says, twisting away. He looks like he's going to say more, then falters and falls silent.

I'm breathing hard, but it's not arousal coursing through me, it's dread. It's how you feel lying in bed as a kid, convinced there's a monster in the dark closet, knowing one wrong move will set it free.

I lean forward and press a kiss to Aidan's jaw, trying to diffuse the situation. "It's been a long week," I say calmly. Supportively. "Want to watch a movie in bed and call it a night?"

I hear him swallow, see his throat move, and know the answer before I hear it.

"I think I'm just going to go," he says, avoiding my stare. "Wes has been sick all week. I might have caught whatever he has." He presses my hips gently, urging me to stand, and I clamber off, feeling graceless and unsteady.

A good girlfriend might offer to accompany him to the pharmacy, make him chicken noodle soup, take his temperature.

But a good boyfriend wouldn't lie.

My bandage metaphor from earlier was wrong. Maybe slowly peeling it off isn't the most painful thing you can do. Maybe the thing that hurts the most is leaving the bandage in place and letting it hide a festering wound while you pretend there's nothing wrong.

* * *

"Think he's cheating on you?" Missy asks with her characteristic bluntness.

We're at an outdoor café in the middle of campus, and her question turns a few curious heads.

"No," I mumble, stirring my tea, wishing the spring sunshine didn't feel like an interrogator's spotlight. "He said he wasn't."

"Do you believe him?"

I study the swirling liquid. "I don't know. Even if he's not cheating, it's something. I don't know why he wouldn't tell me; he knows my secrets."

"Oh yeah? Spill."

I smirk, the closest I can come to smiling today. "No."

"C'mon, I'll tell you mine."

"I'm afraid to hear yours."

"You should be." Then her expression turns serious. "Listen, if Aidan doesn't want to tell you the truth, force it out of him."

"Aidan's not Jerry. He's not guided by a super clean conscience and fear of going to hell."

She sighs. "Lucky you. Jerry washed my whites and darks together and called me to confess."

"To doing your laundry?"

267

"Yep."

"I'm feeling better already."

"Yeah, you dodged a bullet. A doctor-in-the-making bullet."

"My loss, your gain."

"Listen," she says seriously. "Jerry's a sweetheart, but I've dated my share of assholes. Southern men are charming. They make you feel cherished even when they're lying to you."

The mouthful of tea I'd just sipped suddenly tastes like acid and I have to force myself to swallow. "Aidan's not from the south," I protest lamely.

She gives me a look that says I'm a dumbass. "When you're dealing with someone who knows all the right words and all the right buttons to press, you can't beat them by playing a different game."

"Huh?"

"So you beat them at *their* game. You out-charm them," she clarifies, when I continue to stare blankly. "You laugh at their jokes and you buy what they're selling, then you get in close and gut them."

I choke on my tea. "Missy!"

"Not literally," she adds, glancing around for eavesdroppers. "Unless you can get away with it." Her exaggerated wink makes me think of my prison bunkmate, Loretta. She'd tried unsuccessfully to poison her husband for eating all her favorite cereal and taking the toy, even though she'd called dibs. Now that I think about it, she was from the south.

"What's the not-literal version of gutting someone?" I ask, knowing I shouldn't. Knowing this advice is bad, but not having any better ideas. Picturing Loretta in her bunk, recounting the details of her trial as she filed her nails.

"In this day and age?" Missy says, sipping her latte and looking deceptively sweet and delicate in a matching pink sweater set. "You check their phone."

45

Aidan

"All right, Aidan," Mack says, standing and slapping his hand in mine. "The job's yours. Surprise, surprise."

I shake his hand. "Thanks. I appreciate it."

"You kidding? I appreciate you coming back for more suffering each year. We'll see you in a couple of weeks."

I duck out of Mack's cramped office, buried in the bowels of the college maintenance building on the north side of campus. My footsteps are muted by the pocked cement floor as I return to the elevator and start the rickety ride back up to ground level, relieved to see the sun again. The groundskeeping job isn't incredible by any means, but it's exhausting and every night I go back to my room and collapse into bed and stay out of trouble, repeating the process the next day. That's part of the PPP structure: it keeps you so busy you can't find the energy to mess up.

Mostly.

With my summer job confirmed, the next nine days should

be pretty straight forward. Write my second to last exam, compete in the Frisbee baseball tournament, travel back home to Vickers and steal two cars to save Wes's ass, return to Holsom for my last exam, and pray Aster never finds out and still likes me.

Easy.

It's a gorgeous spring day, the trees green and leafy, the sky clear and cloudless. I pass students laughing as they mingle with friends, exams finished for another year, a weight lifted off their shoulders. I keep my head down and my hands in my pockets, my pace slowing to a reluctant crawl the closer I get to home. That's been happening more and more lately. Since finding out about Wes's "situation," I hate going back to that house. Every time I reach the front steps it's a flashback to my childhood, walking into wherever we were living that month and finding some new disappointment, my mother in tears on the couch, my father promising not to do it again.

At the last second I veer into the liquor store a couple of blocks from home and pick up a six-pack to go with dinner tonight. T.J. and Wes are gone for the day, doing their part to find money to make up the shortfall, and I invited Aster over to try to make up for our disastrous last encounter. Fortunately she prefers beer to wine, so I don't have to choke down a glass to pretend I'm sophisticated. One less lie to tell her.

Not that she ever seems to buy them.

The house is quiet when I let myself in, lining my boots neatly along the wall and straightening Wes and T.J.'s. I clear an empty glass and plate from the coffee table, toss a couple of tattered newspapers into the recycle bin, and wipe stray crumbs off the kitchen counter. I've got an hour until Aster arrives at seven, and the evening's menu consists of salad from a bag; frozen chicken pot pies; and a chocolate cake from the bakery T.J. works at that he let me buy with his employee discount.

I get the pies in the oven and set to work on the back deck, scrubbing down the patio furniture and using a broom to fish cobwebs from the eaves. Once it's clean, I fill a bucket with ice and water and stick the beers inside, stashing it in the shade of the patio table just as I hear a knock at the front door.

I wash my hands and grab a small towel to dry off, tossing it over my shoulder as I open the door to see Aster standing on the stoop. She's wearing a blue sundress with little orange flowers, and strappy sandals that wrap around her ankles.

"You look—I mean, hi—you look amazing," I say, unable to stop the grin from spreading across my face.

There's a split second hesitation before she smiles back, her eyes searching mine for any trace of the weirdness from before. She doesn't find it, because it's not there. Oh, sure, I still feel guilty as fuck, but those feelings are firmly squashed when I cup her face in my hands and kiss her the way I should have done the last time.

She kisses me back, her relief evident in the way her fingers dig into my shoulders, like she's anchoring herself. Anchoring us.

We're breathing hard when we break apart, our equilibrium restored.

"Are you hungry?" I ask, hearing the aroused scratch in my voice.

"Famished," she says, the same scratch in hers.

Right on cue the oven timer dings, and I lead Aster back to

the kitchen, gesturing to the limited points of interest along the way. "Living room, dining room, bathroom," I say, flicking a hand. "Bedrooms are upstairs—I'll show you later."

She gives me a lascivious wink that's meant to be funny but nearly makes me trip over my feet. "Can't wait."

I indicate the patio doors. "And I thought we could eat outside."

"Good idea." She wraps her fingers around the frame and takes in the rambling, overgrown yard that's more jungle than garden. "This place is beautiful."

I pull the baking sheet out of the oven, two golden brown pies bubbling in the center. "You think? It's a little messy."

"It's gorgeous," she says. "Imperfect, but…charming."

There's a weird note in her voice, but when I glance at her she's already outside, fishing two beers from the bucket and cracking the tops.

"Need a hand?" she asks, sipping from her bottle as she comes back in to watch me scoop up the salad.

I pass her two plates. "Can you put these on the table? I'll bring the pies."

"Pie for dinner? This is the best meal I've ever had."

"Chicken pot pie. Dessert to follow."

Moments later we're sitting in front of our little feast, making small talk. Aster's completed four of her exams and has her last one next Wednesday; I have one tomorrow and another on Thursday. Just enough time to steal a couple of cars, then come back to Holsom to review my sociology notes.

I pick out the dried cranberries from my salad and stash them on the side of the plate, concentrating on my task as I work up the nerve to lie. "It's my mom's birthday on Monday," I say, stabbing another cranberry.

"Oh yeah?" Aster sips her beer, and I watch her lips press against the edge of the bottle and wish I weren't doing this.

"Yeah. She's turning fifty. They're having a big party."

"That's nice. Are you providing the cranberries?"

I nudge the pile with my fork. "No cranberries. But I am going down there for the night."

"What about exams and the Frisbee baseball tournament—are you still avoiding Shamus?"

I can tell she's trying not to nag, but that's exactly what she's doing. Or maybe it's just my guilty conscience that makes everything sound like an accusation.

"I'll talk to Shamus tomorrow. The tournament is on the weekend, so it's fine. I'll catch a bus Monday morning, go to the party that night, and be back here late Tuesday. My last exam is Thursday, so it shouldn't be an issue."

"And you think this is a good idea?" she asks. "Going home?"

"It's her birthday," I say, hearing how lame it sounds.

Aster looks at her bare wrist. "Do you know the time?"

"Why? Do you need to be somewhere?" I pull my phone out of my pocket and check the display. "It's quarter to eight."

"Nope," she says lightly. "It's just starting to get dark."

I'm not buying her story, even though the sun is rapidly setting, the air around us growing dense and gray. I'd planned for this and turned on the porch lights before we came out, so it's still comfortable. At least, it would be, if I weren't getting weird vibes from my girlfriend. "Is there something wrong with the food? We can go somewhere else."

"The food's great," she says, her smile loosening some of the tension in my chest. I don't know if I'm nervous because I'm guilty or because tonight I'm planning to tell a girl I love her for the first time in my life, but it's taking a lot of effort to keep my fork from rattling against the edge of my plate.

"The company's great," she adds. "The garden's great."

I point at her. "Okay, now I know you're up to something."

She laughs, her head tipping back to expose her throat. I take in the pale skin, the smooth expanse of her chest, her collar bones, the dip of cleavage. She's not hiding anything, because she has nothing to hide. She shook all the skeletons out of her closet, and she's better because of it. And after Monday, I'm going to close that closet door and lock it tight and never think about it again. I'm going all in on *this* life, this opportunity, the one I finally know exactly what to do with.

"Hey," I say, reaching over to snag her hand. Her fingers feel small and fragile between mine, delicate, even though I know she's not. And even though I know she doesn't need protecting, I want to protect her. I want to shelter her from the dark parts of me, and give her only the best parts.

"What is it?" she asks.

I rub my other hand on my jeans, my palm damp. "I wanted to tell you something."

She blinks, her blue eyes made bluer by the dress. Even in the dimming light, I can still see them. Feel them.

"Aster," I say, heart pounding. "I—"

My phone buzzes, skittering across the glass tabletop and startling us both. Aster jumps in her seat, knocking over a beer bottle with her elbow. I snag the bottle before it can topple to the deck, and Aster grabs my phone.

"I know this is Shamus," she says, swiping the screen. "This has gone on long enough. I'm pretending to be you and telling him you'd love nothing more than to be team captain. He'll be delighted."

"No," I say, reaching for the phone, even as she pushes her chair back out of reach.

"Dear Shamus," she pretends to type, fingers flying.

"Aster," I say, louder than intended. "Give me the—"

Her fingers stop moving and I know she's not seeing whatever message just came in. She's searching my inbox, and she's seeing the message from Teddy, my contact in Vickers. She's seeing the only two incriminating messages in my entire phone, each with an unmistakable picture of the targeted car, make and model, and location.

"Aidan," she says, no inflection in her voice.

"Give me the phone, Aster." I stand when she stands, and she darts past me into the house, trying to close the patio door. I grip the edge and shove it open, following her inside. "Aster!"

She runs through the kitchen and into the dining room, not realizing there's no exit. She's trapped herself. But she's still checking the phone, even as she rounds to the far side of Pearl's antique table, breathing hard.

I block the door and start to the left, but she moves to the right, keeping the table between us.

"Give me the phone," I say again.

Her face crumples and she hurls it at me, her aim dead-on. I catch it a split-second before it crashes into my chest, but it's already too late. She knew what she was doing when she picked up the phone; she may not have known what she was looking for, but she was looking for something. She wasn't falling for my everything's-fine-let's-have-a-nice-dinner charade. She played me. Again.

"What are you doing?" she asks, her voice dangerously soft.

"It's not—"

"Don't lie to me!" She snatches a teacup from one of the dusty place settings and chucks it at me. I grab it out of the air and dash around the table before she can destroy anything else.

Destroy everything.

She jumps away, shoulder crashing into the wall, and sprints out of reach. She flees into the living room and I beat her to the small foyer, preventing her from making it to the door. There's no exit through the jungle out back, and she's too smart to run upstairs. Now she keeps the coffee table between us, the permanently unlit fireplace behind her, ornate urns and candleholders decorating the mantel. Everything in this house is too good for me.

"Let me explain," I say through gritted teeth.

"Sure," she says, voice shrill. "Explain. Please!"

"I'm just—It's for Wes. I'm helping him. One time."

"Helping him how?"

We both know she knows the answer, she just wants to hear me say it. "I'm going to lift a couple cars—"

"When?" she interrupts. "During your mom's birthday party?"

My heart sinks. "There's no party."

"No kidding," she snaps. "Is this why you couldn't get it up the other night? Because you're so busy stealing shit again?"

It feels like she hit me with a two-by-four. "Don't you dare—" I stalk toward her, and this time she holds her ground, her fury palpable.

"Don't dare what?" she demands, eyes glittering. "Don't dare wish for something better from my life? Don't dare find someone who wants that, too?"

"I'm not—"

"Don't dare ask you why you're such a fucking idiot?"

"I'm not!" I roar.

"You are!" she hollers back. "You're so fucking stupid, Aidan!"

"Shut up!" My hand curls into a fist, and when I glance down I see four familiar letters, crudely stamped there in a different time and place, when I was a different person. *Hard.*

Maybe I'm not so different after all.

"I'm not scared of you!" Aster screams in my face. "I've been to prison, you fucking moron! You haven't! You have no idea! You got off easy! You got a second chance without even paying for the first one. And now you're throwing it all away because you're an asshole."

"Stop," I mutter, dragging my hands over my face, my whole body shaking. "Stop, Aster. Please."

"You stop," she says, voice breaking. "Don't do this, Aidan."

"You don't understand."

"You're right. I don't. Have you been doing this all along? Stealing?"

"No. I haven't done it since I started here. And I don't want to, but Wes and T.J. are in trouble and if they don't get the money…"

"Their problems are not your problems," Aster says. "You need to focus on yourself."

"Stop quoting the PPP brochure. They're my friends. I have to help them."

"I'm your friend," she says, pressing a hand to her chest. *"I'm* your friend. And I'm telling you to help yourself."

"Aster…" Hearing her call herself my friend on the night I planned to tell her I love her fucking hurts.

"They're not your friends if they're asking you to do this, Aidan. They're not."

"It's just one time."

"You know it's wrong. You know you're better than this."

"It's different, Aster. You don't have anyone. You don't understand how it feels to…"

The tears brimming in her eyes splash over and roll down her cheeks. "My brother is the reason I got caught," she whispers. "Security guards caught him leaving a store, and when the police searched him they found drugs. They threatened to lock him up, force him to get clean, and instead he turned me in. I went to prison because I *understand* how it feels."

I think about her sparse room. Strictly functional. No pictures, no personal touches. Nothing to take away. Nothing left to lose. Just Aster.

"I owe them," I say softly. "They were there for me. The first year at school, when every day felt like torture. Then a few weeks ago, when I needed a place to stay. They helped me. I have to do this."

"You don't," she says.

"Aster."

"Aidan." She steps forward and rests her hand against my chest, over my heart. It's pounding so hard I know she can feel it. "You're better than this," she says.

I shake my head weakly.

"You're smarter," she says.

"You don't—"

"You're different."

I pull in a shaky breath. "It's just one night. Then I'll come back and we'll—"

"No," she interrupts. "There's no 'we' if you do this. I didn't work this hard to have it blow up in my face. I could love you, Aidan, but not if you don't deserve it."

I try to clutch her hand, hold it against me and keep her there, but she takes one step back, then another, and another, until she's at the threshold. She pauses, her hand on the knob, giving me one last opportunity to do the right thing.

"I know you deserve it," she says quietly, pulling open the door.

But I don't.

46

Aster

Aidan doesn't call.

I tell myself it doesn't matter, that I said everything I needed to say—everything I *could* say—five nights ago. I threw him every lifeline I could, I told him about my fucking brother, but he wouldn't grab on. Wouldn't save himself. I know I'm right, but knowing I'm right is cold consolation.

I know from personal experience that saving someone is not in my repertoire. I tried for a full year to get my brother help, but Ramsay wouldn't take it. The drugs were an easier reality than our circumstances. Even after he turned me in, even after I was charged and sentenced, I tried. I thought maybe seeing me in prison beige would spark something in him, but it didn't. He visited me once and never again.

Then he died.

It's not easy, but I make myself get on with my life, even as I swear with each step that I can hear the shattered pieces of my heart rattling around in my chest. It hurts, but I've started over before, and I'll keep doing it until I get it right.

Shamus invited me to come watch the Frisbee baseball tournament today and tomorrow, but I made my excuses, blaming exams, work, whatever. I have to admire the guy's spirit; he never loses hope, even when there's none on the horizon. But there's no way I can go to that tournament and see Aidan, be near Aidan, and not break down.

I thought I was devastated when I ended things with Jerry, but that was nothing. That was an illusion, a mirage, an idea. It wasn't real.

Aidan was real. And I was real when I was with him.

But I was real that night at his house, too, and I'm not throwing away my shot at a better life for a guy who's too mired in the past to see what's right in front of him.

I'm due in Chester at ten o'clock tomorrow morning for the walkthrough of my dad's house. I've already cancelled on Goldman three times, and as much as I want to cancel again, I know I have to do this. It's time to pull off the bandage once and for all.

I fall asleep, the kind of rest that's not restful in the least, waking up even more exhausted than I started. I recoil when I see my reflection in the mirror, unwashed hair and dark circles under my eyes, even less ready for this trip than I was all the other times I postponed it.

A nagging voice whispers that I can still cancel.

Mitch Goldman's probably on a golf course, waiting for my call. He'd been kind and patient the others times I'd bailed on the visit, telling me there's no rush, the house isn't going anywhere.

But that's exactly the problem. If I don't deal with this, it will continue to loom there, the last vestige of the life I left behind, another shackle around my ankle, holding me back. I force myself into the shower, into clean clothes and sneakers, and out the door. The bus leaves from the campus depot in half an hour, and today I'm going to be on it.

My phone rings as I step out of the elevator, and I sigh when I see Shamus's name on the display. I could let it go to voice mail, but I know from experience that Shamus calls three times before giving up. Better to shoot him down on the first try.

"Hey, Shamus," I say tiredly.

"Aster," he replies. His normally upbeat lilt is gone, replaced by stress. "Is, uh, Aidan with you, by any chance?"

My heart lurches. "No. Why?"

"Ah, well, he's not here, and Missy said he might…be with you?"

Missy. I've been dodging her since the fight, too, so she has no idea we've broken up.

I check the time. I know their games started at nine-thirty because Aidan complained about the early starts. It's nine-forty now.

"He's not here," I say, stepping into the blazing morning sun and wincing, everything too bright. Too clear.

Shamus heaves an overburdened sigh. "Right. Do you happen to know where he is, then?"

"No," I tell him, recalling Aidan's lie about his mother's birthday being on Monday, which is tomorrow. "Was he there yesterday?"

"Yeah, he was here, but barely. Really distracted with exams and everything. Kept checking his phone and stuff. Anyway, I guess I'll keep calling him. Thanks, Aster."

I hang up and stand frozen in place for several long minutes, letting the implications sink in. As much as Aidan grumbles about Frisbee baseball, he's never missed a game. Never let his team down. Being there for people is something he does, even when it's not mandated by the PPP.

If Aidan's not at the tournament, it's because he's in Vickers.

And if he's in Vickers, it's because he made his choice.

He chose them.

Not me.

Deep down, I already knew it, but the confirmation knocks the breath from my lungs. I cling to the stair rail to steady myself, trying not to sob.

"Aster?" comes a familiar voice.

I swipe tears from my eyes and look around, searching for Aidan's strong build, T-shirt, jeans, boots, scowl, guilty face. Everything. Anything. I'll take anything.

But it's not Aidan approaching.

It's Jerry.

47

Aidan

Vickers has two bus terminals, one on either end of town, and as we pass the first and travel down the four-lane road that cuts through the center of the city, I peer out the window at the increasingly rundown buildings and shifty people that signify home.

I was supposed to come here tomorrow, Monday, but late last night Wes got a text saying there'd been a change of plans. The deadline had been bumped up and they wanted their money in twenty-four hours. He and T.J. woke me at three a.m. in a dead panic, begging me to do the job today instead. Explaining that I had a Frisbee baseball tournament to attend didn't exactly sway them. So now I'm in Vickers ahead of schedule, and they're off somewhere scrambling to scrape together the remaining cash.

The PPP doesn't forbid students from going home for any reason, but it's strongly discouraged. Still, I know lots of people go back for holidays, and they seem to manage just fine, returning to Holsom and continuing on their chosen path. Sure, heading home for Thanksgiving is a little different than going back to steal cars to help pay off your friend's drug debt, but as long as I stick to the plan, get in and get out, I should be okay.

Well, mostly.

I'm still a fucking heartbroken mess.

I press my hand to the window and count the smattering of people waiting at the depot. I make mental note of the cars in the lot, cataloguing them by value, popularity, ease of entry.

Old habit.

I spot my parents waving eagerly from the edge of the crowd, tall and thin and beaming, just like always. They never change.

I shoulder my duffel bag and force a smile as I get off the bus. The expression feels foreign and wrong, even as genuine happiness fills me at the sight of their faces, the familiar weight of their arms as they do their best to smother me with hugs.

"Goodness!" my mom exclaims, clutching my face. "Look at you! Look at you! You're the most handsome thing I've ever seen!"

My dad gives me a once-over. "Yep," he concurs. "The most handsome thing."

I laugh and duck my head. "Please, stop."

"Are you hungry?" mom asks, leading the way through the parking lot toward the street. "Do you want some lunch?"

"I could eat." I follow my parents, taking in their too-thin frames, the threadbare clothing. My dad has always worn a suit, even on weekends, trying to maintain the illusion that his gambling is a business endeavor, albeit one that always ends in failure. My mom is right there alongside him, with her long flowing skirt and hair spilling down her back, still clinging to life in the seventies, living on love and not much else.

We start down the sidewalk and I glance around. I didn't expect that they'd still be living in the same apartment I'd left, but even when they told me to get off at this station, I hadn't really believed they lived at this end of town. This is the worst end.

"Are you parked nearby?" I ask, scanning the curb for any sign of the rusted out purple VW beetle plastered with my mom's collection of bumper stickers.

"We walked." My dad flashes me his salesman grin. "It's a beautiful day."

"Yeah," I reply, distracted. "It's nice."

It's the same blue sky at Holsom, but I'm not the same guy walking under it. I'm not the guy who feels comfortable in this part of town, hearing cars slow as they cruise past, taking us in. Assessing.

We walk for ten minutes, my mom chattering about old acquaintances I barely remember and most likely never even knew, but I make the appropriate sounds of acknowledgment as my dad holds her hand and indulges her.

We wind through a neighborhood of rundown bungalows, some better kept than others, more than a few with discarded appliances sitting on the dead grass. I feel my throat tighten the farther we go, and when my dad pulls out a set of keys in front of a little brick house with white shutters hanging askew, I try to convince myself it's not that bad. I can re-hang the shutters and maybe get some grass seed for the lawn, and—

But they don't go to the front door, they go around back. Down a tiny dirt rut carved along the side of the house, so thin we have to walk single file. A short flight of chipped pavement stairs leads to another door, and this one opens into their dingy basement apartment, the smell of pot hanging heavy in the air.

"Home sweet home!" My mom beams at me, and when I see her smile I see Aster. I see all the hope and faith I'd seen in my mom's smile growing up, and I finally realize that that's what I saw in Aster. Not just a pretty girl. Not just a hookup.

Hope.

Except unlike my mom's smile, Aster's is real. It's based on something more than a dream. It's based on hard work and dedication and a determination to have the life she wants. The one she deserves.

The one I'd walked out on.

"Have a seat," dad says, gesturing to an unfamiliar couch. I can't even begin to count the number of couches we'd had growing up. How many times my winter coat had disappeared, the time we had a DVD player for almost a full month before that was gone. Before I stopped getting attached to the wrong things.

"What would you like to drink?" mom asks. "I made lemonade. The neighbors have a lemon tree—isn't that wonderful?"

I'm sweating. It trickles down my back, gathers under my arms. I feel the same sick anxiety I'd felt when the cops followed me, sirens wailing, as I drove that stupid bait car. *I fucked up,* I think now, the same words I'd thought then.

Except then it was too late.

"Here you go," mom chirps, setting three cups of pulpy lemonade on the wicker nightstand that serves as a coffee table. There's probably supposed to be a piece of glass that covers it, but it's missing, and now the cups lean precariously against each other, one bead of condensation away from collapsing.

"So how's school?" My dad sits in an ancient recliner, tape holding the arms together, and doesn't dare recline, leaving his feet planted firmly on the ground. "You liking it there?"

I cautiously pick up a cup. "Yeah. It's great."

"Good." He nods. "That's good."

"How are things here?"

"Oh, geez," he says, chuckling. "You know us. Getting by."

My mom returns with a plate of tuna fish sandwiches, cut into triangles, like we're having high tea. She perches on the couch beside me and takes a bite, sighing happily.

I try to keep my expression neutral as I take in the room. The ceilings are low and sunlight barely filters through the smoke-smudged windows, giving it all the appeal of a cave. The carpet is worn and stained in places, the furniture most likely rescued from the side of a road somewhere. It's as tidy as can be managed, my mom's effort to make the best of things, as always.

I sip the too-sweet lemonade, remembering how she always made it this way, like an extra tablespoon of sugar could cover up the sour. "How long have you guys been in this place?" I ask casually.

My parents look at each other, and you can practically hear them doing the math together in their heads, totally in sync. So totally in love, even if it led them here.

"About nine months?" my dad guesses. "Before that we were in the place above the deli on Lennox Avenue—you remember that place? Great corned beef."

"Yeah," I say. "I remember."

My mom must see something in my expression, because she pats my knee reassuringly. "It's not fancy," she says, smiling at me. "But it's only temporary. Your dad's friend has some business out east and is going to rent us his house over near the elementary school—the one with the red door? That's a nice place. I think that's the one for us. We'll move once more, and it'll be the last time."

My dad picks up the story, but I can't hear anything.

It'll be the last time.

The phrase echoes in my mind, all too familiar.

How many times had I heard those words growing up? How many times had my mom made that promise? And how many heartbreaking times did I have to hear it to know it was never going to be true?

When Wes said the same thing a couple of weeks ago, I bought it because I always have, even though I should know better. Even though I *do* know better.

I try to drink my lemonade, but I can't choke it down. There's too much sugar, but it's not enough to mask the bitterness or the shame.

All these years I've been trying not to be my father.

I never thought I'd turn into my mother.

48

Aster

"All right," Jerry says, putting the car in park. "Here we are." Then he hesitates before asking, "Where are we, exactly?"

He ducks his head to look out the passenger window at the large old house looming beside us. My dad's house. It's the same as I remember, two stories, pale yellow, green door. The roses that flanked the steps are overgrown and rambling, my father the only one who'd ever bothered to tend them.

Jerry had agreed to drive me here without question. For the past thirty minutes he'd let me sit in the passenger seat, coping with my anxiety as quietly as I possibly could. He always knew when not to press, when to back down. He never fought for anything. Never had to.

"This is my dad's house," I say. "He died."

His stunned expression is reflected in the glass. "I'm sorry," he says, aghast. "Aster, I'm so—"

"It's okay." I study the house, like my dad might be frowning down at us from the upstairs window, tapping his watch and asking, *What took you so long? Where were you? Who is that boy?* "I haven't seen him since we ran away."

"Ran away? From...here?"

I get what he's asking. *Here* is a lovely house on a lovely street in a lovely neighborhood filled with lovely people. *Here* is exactly the place the Aster he thought he knew would have grown up. But *here* is not who I am anymore.

Before I can say anything, a black sedan pulls up behind us and a well-groomed man in a pricey suit climbs out. "That's the lawyer," I mutter, getting out to meet Mitch Goldman for the first time.

"Aster Lindsey," he says, smiling as he shakes my hand. "I'm glad you were able to make it. I know this is a busy time of year for students."

I feel Jerry hovering behind me, not sure quite what the hell he's gotten himself into.

Mitch makes the first move, extending a hand and introducing himself. Jerry replies in turn and then we just stand there.

"I guess we should go inside," I say, words I'd never dreamed of uttering. Not once after we fled did I think of returning. I hadn't even let myself miss the things we'd abandoned in favor of our freedom, however short-lived mine was.

"Of course," Mitch says. "Absolutely."

He talks as we trek up the long drive, mentioning how the Chester Horticultural Society would like to dig up one of the rose bushes for the public garden, if I would agree. He explains that the wrought iron mailbox is actually a piece of art from a famed local artist and is something I should remove from the house if I choose to sell it. I'm aware of him talking, but I can barely absorb the words, my eyes focused on his hand as he fits the key to the lock and turns it like it's nothing. Like it's just a door.

I don't know what I'm expecting. A bunch of ghosts and demons to come pouring out, maybe. A cloud of old dust, choking us, warning us away, perhaps.

But nothing happens. The door opens and Mitch steps through, then Jerry gestures for me to go, following close behind. It's just a normal entry into a normal old house. Nothing special about it, nothing to warrant the tightness in my chest, the rapid thud of my heart against my breastbone.

I squint into the gloom of the foyer, dust motes hanging in the stale air. It's the same as I remember. A long hall with rooms flanking either side, the hardwood still like new. My dad threw a fit if we ran on it in our shoes, saying he'd take any repairs out of our allowance, not that we ever got one. I peek through each doorway as we pass, spotting the upright piano in the living room, the one my brother would never learn to play, and the glass cabinet in the dining room that still holds my parents' wedding china, neatly displayed. Someone had come by to clean out the refrigerator and take out the trash, so even the kitchen is spotless, no dishes in the sink, no flies buzzing.

It's just a home.

No, not a home.

A house.

An empty house, full of all the things that should have made a home, but didn't.

"Shall I give you two some time?" Mitch asks. "I can come back in an hour or so, if you'd like."

"An hour," I say, my voice sounding foreign. "Please."

"Of course. Take as long as you need."

When the front door closes I slump against the counter, exhausted by the wasted effort of pretending to be someone composed and sophisticated, the same person I've always tried to be for Jerry.

"Are you all right?" he asks tentatively, glancing around. "Can I do anything?"

"I'm fine," I say.

"Did you grow up here?"

"Yes."

"Until you...ran away? From your dad?"

I nod stiffly, taking in the room. The refrigerator door used to be covered with magnets my mom collected, holding up artwork and tests we'd aced at school. Now it's bare, the surface shiny and unmarred. "Yes. He... He was very controlling. He was hard on my mom."

"I'm sorry." He pauses for a second, then asks, "Is she coming? Here? Today?"

I shake my head. "No. She doesn't talk to me. Not since..." I'm clutching the edge of the counter, my fingers white as bone. "Not since I went to prison."

Jerry does a comical double-take. "Say that once more?"

"I went to prison for retail fraud." Jerry is the only person, besides Aidan, to whom I have ever made that confession. "Holsom has a program to help troubled kids they think might have potential, and when I got out, I went straight from prison to college."

His mouth moves soundlessly, like a fish.

"And now my dad died and left me this house and I've been afraid to come back because I've tried so hard to have a new life and I didn't want to be reminded of this one."

Jerry still looks dumbfounded. "I had no idea."

"How could you? I never told you."

"Well... I never asked."

I feel myself soften a bit, the steel spine I've been trying to maintain starting to bend. "Do you ask all your girlfriends if they have a criminal record?"

He smiles sheepishly. "No. But I should probably look into Missy a bit more closely."

I laugh. "Maybe."

"Well," he says, brushing his hands together. Smooth, clean, pre-med hands. Hands he'll one day use to heal people. "Want to give me a tour? I'll ask all the questions I should have asked before."

And that's it. He just...accepts it. Jerry's the poster child for Holsom's clean cut, well-to-do student body, and he accepts me, flaws and all. I wasted an entire year trying to be someone I thought he wanted—someone I thought I wanted—and it turns out I could have been myself the whole time. Maybe we would have fallen in love, maybe not, but it would have been so much less exhausting.

He follows me through the house, each room neat and orderly, functional but impersonal. There are no photos of my mom or my brother or me, nothing to indicate we had ever lived here. Ramsay's old room now holds a treadmill and a weight stack; my room is a half-finished library. Even the master bedroom is nondescript, no alarm clock on the nightstand, no reading glasses, no slippers by the bed. My dad knew he was going to die and hid every trace of the person he'd become from the daughter he would ask to return, as grudging in death as he had been in life.

I trail my fingers down the wooden banister as we descend the stairs, retracing our steps down the long hallway. I don't know exactly what I expected to find when I got here, but I thought there'd be more, somehow. More drama. More history. More pain. But there's nothing.

I tug the door closed behind me as Mitch comes up the driveway.

"Everything okay?" he asks.

"Just fine. Let's hire someone to empty the house and sell it. The horticultural society can have the rose bushes. I don't care about the mailbox."

"Are you sure? It's quite the collector's item."

"Then it's yours," I tell him, heading for the car. "I have everything I need."

49

Aidan

I'm the only resident of the top two floors of Pearl's house.

When I got on the bus to Vickers, I imagined I'd be the one getting arrested that night, tossed in jail and kicked out of the program. But that was Wes and T.J., caught trying to cross the Canadian border with a trunk full of drugs, reeking of fear and desperation.

After finishing lunch with my parents, I'd made my excuses to return to Holsom that same afternoon. Seeing them sitting there, in the mess they'd both made, their co-dependency an illness they'll never cure, I finally understood why the PPP tries to keep its students busy. It's not so we're so physically drained at the end of each day that we can't get into trouble after hours; it's not so we forget where we came from; it's not even to break bad habits. It's to give us perspective. To lift us out of the mire and show us what else awaits, so that when we're confronted with the reality of our past, we see it for what it is—the past.

The first time I caught the bus from Vickers to Holsom, I

wondered how long it would be before I fucked up and got sent back. This time when bus pulled away from the Vickers depot, I knew I was going home.

I'm lying on the antique red chesterfield, reading over my notes for tomorrow's exam, when my phone rings. I scramble across the room to grab it out of my bag, hoping desperately— maybe pathetically—to see Aster's name on the call display. I've texted her a couple of times since returning, but she hasn't replied. Disappointing, but not surprising.

I look at the screen.

It's Jim.

I sigh and answer the call.

I mean, at least it's not Shamus. I'd apologized to him for abandoning the team on Sunday, and he'd used the opening to guilt-trip me into being team captain next year. Now I really don't want to talk to him.

"Hello?"

"Aidan?" Jim says, sounding excited.

"Yep." I take a seat on the couch and wince as a spring digs into my ass. I adjust my position but another spring pinches me. I give up and sit on the floor.

"I hope I'm not catching you at a bad time," he says. Through the phone I can hear him typing frantically, probably calling up my class schedule to confirm I have one exam left before I'm free for the year. Well, free to move out of this place and into the cramped grounds crew staff accommodation for another summer.

"No," I say. "It's fine." With Wes and T.J. in jail, Frisbee baseball over, classes done, and Aster freezing me out, I've spent more than enough time in my own company. Even Jim's too-cheerful voice is relatively welcome.

"I'd like to see you, if you have a moment," he says. More typing. "You've got an exam tomorrow...how about the day after? Can you come to my office?"

I picture Wes and T.J., sitting in jail, turning me in. Explaining how I'd gone to Vickers to steal cars. Selling me out like Aster's brother had done to her.

"Um..." I consider the hole in the toe of my sock, the frayed cuffs of my jeans. I have so little to lose, but I was still stupid enough to risk it.

"It's a good thing, Aidan," Jim says, recognizing my hesitation. "In fact, it's kind of a great thing."

"Really?" The last great plan I had was to tell Aster I loved her and spend the whole night screwing on this very uncomfortable piece of furniture, and that had ended...badly.

"Can I schedule you in for noon? Would that work?"

"Yeah," I hear myself say, still doubtful. "Okay."

* * *

I thought I was nervous about the exam, but the meeting with Jim overshadows that anxiety and leaves me a pacing, antsy mess in front of the PPP building, half an hour early for our appointment.

I would die for a cigarette right now, but instead of using my thirty minutes to jog over to the nearest store to buy a pack, I just keep pacing. Fortunately the campus is dead quiet at the moment, so there's no one to witness my shaking, and when I can't take it anymore, I walk inside, palms damp.

"Hi, Aidan," Becca says, smiling at me warmly. "How are you?"

"Ah, just fine. I'm a bit early."

"That's all right. Let me tell Jim you're here."

I take a seat and stare at my hands, the tattoos I'd felt so badass and dangerous getting inked when I was eighteen. *Ride hard.*

What the fuck was I thinking? Yeah, they probably helped me seduce a few girls, but they have nothing to do with me, with who I am. None of them do. Maybe Aster wasn't hiding her dents and dings because she was ashamed of them; maybe she was hiding them because they weren't her anymore. The new coat of paint wasn't a disguise; it was part of the renovation.

"Aidan."

Jim's voice startles me and I jerk in the seat, making him laugh. "Calm down," he says, gesturing for me to come back. "It's still good news, I promise."

I stand to follow him. "I guess I haven't had a lot of good news lately."

He takes a seat at his desk and I do the same. "I suppose that's true," he says. "I'm sorry about your friends. Wes and T.J. were good guys who tried hard. But sometimes you only get one second chance."

I turn over my hands so the tattoos are hidden. "Right."

"Anyway," he continues. "I won't torture you any longer. I asked you to come in because I pitched your mentorship idea to the board, and they loved it. They especially love that the program has the potential to improve on itself, using senior students to champion the newcomers when they're struggling."

"Oh. Great."

"And they'd like to get started right away. Well, beginning with the next school term. Which means we have all summer to get the details ironed out."

"That's good news." It feels like it's coming a little too late, like maybe if I'd had the idea sooner Wes and T.J. would have had someone else to turn to instead of dragging each other down.

"That's hardly the best part," Jim says, smiling. "I explained that we simply don't have the resources to launch a pilot program without additional funding—and they approved it!"

I'm starting to suspect Jim told Becca this whole story and she didn't get excited enough, so he checked his roster of students to find out who was still on campus and called me, the last lucky bastard still standing. "Congratulations," I say eventually. "That's...wonderful."

"Aidan." He's practically buzzing with excitement. "The funding is for a summer student to help get the program off the ground. And who better to hire than the guy who came up with the idea?"

My mind goes blank. "I—What?"

"I know you've worked with the grounds crew for the last couple of summers, and Mack has only ever sung your praises, but I don't think that's tapping into your true potential."

"He already hired me. I can't just abandon..." I think about what Aster said that last night we fought. That I can do better. Be better. I think about Wes and T.J., sticking to their guns, even if it was the wrong call. My mom championing my dad through every predictable failure. "Can I really just...quit? Before I've started?"

"The decision is yours," Jim says, though it's clear he thinks the choice is obvious. "But the grounds crew job is part of the program, which means the funding is limited, which means you make pretty low pay. The position I'm offering you here is not part of the program—it's part of the school, which means four months with an actual salary. Now, it doesn't come with accommodation like the grounds crew job…"

I picture the brick bunkhouse on the far side of campus, a one-level structure filled with smelly, exhausted men each night.

"…but it pays enough to allow you to find a place off campus. Lots of units have opened up now that school is finished, and rent is reasonable since most of the students are gone. Aidan, I think it's a great opportunity for you and I—"

I think about Aster. I think about her all the time, even though I try not to. I think about her calling me on my bullshit, telling me I can do better. And I try especially hard not to think about her telling me she could love me, if only I deserved it.

"Okay," I tell Jim. "I'm in."

50

Aster

I think I might love IKEA.

For years I've known about it, heard about it, but never stepped foot inside. Never had a reason to think that I should start buying curtains or plates with a mind to making things feel like a home. My whole time at Holsom has felt like a stopover, a temporary resting place until the next part of my life begins. But now I understand that this *is* my life. So even though my summer accommodation is half the size of my resident advisor room, I'm going to decorate. I'm going to buy a duvet cover and a lamp and a throw pillow. I'm going to take home a catalogue and comb through it for things to buy this fall, when I move back into the larger residence. I'm going to get comfortable.

I shop for hours. I examine everything. I consider paintings and bookshelves and potted plants and carpets. My rule has always been to save my income from my summer job at the language school and live off the tips I make working the banquet events at the staff dining hall, but now that my dad's house is up for sale, the pressure of my law school tuition has been eased.

My phone buzzes with a new message, but my heart doesn't pound the way it used to. Aidan texted me a few times after the break up, but I never replied, and after the first couple texts, I stopped reading them altogether. I'm still working up the nerve to delete his number, but I'm getting there. Starting over is a slow process. I should know.

I pull out my phone to find another photo from Missy. She and Jerry went to her home state of Georgia for the summer, and, on Jerry's suggestion, decided to put his newfound survival skills to the test by hiking the Appalachian trail for three months. She's sent dozens of pictures over the past two weeks: posing in front of a large tree, washing her underwear in a river, eating a hotdog off a stick. She's alone in all but the very first photograph, the one where she and Jerry posed beneath the start sign for the trail. That's because Jerry bailed on the hike after four days, and Missy's still going strong. The pictures are a good reminder that it's possible to care about someone—love them, even—and survive without them.

I hate to admit how often I scroll through these photos. With Missy out of state, my only remaining friend is gone. And while most people would complain about working two jobs that keep them so busy they barely have time to breathe, I embrace it. And not because I need the PPP's hectic schedule to keep me on the straight and narrow, but because without the constant preoccupation of my jobs, I'd think about, well... anything.

I stuff the phone back in my bag and push my cart down the next aisle, lined with stylish model kitchens stretching as far as the eye can see. Red and yellow and black and green cabinets beckon, and I let myself get lost in the sea of possibility, a dream that feels just a little more tangible with each step, like the future is almost here.

* * *

It's only nine o'clock when I get off the bus at the edge of campus and make the short trip back to my building. I enter the lobby and take the stairs to my room on the third floor, passing no one on the way. The residences are sparsely populated during the holidays, filling up briefly as summer programs pass through for a week or two, then emptying out again. As it stands currently, there's only me and one other girl on the whole floor, and I haven't seen her in days.

I let myself in and flip on the light, nearly slipping on the piece of paper lying on the floor just inside. I drop the bags on the bed, then frown at the page someone shoved under the door, facedown. I automatically assume it's a desperate attempt at advertising to the only two people who might attend some lonely event, or a flyer asking us to keep an eye out for a missing cat.

Then I turn it over.

51

Aidan

The knock comes at 12:02 p.m. on Saturday, three days after I slid the paper under Aster's door, and three weeks since I last saw her. It had taken me all this time to find out where the hell she was living, then another two days to get into her building since it appears to be deserted and no one was ever conveniently exiting when I needed to enter.

I turn off the television and check my reflection in the darkened screen, then smooth my T-shirt and glance around my new apartment, the one I've been keeping meticulously clean for just this occasion. When Aster came—and I put some admittedly blind faith in the fact that she would—I wanted her to see exactly this. A blank slate. A fresh start.

An opportunity.

I open the door, trying not to grin maniacally when I see her unsmiling face on the other side. I'm on the second level facing the street, and I saw her approaching from the sidewalk. I'd glimpsed just the top of her head as she disappeared beneath the leafy green trees, but it was enough.

She came.

She's here.

Now to get her to stay.

"Hello," I say politely.

She arches a brow and holds up my crumpled poster. "Seriously?" she says. "A *roommate wanted* ad?"

"Are you here to apply for the position?"

She glares down at the "ad" on which I'd worked so hard, the page I'd slipped under only one door, seeking a very specific roommate for the summer. Precisely the one standing in front of me, with her sleek blond hair, white T-shirt and torn jeans, flip-flops revealing unpainted toes. It's the same outfit she had on the day we met, and I wonder if it's on purpose, like she's giving me a second chance to do this, to start things off on the right foot. Or maybe she just likes the jeans.

"*Roommate Wanted,*" she reads, the letters printed in extra large font at the top. I'd even shelled out for a premium print job, so the photo of my smiling face beneath it is full color.

"*Wanted,*" she continues, reading the smaller text at the bottom. "*One roommate for summer months, June through August. Ideal candidate is female, blond-haired, blue-eyed, five-feet, six-inches tall, weight completely irrelevant.*"

She shoots me an unimpressed look, then resumes reading.

"*Totally fine if roommate has criminal record, as long as it is for something non-violent, like retail fraud. Roommate should be smart, ambitious, forgiving, kind, tidy, forgiving, sexual, and forgiving.*"

Her chest rises as she takes a breath, composing herself before forging on.

"About me," she reads. *"Very handsome male, currently gainfully employed as Project Coordinator at Holsom College's Promise & Potential Program. I believe whole-heartedly in giving flawed individuals second—and possibly third and fourth—chances. I am lonely, apologetic and heartbroken, and have not stolen any cars in three and a half years. Will be respectful of new roommate's space and privacy, though openly hoping for less privacy and more sex. Just hoping, though. Totally up to new roommate."*

Her hand is shaking, the paper fluttering like a leaf in a breeze, the picture of my smiling face wavering along with my confidence. I thought she'd find the poster earnest and endearing, but maybe that's not enough.

She crumples the paper in her fist to silence it, then raises her eyes to mine, the blue painfully clear and direct, seeking answers and nothing else. I can give her answers. I can give her everything, if she'll let me try.

"You didn't do it? You didn't steal...?"

"No. I went home and realized it wasn't home anymore. It wasn't me. And I didn't want it to be."

"Why not?"

"Because I don't want that life. I want this life. I want..." It seems wrong to say *you*. It seems unfair to put that pressure on her, to tell her she's my reason. I'm not her reason for waking up every morning, for trying every day to be a better person. She's doing that for herself, so she can be someone who deserves the good things she has, someone who can trust that she deserves them and they'll be there for her. And I guess that's my reason, too. Aster's just the inspiration. "I want better," I finish finally. "I didn't know what I wanted for a long time, but now I do."

She stares at me, considering.

"This apartment has a flat screen TV," I add inanely, like she needs bribing. "The couch reclines. There's a king-size bed and a jacuzzi tub. The fridge makes ice cubes."

"That's great," Aster says after a moment. "Good."

"Do you want to come in?" I step back and hold the door, stomach sinking as she contemplates the threshold but doesn't move her feet.

"No," she says. "Not yet."

"Sure," I make myself say. "That's fine." My heart climbs into my throat, lodging itself there in a nauseating bubble of hope and fear.

Aster smoothes the ad, then folds it carefully and places it in her back pocket. "Let's go for a walk."

"Ah…okay. Sure. Whatever you want." I told myself that if she answered the ad, I'd say and do exactly that. Whatever she wanted. She wants to walk? We'll walk. If she wants to cartwheel around the block, we'll do that too.

I grab my keys off the counter and stick my feet in the sneakers I bought with my first paycheck. I know I'm not rich by regular people standards, but it's more money than I've seen in years. Four digits in my bank account. Money I came by honestly. Money that's mine.

"Those are new," Aster comments, eying my feet as I straighten.

"Boots in the summer aren't very practical," I reply, locking the door. "And I'm a practical person."

She manages to keep a straight face. "Oh, right."

We take the stairs down to ground level and emerge into the

sunlight, the sidewalk empty. Holsom is a college town, and the population dwindles considerably during the summer months. The quiet felt like torture the last two summers I'd spent here, like a vacuum in my head that desperately wanted to be filled by the nearest temptation. It was only the fact that the grounds crew job was so thoroughly exhausting that I didn't have the energy to find trouble.

This year I don't have that need. The quiet feels contemplative, like it's simply time to think things through, consider my future. Sometimes that future extends no further than what shoes to buy, and sometimes it extends past next year, searching online to find information on Holsom's Master of Social Work graduate program. I'm not going to go nuts and picture me and Aster with a hundred framed diplomas lining the walls of our mansion, but it's not totally out of the realm of possibility. The degrees. The house. The girl. I can have those things if I put the work in. I see that now, clearer than ever.

We walk to the end of the block and cross the street, our pace unhurried. I follow Aster's lead, though I don't think she has a destination in mind. She's just thinking. Seeing how this feels. Seeing if it's still something she wants, if it's a risk she can take.

"T.J. and Wes were arrested," I say, when we've covered another block without speaking. "Things don't look good for them."

"I heard," she replies. "That sucks."

"Yeah."

"What about your friend who got married? Was he involved?"

I shake my head, but she's watching the pavement in front of us, not looking at me. "No. They didn't ask him. They knew he had a lot to lose if things went wrong."

"We all do."

"I know."

She picks at an imaginary hangnail, stalling. "I went to Chester," she says. "To my dad's house."

"You did?"

"Yeah. Shamus called to tell me you hadn't shown up for the tournament, and I knew you'd gone home to do...it. So I figured it was time to just get everything over with." There's a pause, then she adds, "Jerry drove me."

The words are three pointy daggers, driven straight into my gut.

Jerry.

There for Aster when I wasn't.

When I was on a bus home to steal cars to pay for drugs.

Seems like an easy choice for her to pick him, when you think about it like that. Like words on a page, a pros and cons list. Steals stuff, doesn't steal stuff. Pre-med, not pre-med. Here, not here.

"I told him everything," she continues. "About my family, prison, all of it."

"How'd that go over?"

"Well, it's Jerry, so he apologized for not having asked about it sooner."

I laugh even though it's not funny. Even when he's such a fucking dimwit, he's still a better man than me.

But.

But he's not here, and she is.

So maybe he's not the *right* man, either.

"How do you feel about everything?" I ask.

"Better," she answers. "It was easier than I thought, being back in that house. He hadn't changed anything. He still had the piano, the china, the hardwood floors. It had a lot of nice things, but it was never a home. Never felt like one."

We've wound our way around several blocks, and now we're nearly back at the apartment.

"I'm selling it," she adds. "It's just a box that holds a bunch of things that have no meaning to me, but at least it'll pay for law school. That's what it's good for."

We stop at the short walkway in front of the building.

"So I guess you don't care about the flat screen television and the king bed and the fridge that makes ice cubes, huh?" I cringe inwardly, thinking about how much I thought that stuff would impress her. *Look what I have, Aster.* But that's not what she values. She cares about who I am. That's the only reason I ever got as far with her as I did. Because she liked me.

"No," she says matter-of-factly. "I don't care about those things at all." I have my keys out and now she stares at my hand, reaching out to carefully snare my fingers in hers. "What happened here?"

I follow her gaze to my knuckles, still red and raw from my first session at the dermatologist.

"I'm getting the tattoos removed," I say, feeling squirmy and embarrassed.

Her thumb strokes my index finger, stopping before it reaches the sore spot. "All of them?"

"Just my hands, to start."

"Did it hurt?"

"Oh, fuck yeah. It hurt more than getting it done."

"So why are you doing it?"

"Because that's not who I am anymore. It never was."

"I like your tattoos."

"But they're so…bad."

She rolls her eyes. "Aidan. I've been to prison. You've got nothing on those girls."

The words make me laugh, ease something inside my chest, transforming that ever-present bubble of hope and fear into two-parts hope, just one part fear. A healthy ratio.

"Do you want to come in now?" I ask.

"Yeah," she says. "Give me a tour."

I open the door to the lobby. It's only two floors up, but we take the elevator, mimicking the day we met, the day I wanted her to be my roommate, not Jerry. My girl, not his.

"Here we are." I wave her into the apartment before me and watch her move, liking the way it feels to see Aster in my home.

"This is the living room," I point out, resisting the urge to demonstrate how the couch reclines. I'd spent a good hour testing it out the night I'd moved in, thrilled by my discovery.

We walk through the rest. "Kitchen, guest bath, master bedroom."

Aster stops at the entry to the bedroom, brow furrowing as she looks inside. I don't know why she's disappointed. The room is huge, the bed is huge, the nightstands match the dresser and there's a ceiling fan. It's awesome.

"Where's your stuff?" she asks. "Where are you?"

"Ah…" I blush a little bit. "It's out here."

I back into the hall and nudge the door to the guest room. It has an unmade bed and a chest of drawers, and in the middle of the floor sits my duffel bag and my milk crates of belongings. Rent for this place is cheaper during the summer when there's no competition for space, but when the price goes up in September and Aster moves back into residence to be an R.A., I'll have to use this room for an actual roommate to cover the cost. But until then...

Aster scratches her shoulder. "Are you sleeping in here?"

"Um, no. Just storing things."

She gives me a scrutinizing look. "What? Why?"

"It's too nice," I mutter, glancing away. "For my stuff."

Aster laughs.

And laughs.

"Aidan," she wheezes. "You're ridiculous."

"How so?"

"That's what you thought about me, isn't it? That I was too good for you? And we know how that turned out."

"It turned out pretty good, if I'm remembering correctly." I take a breath and summon the nerve to address something that's been rattling around in the back of my brain since our fight. "You even said you could love me," I say quietly. "If I deserved it. And I know you don't care about any of this stuff, and I can't give you anything you can't get for yourself, but that night we fought, I wanted to tell you I loved you. I wanted to tell you so that if things went wrong, you'd know how I felt. But now I just want to tell you because you should know that there's someone who loves you, all the versions of you, and is pretty sure he always will, no matter what you decide."

"Aidan."

I kiss her before she can say anything, before she feels like she has to say something just because she's supposed to, because it's expected. I also kiss her because I want to, because she smells like laundry detergent, like the day I moved in, and if we're recreating that scene, I want it to include a kiss. I wanted to touch her hair, so now I do. I wanted to feel her breasts against me, and now I do. She's everything I could possibly want.

"Aidan," she says, holding up a hand when I reach for her again.

"What? You don't—"

"I love you," she says.

Then she kisses me, tired of the talking, ready for the showing. Our clothes come off, T-shirts in the guest room, pants in the hallway, bra and underwear in the master bedroom, the one I haven't felt comfortable in until now. Until I'm lowering Aster onto the 1000 thread count sheets, covering her with my body, my hands, my mouth, rediscovering every part of her and committing them all to memory.

Eventually I'm inside her and she's inside me, her words, her sweetness, her sincerity. All the things I thought I'd never have and never deserve. It goes on forever and not long enough, Aster trembling beneath me as she comes apart, fighting to keep her eyes open to watch me do the same. I let her see it, see me, showing her everything I have, all the flaws, all the truths. She doesn't even flinch.

She smiles when we're finished, her hair messed and cheeks flushed. I'm lying on the biggest bed I've ever seen, with the smoothest sheets I've ever felt, the plushest pillows I've ever touched, and the most beautiful girl I've ever kissed. And that's not even the best part.

The best part is what we have between us, the promise and potential that's always felt like a myth, but is now clear and present. It doesn't feel like something as whimsical as hope anymore, it feels like possibility. Like clean sheets and blond hair and new sneakers. Like stepping stones that reveal themselves after each brave move, paving the way to the future. And for the first time in a long time, I know I'm not walking that path alone.

I reach over to find Aster's hand, linking her soft fingers through my rough ones, and hold on for the ride.

Thank you!

Thank you for taking the time to read *My Roommate's Girl.* The idea for this book came to me as something of a joke, but the more I laughed at it, the more it unraveled itself and became a story I had to write. Then it turned out the joke was on me, because not only could I not stop writing it, I fell in love with it. I hope the joy I found writing this story translates to the reading experience, and I thank you again for choosing to spend your reading time with me.

Before anyone asks: this is a standalone story and I have no plans to turn it into a series. I had actually outlined an entirely different book before this idea came to me, and that outline is sitting on my desk, patiently waiting its turn. (Soon, outline, soon.)

If you enjoyed *My Roommate's Girl,* I'd be very grateful if you would leave a review on Goodreads or wherever you bought the book. Positive or negative, reviews help other readers find my books and I appreciate them all.

If you would like to know when my next book is available, you can sign up for my newsletter at www.juliannakeyes.com/newsletter.html.

You can also find or follow me on the following pages:

www.juliannakeyes.com

http://facebook.com/juliannakeyesauthor

https://twitter.com/JuliannaKeyes

Email: info@juliannakeyes.com

Books by Julianna Keyes

About Julianna Keyes

Julianna Keyes is a Canadian writer who has lived on both coasts and several places in between. She's been skydiving, bungee jumping and white water rafting, but nothing thrills—or terrifies—her as much as the blank page. She loves Chinese food, foreign languages, baseball and television, though not necessarily in that order, and writes sizzling stories with strong characters, plenty of conflict, and lots of making up.

www.ingramcontent.com/pod-product-compliance
Lightning Source LLC
Chambersburg PA
CBHW061934170626
46813CB00006B/2395